# Benjamin Walker

AND THE CASH TRANSACTION HE WISHES NEVER HAPPENED

Alex Barr

Produced by:

# FriesenPress

Suite 300 – 852 Fort Street

Victoria, BC, Canada V8W 1H8

www.friesenpress.com

Distributed to the trade by The Ingram Book Company

*"For the love of money is the root of all evil"*

*1- Timothy 6:10*


*"Drugs destroy lives and communities, undermine sustainable human development and generate crime. Drugs are a grave threat to the health and well-being of all mankind"*

*United Nations*

*To God:*
Thanks for giving me a second chance.

*To my lovely wife Skay:*
Thank you for believing in me; and, most importantly, thank you for being there for me every time I needed you. I have no words to thank you for the two wonderful kids you gave me – Sara and Juan. You three are my inspiration in everything I do. I love you very much.

*To Mom and Dad:*
I couldn't find a way to thank you for all what you've given to me. Now that I have a family, I appreciate more than ever the kind of parents I had. Love you forever.

# Acknowledgements

I WANT TO START WITH A BIG THANK YOU TO PERRY MILLAR and Neil Bailey who edited this book and guided me from start to finish.

Special thanks to Garry Gross who always encouraged me to write.

Thanks to Alejandra Rivera for all the input she gave in this project.

I offer my thanks to all of those who have attended my presentations whose feedback and comments motivated me to write this book.

Sadly, I have to acknowledge that drug traffickers, money Launderers, arms traders, corrupt government officers, and drug users are doing an outstanding job in destroying the lives of millions of innocent human beings. This book was written in honour of their victims.

# Author's note

I was about to start a presentation at a local high school when the principal approached me.

"Thanks so much for taking your time to talk to these teenagers about illegal drug abuse. This will raise awareness about the terrible consequences of drug use. Unfortunately, some of these kids are already victims.

"I'm sorry. I am not here to talk about the victims of drug abuse".

"What are you planning to talk about then?"

"About the millions of innocent people murdered, displaced and caught in the crossfire. They are the victims no one cares about".

"I still don't understand."

"Are you aware of the vast quantities of money made from the sale of drugs on the streets and the profound effect it has on the people and society in the country the drugs come from?"

"No,"

"You should watch this presentation and judge who the victims really are".

# 1
## The Bank

ROSE OPENED THE SAFE SLOWLY. SHE WANTED THIS TO BE her last task before her fifteen-minute break. We'd heard her make plans to meet a couple of colleagues at a coffee shop down the street to talk about the upcoming union negotiations. For as long as I've been a hundred-dollar bill, I've listened to bank staff talk about this. It's their favourite topic.

Rose went inside and quickly took out a small red notebook. It detailed how much money she had to give to each cashier. This was the last Friday of the month and the beginning of the July 4th weekend, which fell on a Monday this year. This Friday was considered one of the busiest banking days. The air conditioning inside the safe hummed along and the dehumidifying machines worked nonstop, trying to maintain a fresh, dry atmosphere.

We were divided in bundles of hundreds, each labelled '$10,000' on a band with a blue stamp in the centre that read CHASE Bank. I was in one of them. She took fifty thousand dollars, closed the safe, walked quickly back to the public area, and left one bundle with each cashier. I went to the third cashier, to the hands of a beautiful woman with green eyes and long, dark hair. A tag on her blouse read "Sara." Her long thin fingers, sparkling with rings on three of them, removed the band and counted us twice with real speed. She then divided us into smaller groups of one thousand and put us inside her cash drawer.

I ended up on the bottom of one of the groups and I hoped this meant I would stay in the bank longer. This thought calmed me. I always felt most secure inside a bank's walls. We're handed out randomly and when money goes out the doors of the bank anything can happen. The streets and the humans scared me.

I'm not that old, born in 2001, but I've seen for myself how weird people can be about money. And, of course, I've heard lots of stories from other bills. For sure, many of my friends have disappeared forever. I've caught up with others that have made it back to a bank I was in but they were often in real bad shape, full of marks or tattoos, tattered or torn, and generally dying from human mistreatment. In some cases the bank decides that destroying them is the only answer and they are shipped out for burning. After all, they can always print more bills. I'd been around a few years––all around the US and to Europe and back––but I still had the crispness and the energy of a young one hundred buck. I was in my prime and I wanted to enjoy every last cent of it.

As a hundred-dollar bill, I'm the currency most respected by bankers and credit institutions. I'm the heavyweight of the financial system and that makes me feel important. What I didn't know was that I am also the currency of choice by drug traffickers, arms traders and all your average criminals because of my light weight and heavy value. A hundred-dollar bill is perfect for illegal businesses.

The morning passed quickly with more luck than expected. Most clients came to deposit money at Sara's station, which increased the number of dollars on top of me and meant there was less chance of being handed out that day. Experience suggested it was unlikely I would leave the bank that day and I'd probably spend the weekend in the safe. Yahoo. But another

Alex Barr

part of me knew that as long as the bank was open and it was a Friday before a long weekend—well, anything could happen.

As the day continued into the early afternoon, business picked up and Sara slowly began to give out more money than she was receiving. I slowly moved up the pile to the top. My hopes of remaining in the bank began to fade, but being on top gave me a wider view of the bank, the clients and Sara. At two in the afternoon something suddenly caught my attention. I glanced at Sara who was suddenly still, all her attention focussed on a man standing at the front entrance. She flushed, she stretched her body taller, she discreetly opened another button on her blouse, and whipped out the clip holding her long dark hair, which she tossed quickly and ran her fingers through. I'd been in the hands of women like Sara before and I knew right away what was up. These young cashiers always did this any time a handsome and important man came into the bank. I'd heard other cashiers in this bank say that Sara dreamed of meeting and marrying a millionaire, someone who'd give her all she needs so that she'd never have to work one more day in her life.

The man standing at the entrance was a tall, elegant, middle-aged man with Latin features.

He walked forward a few steps, removed his dark glasses, smoothed and buttoned his suit jacket, and walked toward the cashiers. I'd been around enough in Europe to recognize elegance and wealth in a glance; believe me he radiated both.

Suddenly, from nowhere I heard this deep rough voice calling.

"Hey, Benjamin…Benjamin!"

I realized the voice was coming from the hundred-dollar note lying under me. "Who are you?" I asked.

"I'm your old friend, the General."

The General. I couldn't believe it. The General was genuine war veteran. He earned his nickname while in the hands of an American army general posted to the NATO Forces fighting in Afghanistan and later to the army in Iraq. The General has also been passed around various New York black markets; racketeers, prostitution, money laundering, you name it; he's been there. He knows more about politics, drugs and wars than any other bills I know. We'd met in several banks before, once in Miami and I think the other time was in New York. Well, the Big Apple is considered a meeting point for high-denomination bills. I didn't know much about the General because we'd never travelled together and wallets are the perfect place to share stories. I was a little intimidated by him, but I liked him and I knew I could learn a lot from him.

"What are you doing back in New York? I thought you were dead." He just kind of grunted at this comment. "I'm sure glad you're not. Heh! We might even walk together this time," I told him.

"Yeah, but hopefully not with the man standing at the door. Benjamin, if we end with him it will be bad. Very bad."

"Do you know him?"

"Oh yeah. He is a renowned businessman in New York. His office is here in Manhattan; he needs to be close to the banking area."

"His accent—where's he from?"

"I'm not sure. All I know is that he's Hispanic and rich. He's got special bank privileges—you know how banks are with the millionaires—special rates, no standing in line…. Hell, we both know money talks."

I looked at him. "For sure we'll talk." We both grinned.

"Good afternoon," the man said to the receptionist at the desk beside the door.

"How are you Mr Gomez? Welcome . Please have a seat while I have someone attend to you."

It didn't take this Gomez customer long to notice Sara. It was hard to miss her stare. The old fox immediately returned the stare and, holding eye contact with Sara, replied, "Thank you very much. What I need to do today is brief," and walked straight to Sara's counter. But before he got to us, a man in a black suit intercepted him. It was the bank manager.

"Mr Gomez! How are you, sir? Can you give me ten minutes of your time to show you our new product specially design for clients like you? I'm sure you will find it interesting".

"Sure," replied Gomez; and before turning back to the manager's office he looked at Sara. He smiled and winked at her seductively. She replied with a smile accompanied by a soft nod. I guessed that they were sealing an understanding.

"Ufff! We were lucky! We have to thank the manager for that one," said the General.

"Now what?"

"I don't know, Benjamin. But one thing I do know is that humans are unpredictable. That's what makes our short lives interesting."

So there we sat in the hands of Sara. She alone controlled our destiny. As a loose bill, she could give either of us to the first client who asked for a hundred bucks, or she could put us in the bottom of the new bundle of hundreds she had just unpacked. She chose to leave the General and me next to her right hand, ready to be handed out. I knew my chances of staying in the bank that weekend were zero.

# 2
## Salida

MOST PEOPLE AREN'T KEEN TO ACCEPT HUNDRED-DOLLAR bills unless they come to withdraw large amounts. Today was no different. It was four-fifteen, and no one had asked for even one of us; everyone wanted their withdrawals in tens and twenties. Only fifteen minutes more and the bank doors would close and I could stay one more weekend inside the bank.

Finally we heard the closing-time bell as the clock hit four-thirty.

"We're lucky today," cheered the General. "But where's Rose,? Is the door still open?"

Slowly we all looked at the main entrance and there was Rose, next to the doorknob, slowly searching through her big set of keys. From nowhere three young men slipped through the door and made it inside. She reacted. "Sorry gentlemen we're closing now. I'm just locking the door."

The young men looked between eighteen and twenty. Two of them were dressed in beach sandals and colourful cargo shorts with dark glasses pushed up on their heads and white New York Yankees t-shirts that showed off their suntans. The third one was dressed casually, in clean jeans, a blue Ralph Lauren shirt, his hair nicely combed to one side, and dark glasses still over his eyes. Jeans Guy came close to Rose, took off his sunglasses and politely said, "Excuse us, we know you were about to close, but we won't take long. I promise. Please let us in."

Rose smiled. "You guys are already in, so go do what you have to do." He turned and winked at his two friends.

"What's going on there?" the General harrumphed. "Rose let those boys in. She always melts when a handsome young man smiles at her."

Sara leaned forward for a better look at what was going on and made eye contact with the one in jeans. He smiled, said something quietly to the others and the three of them sidled together over to her station.

One of the kids in shorts laid a five hundred dollar cheque on the counter. He looked nervous but his smile didn't dim.

"You want to cash this cheque?" asked Sara, also smiling, trying to make a connection with the kid.

"Yeah," he said, glancing back at his friends.

She looked closely at the cheque. "I can see your first name is Robert but I can't make out your last name. Can you please spell it?"

The boy just stood there, saying nothing. He looked nervous and he had a light sweat on his forehead. In a beat, the boy in jeans jumped in and said, "His last name is Moss, M-O-S-S," he spelled.

Sara looked at him sharply. "Sorry, but I wasn't talking to you. He should know his last name."

The General was listening attentively. "These kids don't look like thugs but there's something fishy here, I don't like the one in jeans, there's something phoney about him."

Sara looked again at the boy. "Is your name Robert Moss?"

"Yes, yes." he said hurriedly. I still thought he looked anxious.

"Okay. This is all I needed to know. I'll give you your money in a minute."

Again the one in jeans had something to add. He moved his buddies to one side and approached the counter. "We want all the cash in Benjis," he said quietly, but really now with a faked politeness.

"In what?" Sara asked, looking confused.

"In hundreds," he corrected and smiled. "How long have you been working here?" he asked, continuing with his polite act.

"A few years," she replied, as she opened her cash drawer.

"And you don't know that Benjis are the one hundreds?" Now he was just plain condescending.

Sara nodded and then raised an eyebrow, giving him a look that said stop asking questions.

"See what he's doing? Distracting her? There's monkey business going on here," the General muttered.

I was the first bill she grabbed; the General was the next one, the other three she took from another pile of bills she had recently opened. My illusions of staying in the bank collapsed like a card house. She fanned the notes on top of the counter. "Here's your money," she said, still trying to make eye contact with Robert, but he just looked down at the counter, then his eyes darted nervously everywhere but at Sara, he swallowed hard as he anxiously reached for the prize. Sara stood waiting, looking at him, perhaps waiting for a thank you, but his buddies milled around him, moving him away toward the door. They left without a backward glance.

They rushed us out to the streets of New York. Robert was holding me in his left hand and I could feel the hot wind blowing, roaring like a pack of lions as it funnelled through the avenues of lower Manhattan. It was a dry summer, and looked as if it hadn't rained for weeks.

"When is this kid going to put us inside his wallet?", the General worried. "We could be ripped apart by a struggle between some street thief. There's no way this boy will let us go that easy." The General was right to be nervous.

"Soon, I hope. I don't want to become a half a note with no value, something unimportant and unwanted by humans," I replied.

It was as if he had heard us. He took out a sweaty-smelling leather wallet and slipped in one next to the other, then put it inside the front pocket of his shorts.

Squinting against the dust and walking three abreast into the wind, the boys walked more than four blocks without saying a word. But my mind was racing. I couldn't stop imagining what might happen. I didn't like being owned by young men. I hated bars, and I was sure this was where these kids were going. In bars you get wrinkled; they spill alcohol on you, which deteriorates the paper. After several beers your owner usually feels man enough to pick a fight. I don't like fights. Some owners get so drunk they leave you on the toilet floor, drowning in urine. Anything can happen once you hit the street. I had no choice but to face my destiny––whatever it might be.

After walking a few more blocks the young men came to a parking lot and rushed to a black Lexus, which looked new but was quite dented. Jeans Guy opened the driver's door and was the first one to jump in, then yelled "Hey Robert, Andy, get inside. Let's see the cash." He sounded anxious.

Robert sat in the passenger seat; Andy sat in the back behind the driver.

"Let's get out of here, Tony," Robert said, as he put on his seat belt.

"Not until after I see the cash. Where've you got it?" Tony replied. He seemed to be leading this show.

"Let's go, let's go," Andy insisted from the back seat.

"No rush guys, no rush. We've done nothing wrong. You're both acting like this was stolen money," Tony said calmly. He looked at Robert and laid his hand on his shoulder. "In the end, this is also your money, man. You've done nothing wrong so change that face."

I was desperate to learn more about these boys. I looked around the wallet and spotted a twenty-dollar note laying next to the General *He has probably been inside this wallet long enough to know who Robert really is*, I thought. The note had "I love you" written in red in the upper left corner, under the number twenty. This was a sign he'd been around young people.

We should call him "Lover Boy," the General chuckling. Then he called " Hey, Lover Boy" The note looked startled and uneasily at the General. "Yeah, you, the twenty note," the General said again.

"How can I help you?" the twenty note replied stiffly.

"Can I ask you few questions?"

"Sure. Start fast before these guys start spending," Lover Boy replied, relaxing a little.

"Do you know who these kids are or what they plan to do?" I asked.

"Robert and Andy are cousins, and they've been best friends since they were ten. They're both civil engineering students at NYU. They met Tony in a bar a few months ago and they've been hanging out with him since then. The deal is, Tony knows girls and has introduced them to several. Until then, Robert and Andy had thought university was taking up their extra time, time that could be spent meeting nice chicks but they kept studying pretty much all the time so weren't really meeting girls. But with their new friend introducing them to girls, they no longer spend as much time studying and think their problem is solved," Lover Boy explained.

"So how come you know so much about Robert?" the General asked. "Twenties are one of the fastest moving bills in circulation."

Lover Boy smiled. "Well, it was like this. One night Robert was with his girlfriend at a restaurant celebrating the end of Robert's first year of university. He got outstanding grades. She took out a twenty-dollar note from her purse, which was me, and laid me on the table, then slowly drew a heart with a red pen and wrote 'I love you,' as you see. She also wrote her name, "Amanda," at the bottom. She gave it to him and asked him to keep it forever because her love for him was endless and nothing in this world could break it. They kissed, then he put me inside his wallet and I've been with him ever since. He loves her so much that I don't think I'll ever leave this wallet. I'm sure he'll keep me forever."

"Silence, silence!" I yelled. "Something's going on out there."

"Who's got the money?" Tony asked insistently.

"I've got it," Robert confirmed, with the confidence of having done a good job.

"Let me have it." Tony ordered. All his politeness had vanished. Robert opened his wallet and handed Tony the five one hundred-dollar bills out of his wallet, making sure Lover Boy stayed with him. Tony slowly counted us, rubbing each of us between his fingers. "I'm glad all this came out well. I don't know why that bitch was asking so many questions at the bank. But we'll talk about that later, now it's time to celebrate." Tony grinned; Robert and Andy also looked happy.

Tony started the car and veered sharply to the left. I could hear the squeal of the burning rubber. I could also hear Robert ask Tony "Where are we going?"

"We're heading to Queens."

"What're we going to do in Queens?" Andy asked.

Tony eased up on the gas and replied, "We're going fill up the car—the tank's nearly empty—and then we're going to buy some good stuff for us." He turned off the radio, "Don't ask so many fucking questions. Today we're going to have fun." For sure, Tony called the shots in this group

"This wallet smells like fermented milk," the General said. He'd been quiet for a while. "I need to get out of here. I sure hope that after they gas up they go for a beer and we'll have a chance of getting out of this shit hole. I'll take any bar over this place."

I wasn't too sure about this after seeing Tony's attitude, and I began to worry. Since I was inside his wallet, I decided to sneak around and get some information. My doubts were quickly confirmed. His driver's licence showed he was much older than Robert and Andy––he was 26. There was an expired credit card and five parking tickets. But what caught my attention were the traces of a white powder sticking to the wallet leather. "This is what probably gives the acidic smell to this wallet," I told the General.

"You don't know what that is? I should call you Innocent Boy," he said with a wicked grin.

Tony stopped at a Shell station and told everyone to stay in the car while he filled up. Then Robert's phone rang. He quickly checked the number. "Shit, it's Amanda. We were supposed to catch a movie tonight."

"Answer it or she'll just keep calling. Make an excuse she'll understand." Andy said.

Robert answered. "Hi, Babe... Yeah, well, sorry I didn't call sooner. I forgot that today the summer temps had to stay and help set up the new backup systems on everyone's computer... Sure... I'll call as soon as I finish... I love you." I couldn't hear her reply, but considering the conversation ended ten seconds after, I am sure she was not very happy.

I already had a feeling about where all this was going to end and I didn't want to be part of it. Like the General, I wanted to be one of the bills chosen by Tony when he paid for the gas. I wanted to stay in the cashier register of the Shell station and find a new owner. But Tony opened his wallet in a hurry and chose the bill that separated me from the General. He scooped up his change, got in the car and began driving.

Andy, probably thinking this was going to be the best night ever, suggested they go to a nearby bar he knew. "It's a cool place and there're always hot girls," he said, probably thinking they would all like the suggestion.

Tony immediately interrupted. "First we're going to buy stuff for us, and then we can go to any bar you guys want." No one inside the car contradicted him, and I was pretty sure I knew what he meant by "stuff." The General heaved a huge sigh. I think he knew, too.

## 3
# Droga

TONY KEPT DRIVING, IGNORING ANDY'S SUGGESTIONS. WE headed up to the Bronx and, after about half an hour, he slowed down and stopped the car.

"Why are we stopping here?" asked Robert.

Tony got out of the car and opening the passenger door said, "Don't worry guys. I need you to come with me. I want to show you the cool side of New York."

Andy was the first to reply. "This place isn't safe; I don't know what we're doing here." Anyone who lived in New York knew that the area was known for drugs; even the General and I knew that, so for sure Robert and Andy knew it. But they both followed Tony like a gaggle of goslings behind the mother goose.

By now, the sun had set. The streetlights shone over the pavement of the narrow streets and back alleys that made this place a labyrinth for drug dealers to hide in and escape. Men speaking Spanish patrolled the street corners in loud cars. Through the open windows we could hear traditional Latin music coming out of their car stereos. Some lounging on street corners in groups pretended to dance salsa as they checked out the people walking by. Coiling tattoos could be seen on some men's arms, necks and chests; others were not wearing shirts, but I knew from my own experience that every one of them had a hidden gun ready to use if necessary. Everyone in the vicinity stared at the group of white boys and smiled and joked about it as experts in identifying who was coming here for the first time. From the way someone walked, the way someone moved around the area and from the look on your face, these men knew in seconds if you are regular user or had never tried drugs. Strangely, the white kids were not questioned or stopped. I knew it was because one of them was a regular user and for sure that was Tony.

Robert and Andy followed Tony until he slowed in front of a house with a small front yard. He walked up to the low steps to the front door and rang the bell four times. The men on the corners continued to stare at the group. A short man with dark hair and prominent Hispanic features opened the door and in accented English said, "Come inside the house fast." The man then went outside, down the stairs and halfway down the front walk stopped and waved his hand up and down to the men standing in the street. He returned to the house, closed the door and shook Tony's hand.

"*Hola* Hilario," said Tony. I was surprised he knew some Spanish.

"*Hola*, Tony. How are you?" Hilario replied in Spanglish.

From the way he talked to Tony it was evident they knew each other well. However, this Hilario put his hand firmly on his shoulder and said, "Tony, next time make sure you come alone or one person at a time. This is too many people. Police have been patrolling the area recently. You be careful next time." He seemed to be practising his intimidating stare. Andy and Robert were silent; they were out of their depth and afraid.

The place looked like a small slum. Boxes with china, clothing, crystal, TVs, PlayStations, and computers cluttered the entrance hall. They moved into a dimly lit large room off the entrance. All the windows were boarded so you could not see outside and nobody could see in. The room had small cubicles, each separated by drab curtains made from pieces of different coloured fabric that hung from rusted wires. Each cubicle had a filthy mattress on the floor; most were empty but some had a comatose person, completely drugged, lying on a filthy mattress with his pitiful possessions next to him. None seemed conscious of what was happening around them. Because of the boarded windows there was no circulation of fresh air and the odour of weeks of accumulated human sweat penetrated deep into your sinuses. I couldn't smell anything but alcohol, sweat and dust that tainted every corner of that house.

In a moment of bravado Andy said to Robert, "What are we doing here? Let's get out now. This place is only for drug addicts. That's not us, man."

Hilario responded aggressively. "No one leaves this place without my authorization. If any one of you leaves without Tony, the men outside will think you did not come to buy drugs and will react. I don't want to tell you what can happen to you."

Robert and Andy had no choice but to stay. The dealer then asked Tony, "How much do you want?"

"Whatever I can get with two hundred bucks," he replied, opening his wallet.

I didn't want to be chosen by Tony. I was afraid to be with drug dealers after all the stories I heard from other friends. Tony opened his wallet and took the two bills on my left; his fingers brushed close to me and barely touched the General. He gave the two bills to the Hilario who accepted them with a smile. He then checked both sides of each bill under a fluorescent light he had on top of a rusty metal desk.

"Counterfeit currency is common in these places," the General pronounced knowingly.

Hilario took the money and disappeared into the back of the house, moving curtains, jumping over mattresses and moving bodies aside as he went. He returned in a few minutes with two small bags of white powder. This time Tony was the one who

Alex Barr

needed to verify the merchandise. He opened one of the bags and using a miniature metal spoon he took out of his pocket he scooped as much powder as the spoon could hold. He brought it straight to his nose and sniffed with the force of a vacuum cleaner. "This shit is really good," he said, wiggling his nose from side to side.

The General weighed in again. "I'm sure Robert and Andy realize they have make a big mistake hanging with Tony, but it's too late." Not for the first time, I wished I could communicate with people. I would have told them to run from that place because this is just the beginning.

Tony was now euphoric as the cocaine sped through his system. I could feel his heart rate accelerated, rushing more blood to his body and expanding his capillaries. His face turned red, his pupils dilated and his mouth dried. He moved and hugged Andy, saying, "It's your turn to sniff some of this good stuff."

Andy was not impressed with what he had seen. He looked Tony in the eye and replied, "*No*, I don't use drugs. I don't care if you do, but I definitely don't."

Tony insisted but Andy firmly said "*No*" again. Tony realized Andy had a strong personality and moved on to Robert, who started smiling nervously as he approached him. "Here's your portion," Tony said, showing him the small spoon loaded with cocaine.

Robert quietly and hesitantly said " No." then rushed on "No I don't use drugs."

Tony didn't give up easily, he tried a second time hugging Robert and whispering in his ear, "Don't worry. All the cool people use this stuff; it makes you feel good. Apart from that, girls like cool guys."

Robert looked at Andy who widened his eyes, trying to tell his cousin not to do it. Tony kept hugging Robert and insisted again. The third time he used a different strategy and in an aggressive tone said, "You're a pussy, you don't act like a man, you have no balls. It's harder to steal a five hundred dollar cheque from your dad than trying a little bit of this." Bingo! Now I knew where that cheque had come from.

Tony stood close to Robert, his body language urging him, the spoon of cocaine held ready. Robert had tried to say no but now he wavered, seduced by the thought that he had to show his friend he did have balls. He took the spoon. Inside that wallet I was trying to will him not to. *Don't Do It, Please Don't Do It! Having balls has nothing to do with using drugs!* But I had no voice that a person can hear. I'm simply money.

Robert sniffed the cocaine once through each nostril, "I do have balls," he said, looking at Andy as if he was now part of another group. Andy didn't say a word. "This merchandise is perfect," Robert said, pretending he was an expert on the topic even though it was obvious he'd never tried coke before.

After seeing Robert empty the spoon up his nose, Tony opened his wallet and told Hilario, "This is not going to be enough now there're two of us consuming. We'll need another two hundred dollars' worth." I knew our luck was finished.

"Shit," exclaimed the General as we were handed out to the Hispanic dealer. Even though at that moment I was not sure of what was going to happen to us, I was sorry to see Robert didn't have the strength to say *No*. I never saw him again. I was now embarked on a voyage that according to the General would take me deep into the dark world of drug dealing. We both knew Robert had started a decline that would probably ruin his life forever.

Hilario again checked us under his lamp and took us to a small, dark room where he slept, ate, and hid his money. He left us on top of a small bed and went back with two more bags of cocaine.

Alex Barr

I heard Tony testing, sniffing some through his nose then we heard Tony yell, "Let's get the fuck out of here; we have a good supply for the night."

We could also hear Andy trying to persuade Robert not to use any more "Don't be stupid man, this stuff is toxic. You start this you'll blow everything––school, Amanda, your job. You're already in big trouble when your dad figures out you took that cheque. I don't know why we came so far!"

By now those were just words for Robert; his body and mind were asking for more coke, and Andy's arguments made no sense to him now.

"Stop worrying, Andy. It's okay. I can handle this. So stop lecturing me. You think I know how to deal with my dad? I know I can control dope, I'll only use it this time and no more, I promise." Andy said nothing more, but something about his silence made me think he wasn't convinced. Tony said goodbye to his Hilario and left with his little gaggle of white boys following him.

With his customers gone, Hilario returned to the room where he had left us. He turned the light on and stacked us with other hundreds lying on the bed. I couldn't believe what I was seeing. In that slummy room there was enough money piled to buy the biggest, most expensive mansion in all New York City. The money was stacked in boxes and wrapped around with thick plastic.

Hilario grabbed the money from the bed, the income from his most recent sales, and counted us faster and with more skill than any bank cashier. He then organized several stacks of ten thousand and dropped all of us inside one of the boxes. Our stack was in the upper part. He then grabbed a couple of hundreds he had on one side of the bed, opened a drawer and took out a small metallic box. The box had some money inside and the pictures of two little boys and a woman around his age. He looked at the pictures then gave each picture a kiss. After whispering some words in Spanish he put the cash inside the box, closed it and put it back inside the drawer.

Two hours later the doorbell rang four times. Hilario jumped off his bed and walked to the door. "I can only give you two bags for this," we heard him say. A few minutes later he showed up in the room with one twenty-dollar note and a beautiful stainless steel watch I was sure I'd seen before.

"That's Lover Boy," the General said. "Why're you here"?

"You guys won't believe it! Robert and Tony kept snorting cocaine until they finished it all. After sniffing the last gram, Tony harassed Robert for more money but all he had left was me. I never thought cocaine could change someone so much and so fast. He just handed me like I was any old twenty. 'This isn't enough. We can't buy shit with this! We need more money,' Tony told him when he saw me. Then he noticed Robert's watch. 'Is that a Tag Heuer original?' Robert told him it was. 'My mother gave it to me when I started university. I'm not going to give my watch for more coke. Forget it.' That's when Tony turned on his slimy charm. 'I understand why you like your watch so much. I'd do the same if I were you. But don't worry man, we'll give it to Hilario for some more coke, and tomorrow I'll give him the money back and get the watch for you. Simple, simple. I've got the money at home but I don't want to go there now. Come on let's go man. Tomorrow your Tag will be back on your wrist.' Robert bought the story and they drove back to this horrible place."

"So what happened to Andy? What happened after those kids left this place?" we asked Lover Boy.

"Same old, same old you see when people use drugs," he said. "They drove off heading downtown. Finally Tony said, 'Let's go to a friend's apartment and continue partying there.' I guess he expected Robert and Andy to agree. Robert, of course said yes. But Andy had had enough and even though you could see Robert's answer depressed him, he asked Tony to drop him off so he could catch a bus home.

"I figured this was what Tony wanted. He knew Andy had a strong personality and wouldn't change his mind. He needed to dump Andy before he could convince Robert to stop using drugs. Tony stopped at an intersection. Andy had the door open and one foot in the pavement, and made one last try. 'Robert, come on, man. Come home with me, enough is enough. Don't screw your future.'

"You could tell," Lover Boy said, "that Andy knew it was now or never. I knew this, too, cause I saw the look in Robert's eyes when he looked at Andy. Robert's eyes had that gleam when you're in the grip of coke. His body only wanted to inhale more. 'I know what I'm doing,' he told Andy. 'Go on—go home. Who needs guys who aren't cool?'

"So, Andy had no choice and got out without saying goodbye. He looked like one depressed guy as we watched him disappear into the distance behind us. I can understand it. Those two had dreams, I've listened to them plan how they will build up their own construction company, build the tallest building in New York. Robert was going to be the godfather of Andy's future kids. Now none of this will happen."

The General, as usual, interrupted Lover Boy. "This is what happens when humans use cocaine—it grips you fast. It's seductive and makes you feel so great you never want to feel any other way. It grabs you like a boa constrictor—except you don't notice until too late how it eats into your decisions and judgment and turns you into an idiot. Then one day you've lost your job, lost your best friends, maybe your girlfriend or wife, and the only people you have for friends are other cokeheads. Now you don't have any money but you feel as though you're constantly being gnawed from the inside by your need to get more, whatever it takes. Sorry for interrupting, Lover Boy, but sometimes I just can't contain myself. I've seen too much."

"That's okay, General. There's not much more to say. Tony and Robert used up all they bought on the first trip here in a few short hours. It was Robert who took me out of his wallet and passed me to Tony along with his watch. 'Let's go buy more' were the last words I heard from Robert, and here I am with you guys."

## 4
# Colombianos

We were kept in a box that held $100,000 exactly for more than four days. I dreaded the future but even then couldn't imagine what was in store. As it turned out, I would be making the bloodiest voyage a hundred-dollar bill could make.

I, and thousands of other bills just like me, would enter a currency stream for a black market commodity. The sums of money involved meant that the commodity dealers would stop at nothing to protect their crops, their processing facilities, their distribution chain, and their personal bank accounts and all that that could buy: women, land, swimming pools, social and political position, prestige. Anyone who stood in the way was tortured and slaughtered. These commodity merchants are drugged on money. They are merchants of death. I came to understand how the trade for drugs, particularly by young people with disposable incomes who "just want to have a good time" in developed countries like the States, Canada, Britain, Holland affected not only their own lives but also destroyed families and killed innocent people in countries like Colombia. All I saw on this voyage and the way it began with Robert and the way it ended compelled me to tell my story.

Hilario never left the house and only turned on the lights when he packed money. The necklace of keys to the three locks that protected the room never left his neck. He had breakfast early in the morning before the smaller dealers and addicts started to arrive. But mostly he loved to sit and look at all that money piled in boxes. I could see how he let his imagination fly as he stared at us.

He received no phone calls. The landline was disconnected so nobody could trace his calls. He used his cell phone instead.

On the fourth morning something unusual happened. Hilario dressed up. He put on a decent shirt and sprayed on some Calvin Klein lotion. It was the first time that room smelled anything but awful.

Then he sat on the bed expectantly. Finally his cell phone rang. "*Hola, habla*, Hilario," he said when he answered it. "*Si señor. Si señor.* Everything is well packed and all in hundred bills."

As an American dollar spending most of time in New York I'd learned that knowing Spanish was essential. You hear it daily in the streets, inside buses, banks, and wallets. My Spanish was pretty good, but recently I had the chance to really polish it when I ended up in the tip jar of a Hispanic nightclub dancer. (She did more than just dancing; but that's what she called herself.) At home she only spoke Spanish; her boyfriend was Spanish and her clients were all Hispanic. From the moment I fell into Hilario's hands, I'd be grateful to that dancer for the time that she kept me.

At first I was puzzled by some of what I heard. I understood the words but they didn't seem to make any sense. As always, the General filled me in. Part of the conversation was in code, "something very common with criminals," he told me. "But I assume it has to do with the money piled here. I'd bet myself that today is going to be collection day."

"Collection day? What do you mean?" I asked him.

"I mean the Cartel will be sending some very hard men to pick up their money."

"Cartel money? I thought all this cash belonged to Hilario?" I was confused.

"Don't be stupid. Do you really think a humble guy like Hilario, with zero education, owns all that dough? He's just an illegal Colombian immigrant who is used by the Colombian cartel to sell their drugs. He's paid to never leave this place and look after their drugs and money. But it's the guys like Hilario that end up in prison. He's just a tiny fish in an ocean of sharks."

"Hilario should run away with a few mill from this room and never be seen again." I was trying to be funny.

"He'll never take one cent of it because his family would pay the consequences in Colombia. I can see you have no idea what the Cartels are, but I think you'll be finding out soon," the General added dryly.

That morning, Hilario didn't open the door to any of his clients. Punctually at two in the afternoon the doorbell rang twice. Hilario didn't even have to open the door because the collectors had their own key to the house. I could hear them greeting one another. Beyond greetings we could hear there were no formalities; they all knew why they were there. In moments, Hilario brought three well-dressed men straight to the back room. One of them was a Caucasian with a strange English accent that I never figured out the origin of, and the other mainly two spoke Spanish. The one who gave the orders was a man with dark Armani glasses, dark hair loaded with gel and pulled back into a tight little ponytail. He wore a thick golden chain outside his shinny black shirt. He pronounced his words a little strangely. I looked hard at him and could see he had a slight part in his moustache that looked like a scar.

"I know that guy," the General said. I'd never seen the General look so wary. "I don't want to begin to imagine what will happen to us if we end with him. He's a known assassin. His co-workers call him Half Lip behind his back—because no one would dare say it to his face. No one ever jokes with him because if you do, you always loose. The Colombian cartel put him in charge of looking after their drug shipments and moving their money. Besides being a good organizer, he's a ruthless killer and no one under him would ever contradict him. One of his duties is to threaten and if needed, finish off the lives of those who don't follow cartel orders."

This was definitely not what I wanted to hear. I was so scared and overwhelmed by all the General told me that for once I had nothing to say, no jokes to lighten the moment. And as if what he'd already told me wasn't bad enough, he had more.

"See the other two? Watch them. Check how they never take their hands away from their waists. They know Hilario is one of them and wouldn't betray them, but they still carry guns in case something goes wrong. In this business you don't trust anyone, especially when there's this much money involved. There'll always be someone ready to steal it and these guys know this very well if only because they've done it to others. So they always come prepared for the worst-case scenario."

Hilario showed them the boxes of cash. "This is the money, all in Benjamins and one box of twenties. Please count it before you leave."

The guy called Half Lip stepped closely in front of Hilario, took off his dark glasses, and replied loudly, making his lip defect more evident, "Why do you want us to count? It looks like you are not sure."

"No, no." Hilario said. "I just want you guys to count it so things are clear." Hilario tried to appear confident, but I could see he was scared. I was trying to stay calm even though I knew I was going to end up in their hands. Hilario tried to smile but the three men had faces of stone and stood with an eerie still-ness with their hands close to their waists. The atmosphere was tense.

"Check a stack," Half Lip ordered one of the men, who grabbed my stack and counted us dollar by dollar.

"The amount is correct, boss."

Half Lip turned and looked at Hilario. "There are many stacks here and we don't have enough time to count them all." Now he lowered his voice and said in a quiet and menacing way, "Hilario, if we find there is even a dollar missing we will come back and get you. And if you are not here we will go and get your family in Colombia and you know what will happen to them."

Hilario's eyes widened. He knew this was a serious threat, and he quickly reassured them. "Don't worry. I counted the money and is okay and please tell the boss to send more drugs. Demand is growing. Gringos love dope."

The three men opened all the boxes and dumped us into blue heavyweight plastic bags. When each bag contained $1,000,000, it was tied off with a plastic strap and numbered with a tag. The men took the bags out to a waiting van parked out front where they loaded them into the cargo area of a van. The van was white with tinted glass and had a Plumbing company sign painted on each side. It all happened so fast that we didn't even get to say goodbye to Lover Boy who had been left behind in a box with only a couple of hundred dollars in it.

Half Lip's two underlings got into the van. We noticed a car parked in front of the van with a fourth person sitting at the wheel. "Ah, the watcher," the General said. "He'll stay two blocks ahead of the van and will report police road blocks or anything suspicious. This'll give the guys in the van the time to take an alternate route without drawing attention to themselves."

Half Lip got into a dark BMW sedan parked behind the van. "He's escorting and van and monitoring it's movements," the General told me.

By now, I knew the General knew way more than he was letting on. But in a way, that was okay with me. I'd already had enough information for today. But, still, I was sure glad he was there.

The three cars drove several blocks until they came to cross Bronx Expy, where they joined the flow of traffic. They drove for more than twenty minutes, staying in phone communication and getting instructions from Half Lip. Inside that bag it was impossible for me to know exactly where we were heading, but seeing the way we were packed I was afraid this was going to be a long trip and I was going to be packed and tied for a long time.

Then we heard Half Lip tell the van passenger who had left his phone on speaker. "Go to the boat warehouse." I looked at the General, but he had nothing to say. As we approached I could hear the gulls and the wind, and I could even smell the ocean. We slowed and I heard a large door rolling up. We slowly crept forward. I assumed we were in the warehouse.

We stopped and could hear car doors opening and Half Lip yelling to the drivers, "Get bag number one here. Now." Fortunately, we were in bag number two.

The place sounded echoing and empty but as if by magic, we heard new voices as they said hello to Half Lip with kind of nervous respect. Someone grabbed bag number one and walked away.

"Do you see no one counted the money?" the General said. "Apparently they believed in Hilario's word. But if for any reason one dollar is lost Half Lip is there to recover it any way he can."

Minutes later, one of the men came back and said, "Everything is okay. The area is clear, so you guys can go."

# 5
# Money Launderers

"TIME TO LEAVE! WE HAVE ONE MORE STOP TO DO." HALF LIP yelled as he approached the driver's side of the van. "Take the second bag and pass it to the front and have it ready when I ask for it," he said, turning his attention to the car passenger.

"*Si señor,*" the man said as he stretched his reached into the back seat and moved us to the front. He laid the bag half open between him and the driver, giving me a little to peak out to the outer world.

"Take Cross Expy, turn left on Broadway and follow me from there," Half Lip instructed.

"*Si señor,*" the driver replied as he turned on the van and punched the accelerator, steering with one hand and holding a cigarette with the other. Once en route he glanced at the passenger. "This is the way to Manhattan."

"*Si.* Probably we are going to that same office in the financial district, where that nice lady is … you know who I am talking about," the passenger replied as he lit a cigarette.

"You better not mention her name. She is the wife of a big boss." The driver sounded respectful.

"*Si.* I know. But still she is nice"

" Yes, she is beautiful, but remember the rules when we started working here. What is not yours; you do not touch, you do not take, you do not mention, you do not even dream about. And remember that rule not only applies for money and drugs. It also includes their woman. Man, I don't want to end like Antonio." The driver's voice thinned out as he said this name.

"Don't tell me you also believe Antonio was murdered by the bosses. Antonio just did not want to live in New York and that is why he disappeared. I bet he is some place having fun. Vegas probably." The passenger laughed as he said this.

"Don't laugh, I know he was killed."

"What? But he didn't do nothing," the passenger protested, grinning.

"For you and for me he probably did nothing, but for the bosses he did when he alerted one of his friends that the *señores* wanted him dead and they considered it as treason. After being killed the office made this rumour that he is still alive."

"How you know all this?" The passenger's eyes narrowed with suspicion.

"I was the one who threw Antonio's remains into the Hudson River. Antonio is dead, dead."

The passenger looked perplexed. He probably didn't have the nerve to ask for more details, but hazarded question. "Did you know he was going to be killed?" He didn't take his eyes off the driver.

"Yes, I knew. But I had to stay quiet."

"But he was our friend. You could have warned him." His voice was tense—maybe because he was confused.

"Man, there is no friendship in this business. None, *nada*. I am going to give you advice. Shut your mouth if you do not want to end with him in the bottom of that river. Forget what I told you and pretend you believe he is still alive."

The passenger just sat there. He looked pretty stunned, unable to believe what he was hearing. The General and I looked at each other. I expected him to say something, but he didn't say a word. Later, I wondered if he was quiet because he wasn't surprised by this story or because he was surprised that the driver had told him what had really happened to their friend.

They drove in silence for at least half an hour as they negotiated the traffic. I wondered what each was thinking. Perhaps the passenger was wondering what he had really gotten into; maybe the driver was regretting his life. Who knows? After veering sharply to the right, the driver slowed and carefully looked at both sides of the street, his head slowly moved from left to right. "This is the intersection where we are suppose to meet Half Lip," he said.

"Hey, don't worry. There's Half Lip in his new BMW."

The passenger pointed his finger to the other side of the street. I heard two honks. One was our van; the other I suppose was the BMW.

"Follow him, follow him," the passenger said hurriedly.

The van made several turns and then, unexpectedly, the driver hit the brakes.

"Here comes Half Lip,"

Suddenly, Half Lip was standing beside the passenger side of the van. "Give me the bag, fast," he snapped.

The passenger handed him the bag through the open window, giving him a tentative smile. I could see the passenger was nervous, but he was trying to remain calm. Half Lip grabbed the bag, giving the passenger a hostile look.

"You can go now. Tomorrow we will do some more merchandise movement. Meet at the usual place, ten o'clock."

He walked away, our bag gripped under his arm, pressing us against his body as he headed to an office entrance. He pushed open a double door and walked down a long corridor. The place sounded like a huge office; people typing, phones ringing, names being called through intercoms, the type of atmosphere you feel in busy offices in New York.

"You guys know where we are?" I asked the other bills.

This time the General replied. "Honestly, Benjamin, I have been in this place before. I knew we were coming here since day one with Hilario."

"Why you didn't tell me? I thought we were friends!" I felt betrayed.

"There're certain things in this dark business that you don't understand unless you go through them," the general replied. "I have to let you learn by yourself. You're still too naïve about the drug trade."

*Here we go again with the General and his professor attitude,* I thought. But I bit my tongue. I needed him and I knew he meant well.

"So what are they going to do with us here?"

"We'll be sent to Colombia; that's when we'll see our real owners."

"The Cartel?" I asked timidly.

"The Colombian cartels, which are a *bit* different," he said, emphasizing the 'bit'.

"So what's this place, then?"

"Actually," the General said, "this is a legal business."

"How can this be legal with a man like Half Lip walking through this place with one million dollars made from drugs under his arm?"

"Good question, son. This is a money exchange and wiring office. Immigrants come here to wire money to their families in South and Central America. It's kind of like Western Union, but with better rates and fewer questions. All transactions made here are legal. The Cartel uses this legal business as a cover to their multimillion-dollar money laundry business they run on the side. Half Lip isn't here to wire all that money the legal way. In places like this, you're only allowed to wire two thousand dollars before you have to explain the origin. Half Lip is here to send that million dollars the illegal way."

I was still confused. "How can a business be legal and illegal at the same time?"

"Benjamin, better you see firsthand how this unfolds. You'll understand the magnitude of what they do here better. Take my word for it, you have to go through it, you definitely have to go through it. And the good thing is you will." Now he was being sarcastic again.

Half Lip walked straight to a door at the end of the corridor. I could sense how he opened it and slowly popped his head in, turned the lights on, then opened our bag and put it on top of a table. He pulled out a wooden chair and sat next to us. The room seemed to be located at the opposite end of the office entrance. It looked like an old and unused kitchen, probably used as storage now, a place not many people had a reason to come into. Chairs were stacked in the corners; piles of folders lay in open cabinets, and the air felt heavy. A few minutes later a young man in his early thirties and a beautiful woman with big brown almond-shaped eyes and long straight brown hair came in. The woman was dressed in pale blue from head to toe. She was the kind of woman who attracted everyone's attention when she entered a room. The room was sweetened by the scent of her perfume.

"*Buenas tardes,*" the woman said, trying to keep her distance.

"*Hola,* Sofia *Como estas*?" Half Lip replied, also with some distance. Half Lip then set us on the table. He was here for business.

"Give me a second," she said. Then, with the help of the other man, she slid a bookshelf to one side. It covered a small entrance. She took out a pair of keys from her purse, opened a narrow door, went in first, and flicked on the lights. Half Lip followed her, carrying the bag holding us. The other man took a position guarding the narrow door. We were in large windowless office with a desk to one side and four counting machines sitting on a table in the middle of the room. The doors to three huge walk-in safes on one long wall were closed but they were clearly big enough for a man to stand inside. Quality leather chairs, original paintings, antiques, a tiffany lamp in the middle of the ceiling illuminated the whole furnished room. The wooden desk shone like crystal and beside the desk was a brown leather sofa with cream cushions. It was all very expensive and tasteful.

The woman sat at the desk and removed some documents from a drawer. "Bring me the money," she said, as she fastened her long brown hair into a ponytail. "How much money is here?"

"Each stack has $100,000. Ten stacks; a million dollars," Half Lip replied confidently. "Tomorrow I will bring you more or less the same amount. We didn't bring it all today because the boss does not want to take chances."

"Yes, I know what you mean," she said. "Police roadblocks are more common each day. They are not always searching for drugs, more for terrorists and bombs. But looking for them, they can find us."

"Yeah, I know," Half Lip responded, glancing at his watch.

Sofia walked over to the table, rapidly unwrapped the money and placed us in the counting machines. I was okay with that. I love the tickle these machines give. Still, I'd never object to being counted by those beautiful, delicate and perfumed hands, either. Four machines at high speed don't take long to count a million dollars. She put the money back on her desk and said, "The amount is correct."

Half Lip nodded. "What do I tell my boss about arrivals?" Half Lip asked.

The woman opened her purse, took out a small calendar and flipped through it with a tiny silver pen. "Tell him we will deliver this money and the money you brought yesterday to Colombia in ten days. Make sure he knows we charge fifteen percent."

"We know that, Sofia," Half Lip drawled.

The man who had accompanied the woman stood quietly in the doorway, his eyes on Half Lip. He didn't have that obvious criminal look that Half Lip had, but I knew he was there to respond if the situation ever got out of control for some reason.

The woman stood up and gave Half Lip a small piece of paper with some numbers, her signature and some kind of stamp on the bottom.

"She's giving Half Lip proof that he has given her a million dollars," said the General.

"That's it?" I exclaimed. "You can't prove anything with a piece of paper."

The General smiled. "Benjamin, Benjamin; this is a business where people believe in your word. That is why 'you lie, you die.'" He smiled again.

Half Lip folded the paper and put it into his wallet. Then he asked casually, "How is your husband?"

Sofia's eyes widened a little in surprise. "He is okay."

"*Señora*, my boss asked me to send many regards to your husband."

Sofia smiled. "I will let him know. But please excuse me now, I have to leave." It sounded like she was trying to end the conversation.

Half Lip nodded to the man standing in the door, put his black glasses on and walked over to him. They chatted in low voices then stepped out into the outer room, too far for me to see or hear. Then Half Lip silently closed the narrow door.

A few moments later the man came back to the office.

"Is that disgusting man gone?" Sofia asked.

"*Si*, don't worry. Half Lip is gone."

"Why was he talking to you? Remember he is a remorseless assassin. No friendships with people like that!"

"No Sofia. It was something completely different."

She looked at him still standing at the entrance, then gave him a sexy look and said in a seductive voice, "Francisco, come in closer. But first—lock the door."

He smiled, resting his right hand on the doorknob. Sofia, sitting on top of her husband's desk with her legs crossed, opened her arms to embrace Francisco as he walked toward her. He pressed his body to hers; they kissed as if they were given only two minutes to love in life. Sofia nestled into his arms. Her sighs and accelerated breathing filled every space of that office. But I knew that wasn't a problem, because the General had told me he knew it was soundproof.

"Calm down, calm down," Francisco said as Sofia passionately kissed him. "Sofia, you must listen. There are rumours about us." He tried to gently disentangle himself a little. "That is what Half Lip just said to me."

"What?" she shouted, her body now stiffened. "What did he tell you?" Now she was taking deep breaths and her eyes had widened.

"He said how lucky I was to be always next to a beautiful lady like you. But then he said that I was taking too much care of you, and that I should be careful. He finished by saying, 'Walls can see and hear.'" I could sense anger in his voice, "Sofia, Half Lip and your husband are friends. If he finds out about us it will be Half Lip who will come calling. I know he is merciless."

Francisco hugged Sophia hard and then, with one arm on each shoulder, he asked her to listen. He spoke gently.

"Sofia, I love you, but we have to get away before Carlos finds out what is happening between us."

"I don't think he will care," she replied, but I could see a growing wariness in her face and her eyes glistened with tears. "I know he goes out with other women. I even know one of his mistresses is pregnant! It is his turn to feel like I've felt all these years."

"Yes I know. But don't forget he will kill us just for pride. Sophia, we have to be very careful." He looked at a picture sitting on the desk. It was Sofia and her husband on their wedding day.

"Hey Benjamin" said the General, " have a look at that picture. You recognize that man?"

I looked and the penny dropped.

"Shit, it's the elegant old fox who flirted with Sara at the Bank! Then she must be his wife!"

"Yes Benjamin, she's his wife, I know them both."

"Those two are a pair of cheaters," a fifty dollar note from a bundle next to ours chimed in. "I know her husband very well. His name is Carlos. I've been in this office many times. The Colombia cartel calls him Whirlpool, for his ability to clean money. Many's the time I've heard Francisco and Sofia plan to escape to an island in the Caribbean and take a big amount of money with them so they don't have to work one more day in their lives. I think Sofia loved Whirlpool when they were first married, but he cheated on her so much that she looked for love somewhere else, and now she seems deeply in love with Francisco. She's in charge of the legal money transfer business, but when Whirlpool is not around she comes to this office and deals with people like Half Lip.

"What's your name?" I asked the fifty-dollar note.

"Ulysses."

"Thanks for the info, Ulysses."

The table rocked back and forth for a while, then a few minutes of silence. "Go outside and wait for me in my office," Sofia said, buttoning her shirt. She let her ponytail down, ran her fingers through her hair, and quickly applied some lipstick. Then she grabbed us from the table and put us in one of the safes, checked it twice to be sure it was locked, and left. All would be quiet until the next day.

I used the silence of the night to get more information about money launderers. I was still confused. Fortunately the General was in a talking mood. When he wants to he's good at explaining things clearly. "General," I said, "I still can't picture what money launderers are, or how money laundering works."

"Don't worry Benjamin, it took me awhile to figure it out, too. Money launderers are people and companies that use their reputation and company infrastructure to disguise the origins of money gotten through illegal activities. They make it look like it was obtained from legal sources. Take us. We and all the other bills here are money made from drugs sold in New York. We're called dirty money. When we reach Colombia we will be clean money."

"But how can these companies be considered legal?"

"The money launderers have companies like the money exchange, which in theory are profitable. But most of the money this money exchange makes comes from the 15% they charge to clean the money the drugs dealers bring them. Just think about it. If they clean two hundred million dollars, they will earn thirty million just like that. Believe me, there are money laundry offices in New York that clean way more than that a year. Are you still with me?" the General asked.

"So far, so good," I told him.

"Money launderers' offices have nothing to do with that dive where they sell drugs. These are stylish offices, located at prestigious addresses in the most elegant areas of New York and the other big cities. They're a perfect front, because few people question their activities. I mean, outwardly they are successful and legal but the reality is they move billions of dollars made from the sale of illegal drugs."

Finally, I began to see that the drug business is a chain of intermediaries that make billions from the bad decisions of young kids like Robert or from desperate people who turn to drugs to numb out misfortune. Even though it pissed me off when the General called me naïve or talked patronizingly, I now knew he was right. I had just begun a journey and already

I had passed through the hands of consumers, drug sellers and now I was in the hands of money launderers. Sheesh, I hadn't even reached real owners yet!

I was not a happy camper at the thought of going to Colombia. I didn't know much about the place, but what I had heard was not inspiring. Even I knew my hope of being deposited in a bank account was naïve. I'd heard what Sofia said. We were on the verge of being physically transported to the Colombian cartel so they could avoid being tracked by police through bank deposits, cheques or money transfers.

# 6

## Exposed

THE NEXT MORNING WE HEARD THE SAFE HANDLES MOVING.
"Hey guys someone is opening the safe," the General said. In
seconds a tall, thin man in his late forties entered the vault. I
recognized him from the bank, the same elegantly dressed man
wearing little round glasses, a crisp white shirt with the sleeves
rolled loosely up his forearms, and a blue tie with stripes of
different colours. It was Carlos, or Whirlpool, as I now also
knew him. Definitely the old fox who had flirted with Sara
at the bank. Even though I had a better idea of what he was,
I had to admit he didn't look like a cartel gangster. He wasn't
showy––no Rolex limited editions or gold neck chains. He
looked like a New York CEO, not a man who would attract the
attention of investigators. He rapidly moved bundles of money
to his desk. As he laid our stack down I saw a framed university
degree on the wall behind his leather chair. It was from Stanford
University, a degree in economy to Carlos Gomez. Whatever
else he was, Whirlpool was a well-educated economist, a gradu-
ate from a prestigious university.

"How can a guy like him be involved in this type of business?
I asked the General. "I mean, he's a Stanford grad!"

"Benjamin, humans are driven by greed. They love money because we're the motor that runs this world. This means money has the power to corrupt."

Suddenly, the door to the office opened and in a swirl of colour and a haze of scent, Sophia entered and walked over to the desk and stood next to Whirlpool who was seated with the money in front of him.

"Did you count the money?" Whirlpool asked.

"Yes, honey, I did. It's all ready to be sent."

"Did you use the machine or you counted by hand?"

"The machine," she said smiling.

"I always like to count it by hand, I don't trust those machines," he said as he began swiftly working his way through the bundles.

Standing behind, Sofia massaging her husband's head lightly, running her fingers delicately through his hair with her fingers,

"I love you," she leaned down and whispered in his ear. "I love you."

He stopped counting, looked at her. "I also love you." He held her gaze and smiled, but he seemed distracted, a little distant. For sure not sincere. He started counting again then stopped and looked at her.

"It is better if you go home, Sofia. There is nothing urgent here. Go have lunch with a friend. I will be with you later. But in thirty minutes I have an important meeting so you will have to drive yourself because I need Francisco here."

Sophia looked uneasy, but I could see she was trying not to show this. She swallowed hard and kissed her husband on the forehead. "Don't come home late tonight, my darling," and she smiled provocatively.

Whirlpool ignored her comment and smile and just looked at her through the upper part of his glasses. She stopped at the door and glanced back "Is there something wrong?"

Whirlpool stared at her, looking like he'd like to say more, but eventually settled with "No honey. Everything is okay. Just go home. I will see you later. *Te amo.*"

She stood looking at him thoughtfully for a moment, and then walked out of the room. As she was leaving I saw she was pushing button on her phone. I was sure she was trying to reach Francisco.

Whirlpool finished counting and stacked all of us neatly on his desk. Then we heard the doorbell ring three times.

Whirlpool checked the security camera next to his desk. "Come in," he said.

The door opened slowly and someone I thought I was never going to see again entered. Half Lip with two men in tow came through the door looked every inch the assassins they were.

"I don't like this one bit," the General intoned.

Half Lip shook Whirlpool's hand. "*Hola señor. Como esta?*"

"Not too good; not too good," Whirlpool replied, looking at the other two men. "Are they the ones doing the job?"

"Yes sir. And also I am going to help because I do not like that son of a bitch."

"I want you to tell me what is really happening between my wife and Francisco," Whirlpool said calmly and seriously.

"I am sorry to tell you *señor* that Francisco is sleeping with your wife. She has been seen going inside a motel room with him." Half Lip sounded sure of himself, and he looked a bit smug.

"Have you seen them?"

"No sir."

"Then all are just rumours?" I heard a sigh of relief coming from Whirlpool.

"Many people have seen them, believe me." Half Lip was trying hard to sound convincing.

"Let's bring Francisco here," Whirlpool said. "I will ask him to phone Sofia but not tell her he is with us. How they speak to each other might tell us if they are really having an affair." I figured he was grasping at straws but his voice was hopeful.

Half Lip looked unhappy with this. "Sir, do not go around this issue so much. Just do what you have to do."

Whirlpool looked lost. "And what is I have to do?"

"The Colombian way. Kill the son of a bitch. Why do you think I brought these guys?"

"Listen, listen," Whirlpool said. "You know I use violence as a last resort and these are only rumours. Apart from the fact my wife is involved, I have to act with prudence."

"Boss, I am sure Franscico will kill you if he has the chance. You can not let that rat live."

Whirlpool sat in silence, thinking. Silence and tension filled the air for a couple of minutes. Then he got up, walked into the outer office calling, "Has anyone seen Franscico?"

"*No señor,*" could be heard from various people, and we heard the voice of a young woman say nervously, "He went to buy some lunch at Latin To Go. Is over by Union Square. He said he would be back soon."

Now Whirlpool was really irritated. "I need someone to go find him and tell him to come back to the office. Now. I've been calling his cell phone and he doesn't answer."

The young woman, without knowing what she was about to unleash said, "Francisco, he left his cell phone here and it has been ringing all since he was gone."

"Give it to me" Whirlpool ordered and returned to the office, his eyes gleaming as if he had just discovered a treasure. Then, as if afraid of what he had found, he handed it to Half Lip, who turned on the call history display.

"There are twenty unanswered phone calls made from Sofia's phone in the last two hours." He showed the list to Whirlpool. "*Señor,* does this tells you something?" Whirlpool grinned. Suddenly the cell phone rang.

"It's Sophia," Whirlpool said softly as he glanced at the call display. It rang several more times. "I don't want to answer it without having Francisco near." They let the phone ring. A moment later it rang again, but it was a text message tone.

"Give me the phone," said Whirlpool. In a soft, haunted tone, he read aloud. "'Don't go 2 offce thnk C knows call begn plan 2day.'"

One glance at Whirlpool's face, both emotionless and ruthless, anger flickering in his eyes, told me what would happen. I suppose Sofia, possessed by anxiety and desperation, had sent a text message. But it only made things worse.

Half Lip and his friends looked like rabid dogs waiting for their prey. Fifteen minutes later the office door opened, and Francisco walked in with the innocence of a lamb not knowing it was to be slaughtered.

"Do you need me, boss?"

Whirlpool looked at Francisco, his face poisoned by jealousy and rage.

"Sit down, Francisco," Whirlpool said.

Francisco looked to one side of the desk straight at me lying on the top of a bundle, but there was nothing I could say. I felt indescribably helpless. Then he noticed his cell phone lying open. His face filled with confusion as Whirlpool yelled at him, "Are you going to sit or not?"

Francisco quickly sat and looked at Whirlpool. You could see Whirlpool struggling to stay calm. He drew a deep breath and pressed his lips into a hard line. His face was red; his jaw trembled. He was a man ready to act from the hate in his heart and not with his mind. And whether we wanted to or not, we were in a perfect spot to watch events unfold.

Half Lip rubbed his hands together, as if anxious for the job to start. "Bring me two tablespoons from the kitchen drawer," he ordered one of the men.

*Spoons?* I wondered. *Two spoons?*

Alex Barr

Francisco sat there, looking confused. He still didn't realize his relationship with Sofia was out in the open, but he knew something was wrong. Whirlpool's hands formed tight fists; his breathing grew heavier as he stared at Francisco.

"Do you know that beautiful things usually have a high price?" he asked him.

Francisco had no clue what his boss was talking about.

"How long you have been fucking my wife?" Whirlpool cried out. "I am talking to you." Whirlpool's eyes met Francisco's for the second time

"I don't know what you are talking about," Francisco said as he tried to stand up. But his denial lacked conviction.

"Where are you going?" Whirlpool screamed as his left fist hit Francisco's chin with so much power it knocked him to the floor. Whirlpool was transformed into a raging bull. He kicked Francisco's head and face repeatedly. He didn't want to hear the truth coming from the mouth of his wife's lover. Francisco just lay on the floor bleeding. He'd probably realized he wasn't going to come out of this alive.

Whirlpool grabbed Francisco's cell phone then picked up a chair and smashed it against a wall until it broke.

"How could Francisco be so stupid as to think Whirlpool wasn't going to find out someday?" I asked the General.

"Humans are like that," he replied. "They usually regret their actions when it is too late."

He was right. I'd seen this myself all too often. Humans bull-dozing along without a thought for the consequences, acting with their hearts and not with their minds, not noticing the danger until it is too late.

Francisco was lying in the floor, his hands covering his head, waiting for whatever was next. Half Lip and his two men were prowling around the desk like wolves tiring their prey, anxiously waiting for the pack leader's final order.

With hate blowing out of his eyes, Whirlpool stood over Francisco.

"Who helped you when you came with nothing to this country?"

"You, *señor*," Francisco choked out in a gargling sort of way.

"Who used his contacts so you could get accepted at NYU?"

"You, *señor*"

"Who helped you buy your first house?"

"You, *señor*"

"Who always told you he loved you like a son?"

"That was you, *señor*. *Por favor…*" Francisco was making whimpering sounds now.

"Shut up," screamed Whirlpool. "You think fucking my wife is the way to repay me?"

Francisco just whimpered. What could he say? Suddenly Whirlpool's anger seemed spent but he seemed even scarier as he looked down at Francisco in a cold and calculating way. Finally, Half Lip couldn't contain himself and stood up.

"Don't delay this shit anymore. Let me finish the job."

"No, no, no," Whirlpool replied.

"Carlos, do not let these criminals kill me, please! I beg you. I can explain to you what happened!" Francisco pleaded from the floor. He must have known he was walking on thin ice. Whirlpool grabbed Francisco's cell phone and dialled Sofia's number and put it on speaker mode. She picked up after three rings.

"Hi, finally you called me!"

Whirlpool, once again straining to hold his anger, passed the phone to Francisco who was still bunched up on the floor. He refused to talk and closed his lips tight. Whirlpool opened his drawer, took out a pistol and pointed it at Francisco's head. I heard a metal 'klink'.

Whirlpool then whispered in his ear. "Tell Sofia to calm down because your relationship is not known yet."

But Francisco, probably knowing he wasn't going to leave the office alive, screamed, "Sofia, I am in Whirlpool's office. They are going to kill me. He knows everything." He was still screaming his message to Sophia when Half Lip and one of his killers went into action.

"They are going to kill me; they are going to kill me," Francisco kept yelling, but it was in vain.

The third man jumped in. While the other two men held Francisco down, he stuffed a wet rag into his mouth, and then covered it with duct tape. They struggled as Francisco writhed but they soon had him face down with his hands tied behind his back and shoved as high to his shoulders as they could.

Whirlpool picked up the cell phone. "The bitch hung up." He threw the phone against the wall.

Francisco was rolled on to his back. Whirlpool tried to relieve some more of his hate by kicking Francisco's head, face, and stomach. Tears and blood streamed down Francisco's face, and his muffled grunts told me that his nose was broken and the blood flowing from it was making breathing difficult. He looked terrified.

Whirlpool stopped kicking him and turned to Half Lip. "This is enough."

"What do you mean with this is enough? Are you trying to tell me you are going to leave this guy alive? He knows too much about the organization. The upper bosses will come to us if they know we let someone walk away alive." He paused, looking hard and somewhat disdainfully at Whirlpool. "Whirlpool, you know this man cannot go out alive from here. You know that."

Whirlpool sat on his leather chair and shook his head.

"He's in a bind," the General said. "If he kills Francisco he has to kill Sofia, too. But if he doesn't kill them, the cartel will kill him. Not an easy decision." The room was silent except for Francisco's laboured breathing. Whirlpool stared blankly at

Francisco but I could see a look in his eyes that I had seen in good people.

*Please rethink what you are going to do,* I silently implored. I kept watching his eyes. *You are a good man. Let him live.* But my thoughts had no effect. He gave his former friend one last glance then looking Half Lip straight into the eye, screamed "Do what you have to do." Then he stood up and walked out of the office.

Half Lip, looking at Francisco, said in a light-hearted tone, "He is done with his part. Now comes my part."

Francisco raised his head groggily, but Half Lip forced him to remain face down, his right cheek pressed to the ground. It was then that I knew what the two spoons were for. He opened a bag he always seemed to carry, took out a pair of surgical gloves, and donned them with the skill of a doctor and with the coldness only criminals have. He walked toward Francisco, beating out a rhythmic tattoo with the backs of the two spoons. Francisco squeezed his eyes shut.

"He's squeezing his eyes closed because he knows the Colombian cartel uses spoons to take out the eyes of their enemies while they are still alive." the General told us.

"What? He's going to do that now? In front of us?"

"Yes, I'm afraid so" the General replied.

I wasn't ready for something like that. I never would be.

Half Lip moved efficiently and pried open Francisco's left eye, his thumb on the lower lid, his index finger on the upper lid. He inserted the spoon behind the upper part of the eye, pressing down in a scooping motion, lifted the eye from Francisco's socket, the eye ball balancing on the spoon.

Francisco was still conscious and even though his screams penetrated the wet rags in his mouth, no one helped him. His muffled screams filled all the room. His body trembled while his executioner, grinning, showed his left eye to the rest, as if it was a trophy. He passed it in front of Francisco's right eye. "Let's do the other," he said, matter-of-factly.

I couldn't believe what I was seeing.

"How can humans be so cruel?"

"This is nothing," said the general. "Wait until you see Colombia."

Francisco could hardly see through his right eye with all the blood flowing from the left eye socket and the tears of pain and impotence flowing from his right eye.

Then Half Lip's cell phone rang. "See who is on the phone," he told one of his men. He peeled back the gloves and he dropped them on the floor.

"Boss, is Whirlpool."

"Answer and tell him I am busy. Ask him what he needs." He was looking for something in his bag.

"He said, 'No more torturing. Just finish with the job.'"

Half Lip sighed. Then he pulled on another pair of gloves and grabbed a short rope from his bag. He rolled in his hand and leaned over Francisco, saying coldly, "Your suffering is going to finish." He tied the rope around his neck and strangled him until his hands and legs stop struggling and his heart slowly stopped beating.

Half Lip again peeled off the gloves, closed his bag, and smoothed and straightened his clothes as if brushing off what he had just done. He called Whirlpool. "Don't worry *señor*. The man is gone." He listened for a moment. "*Si*, I will look after it." He paused then said, "About Sofia, *señor*. She is not going to make a fool of you. I will find her myself and make her pay for what she did."

Francisco's lifeless body lay next to the feet of his killer. Half Lip looked at him, moved the body a little with his left shoe. "You looked for it man," he murmured. He turned to his men. "Okay, wrap this *mentiroso* for the morgue." The two men rough-handed Francisco on to sheets of plastic they already had laid on the floor.

Ulysses, too, had seen this before. "They will take the body to the morgue that Half Lip referred to. It's a house a few blocks from here. There they will open his stomach and put heavy rocks inside, close it again and late at night they will throw his remains into the Hudson River. His body will sink because of the rocks and soon enough there will be no evidence left of the torture or even of the body itself. It will be business as usual in this office, as if nothing had happened."

I had nothing to say. I was so shocked by what I had seen that I needed time to recover. What was really beginning to gnaw at me was the General's comment that this was nothing compared to what I would see in Colombia. It chilled me every time I thought about it.

But right now, I needed to remain calm.

# 7
## Customs

EARLY THE NEXT MORNING WHIRLPOOL AND HALF LIP MET at the office. They opened two safes and I was lying on top of a stack at the front. Neither mentioned what had gone down the day before. Half Lip opened a bag he was carrying and took out several hundred-dollar stacks. All together there was about thirty thousand. He walked into the safe where I was and exchanged those dollars for several stacks near me. He looked at Whirlpool, who smiled and winked.

I wanted to know where these new dollars had come from. The General also looked intrigued. "Hey guys, where're you from?" he called out. None replied. It was as if they were deaf.

"Let it go," Ulysses said. "Those bills'll never reply. They're counterfeit. They're dead." I looked at them more closely. Who better than one bill to identify another and sure enough, they were counterfeit.

"Half Lip and Whirlpool always change a few legit bills for counterfeit bills. They exchange small amounts to avoid being caught. About twenty to thirty thousand from every two million," Ulysses told us.

All the same, one of the stacks placed by Half Lip didn't look like counterfeit bills to me. They looked crisp and not overly used. I tried to start a conversation with them but something stopped them from speaking. I looked more closely. Light reflected from a lamp in the ceiling of the safe let me to see their faces clearly and I still couldn't see anything wrong with them. I asked them again if they were okay and some replied in soft, thin voices, "No."

"But you all look in good condition."

The General, our battle-seasoned veteran waded in, "What's wrong with you guys? Why aren't you well?"

In a creepy, thin voice one replied, "We've been skinned alive. Some criminals have put a different skin over us."

The General didn't need to hear more. "Now I know what's happen to them. They're another form of counterfeit money. They started as legitimate one-dollar bills. They've been washed with acid to erase all their color and numbers and then on that same original paper they've been printed with all the marks and signs of hundred-dollar bills. This type of counterfeiting is much harder to detect."

Our conversation was interrupted by Whirlpool's ringing phone. He spoke for a few minutes then told Half Lip, "We have to organize the money. They will soon be here." Stack by stack, they emptied all the money inside the safes included the counterfeit and stacked it high in the middle of the table in the office.

Around noontime we sensed some movement of people outside the office. Whirlpool sat in his leather chair and watched the surveillance camera.

"Get prepared," he finally said, "the customs guys are here."

Half Lip seated himself at one of the back corners of the table, facing the room. Whirlpool stayed in his chair and called, "Come in. The door is open."

Two men stepped through the doorway. One was a white-haired, white American, the other was Hispanic and looked a bit younger, probably because of his dark hair and brown skin tone. They might have been the same age, early fifties, casually dressed.

Alex Barr

"*Hola, señor* Carlos," the Hispanic said. The other guy didn't seem able to even say *hola* but they all greeted each other with embraces. I figured the white guy couldn't speak Spanish because they all switched to English.

"How are you?" Whirlpool asked them both. "Why do you came so late? I was waiting for you since early in the morning. Are there any problems?" Whirlpool can look intimidating when he wants to––like right now.

"Sorry, sir," the American said, "we didn't come earlier because the boat isn't leaving tonight. It's been rescheduled to leave tomorrow night."

Whirlpool took his glasses off. "Listen to me, Eric. We are not dealing with eggs here. This money belongs to the Colombian cartels and when there are any changes of plans you guys have to inform us. Is that clear?"

"Yes, sir." Eric said, trying to swallow his fear.

Whirlpool then looked at the Hispanic. "*Esta claro?*"

"*Si señor,*" the man replied, looking at his partner.

"People can get killed for doing shit like this," Whirlpool said, speaking to himself more than anyone else.

Half Lip was quiet throughout this exchange, almost like a cold statue. But his eyes recorded every single movement.

The two men looked at each other nervously. Then speaking politely, if hesitantly, Eric asked Whirlpool, "Is that the money, sir?" He pointed at us.

Whirlpool nodded. "Please count it."

Both men rapidly counted through the two hundred stacks of ten thousand dollars each. Half Lip glowered in his dark glasses on the opposite side of the table, his hands close to his waist. The visitors' glances kept returning to him. They seemed to be intimidated by Half Lip. They probably sensed, like me, that he enjoys assassinating any human being.

The visitors recounted the money and put us into sort of sports bags. In the hurry, our bag was not zipped to the end, and that short narrow opening allowed me to see and hear better. They shook hands with Whirlpool—no embracing this time. Both tried to ignore Half Lip as they left the office, but turned back when they heard him say from across the table, "Hey guys, be careful next time. One mistake in this business can cost a lot … *a lot.*" They both nodded and left. Neither said a word as they made their way out of the building.

They walked to a nearby parking lot and headed to a black sedan parked in the most isolated spot. They crammed themselves inside. Eric took the driver's seat.

"Let's head to the port now," he said.

"Goofball. We're not in uniform. You know we can't enter the port without uniforms," his partner replied.

"Shit Juan, those guys make me so nervous I forgot I didn't have my uniform on." said Eric, smiling.

Both stepped out of the car and put on light blue jackets they had hanging from the roof handles in the back seats.

"Now let's go. We gotta make sure this cash goes inside that container tonight." Eric said. And we were off to what I assumed were the New York ports.

"So these guys are what?" I asked the General as we sped along.

"They're customs employees," the General muttered.

After awhile the car stopped at a red light and Eric looked at Juan. "Y'know, I didn't like the way Carlos talked to me at the office. Those Colombians think they can intimidate anyone. He knows as well as I do that ship scheduling changes. He could've called if he was so worried. You know, man, I'm thinking I'll ship this money and that's it. I'm done. I don't need this anymore, Thing is, I've been thinking about this for a while. I mean we could end up in prison!"

Juan stayed quiet. "What'd you think?" Eric asked.

Juan said nothing for a couple of beats then, "Listen Eric, we have been receiving money from the Colombians for quite a long time. We just can't walk away like that, not with them. I want to get out of this and go back to Puerto Rico with my people. I have saved enough to go there and live like a king. But we have to act with discretion. If they get to know we plan to withdraw, we will not be able to enjoy one penny of what we have made."

Eric didn't look totally convinced. Apparently Juan's answer took him by surprise. "You didn't tell me that when you introduced me to them," he said.

Juan looked impatient. "Eric, you are acting like I had forced you into this. Remember how happy you were when you got your first payments? You act different now because you do not need the money anymore. Tuitions are paid, mortgage is paid. You have money in the bank. You have travelled the world. You even helped your sister pay for her house. But tell me, where did you get the money to do all this? Not from Custom's paycheque. It was with the money those Colombians pay us. And only now you are thinking on the consequences?"

Silence hung in the car for a while. "So you're telling me we can't get out of this?" Eric asked. " I mean this isn't drugs we're shipping. We just ship out money." Eric sounded disappointed.

"That means the same to them. In the end, all is about money, isn't it?" Juan said, smiling.

Eric punched the steering wheel with his right fist. "Why the fuck did I end up doing this?" he yelled.

"Some people call this easy money, but I don't think it's that easy when your life is always crossing the line," the General whispered to me.

The car continued on for several blocks, made a few more turns, and then stopped in front of a huge gate.

"Juan, your turn to swipe the card. I've used mine more than yours and I'm worried about drawing too much attention."

"Who is on today?"

"Garry."

"Okay, but what is the story this time?"

Eric thought for a moment.

"If he asks where we're coming from, say we were at a meeting. He won't ask. He's not a keener, just moonlighting for some extra dough. But don't forget he can search our car. Be careful."

"Always am, man," Juan went out and seconds later I heard the sound of metal gates moving. For sure, we were at the main entrance of the New York ports. Juan was back in moments. "Did Garry see you?"

"Yes, but he just waved at me."

"Cool," Eric said.

Juan nodded. The car moved slowly for another hundred yards or so and stopped again. "I don't like this second gate; they search every vehicle no matter who you are." Juan said. "But don't worry. Howard works this shift, and he knows we are coming. He is also on the Colombian payroll." Both their eyes met and they smiled. The car stopped moving and we sat waiting.

After about five minutes Eric and Juan were really impatient.

"Come on, come on," Eric said in a low nervous voice.

"Here comes Howard," said Juan said finally, in a low voice.

Eric rolled down the window and a figure rested his arms on the open windowsill. "Hi guys. You loaded?" a voice whispered through the window.

Eric nodded.

"Okay here's the drill. You pretend you open the car trunk for a search. We've got a new guy today. I don't want him to think I let you through without a search. So let's do this." In a louder voice, he said, "Open the trunk."

Eric winked at him, opened the door, and was gone for less than a minute. The search was fast, but probably long enough to appear thorough.

"Looks good. You can go now. Thanks!" I heard Howard say loudly.

In seconds Eric was back inside the car.

"Howard was scaring me," Juan said.

"Yeah, I know. That's why we have to stop doing this soon." Eric said firmly, as he turned on the car.

Juan just nodded. They drove slowly as if trying to go unnoticed and stopped at the main door of an office building with a sign reading "International Customs Brokers." Juan snapped up one bag and Eric grabbed the other. They made their way quickly toward the front office door. Eric looked at Juan and turned the knob. The door was open. They walked in, put their bags on top of a round table sitting in the center of an office. The table had remnants of delivery food: open soda cans, two empty pizza boxes and used napkins.

"The boys were here already," Juan said. "They must be around."

Eric checked his watch, walked to the window and punched some numbers into his phone.

"Julio, where are you guys?"

The rest of the conversation was in code and I had no clue what they were arranging. Eric hung up and looked concerned.

"What happened?" Juan asked.

"We have to leave the bags in here and lock the doors. They can't come now. They've had word that DEA plans a sudden check today on several containers. They can't take the risk."

"So what will happen then?" Juan asked.

"They'll move the money after the DEA have gone. Once the heat is over they'll get the call from inside--you know what I mean?" Juan nodded and looked at the bags on top of the table. They each grabbed a bag and put us inside a small closet, turned the lights off, closed the door and disappeared.

*Now what? What's next?* I wondered anxiously. A thousand different scenarios bombarded me at once.

"Calm down, calm down" the General huffed. "We're money. Those guys have no intention of abandoning us here. No one in this world abandons two million dollars. They're just waiting."

It was nearly midnight when we heard a noise from rusted door hinges along, with two voices. "Don't turn the lights on," one said.

"Eric told me they left the bags in the closet. Go get them," the other voice ordered.

The closet hinges were loud. I didn't know if it was rust from the sea air or that the place was so silent that any noise was noticeable. Holding the closet door with one hand and moving a flashlight with the other, a man found right away––well two sports bags of money are not that hard to miss, lying on the closet floor.

"Here they are," he murmured quietly to his friend.

"Open them and have a look, just to be sure the money is what's inside. I don't trust no one." his partner replied in a whisper. Our bag was the first one he opened. A small light coming from above pointed at us. All was dark behind that; the man, the office, everything. Identifying his face was impossible with his flashlight in front of his face. But I was able to see he was wearing a dark blue, or maybe black, uniform.

"It's all good. It's money," the man said as he grabbed the bags and pulled us out.

"Bring the money here. We have to do some planning first," the other man said. I guessed he was the leader since he was giving the orders.

"Listen up," he said. "Howard's going to cut the power to the security cameras at exactly one a.m. We only have twenty minutes to remove the security locks from the container, unscrew a twenty-by-twenty-inch metal plate from the container internal left wall, place the money inside the hole, screw the plate back, close the container and place new security locks. Remember only twenty minutes to do that. It's all the time

Howard can give before this section of the port goes into an alarm mode and we don't want that. Now take the money from each bag and put it inside these transparent plastic bags." He took out a roll of bags.

"What're these for?"

"They're a new type. They seal perfectly and are specially scented in case money search dogs are brought in. They're also used to smuggle cocaine. This is the latest technology in Colombia." Both smiled.

"Split the money into six bags," the leader continued. "It'll be easier to fit six small bags inside a hole than two big bags."

The man rapidly redistributed the money into the six plastic bags. At least we could see through the transparent plastic. Each man took three bags and walked out of the office, heading north toward the docks. They stopped in front of a massive stack of containers ready to be shipped, stowed under a lifting crane. They slowly approached the bottom one.

"Check the bill of lading. It should say Cartagena," one of them whispered.

"This is it," the other said."It says it's carrying two new Mercedes Benz, final destination Cartagena, Colombia."

"Yeah, this's the one."

They looked at each other and smiled and laid the bags beside the container. While one held the flashlight, the other removed the security locks placed by customs personnel, which could be easily have been one of their colleagues. He also removed a red sticker that read in big letters INSPECTED. Then he pulled the doors open. He quickly took a small screwdriver from his pocket and used it to remove four screws that held a metal plate covering a hole in the container's left sidewall.

"That hole is going to be our home until we reach Colombia," the General said.

The man put in four bags with no problem. He pushed hard to fit in the fifth. Ours was the last one. "There's no room for this one," he said, showing our bag to his partner.

"That hole is made for two million dollars in Benjamins, and that stack has to go in!" the leader insisted. The man pushed and tried again, but nothing

"What's wrong? Put that bag in! We've only got eight minutes left!" His partner was visibly worried. The man's hands trembled slightly. I could sense the blood rise to his face. He took all the bags out of the hole.

"If they don't fit now this container will go with just the five bags," he said.

"That's not gonna happen," the leader replied. The Colombians already paid for two million dollars. You better make this work. Push harder!"

This time our bag was the second to go in, and three more went in easily. The man pressed the last bags hard until he finally managed to fit that sixth one in.

"Screw that plate fast, we only have four minutes left. Time's running out!"

With some help from his partner the man screwed the plate back into place. His partner closed the doors and I heard them place the security locks. "Let's go! Two minutes left." We listened as they walked away.

Speaking from experience, the General told us all that the new locks would be identical to the ones the men had removed and would even have the same serial numbers. The idea is that these locks can only be used once, and each has a different code and seal so that they are unique. However, if you have access to counterfeit money, you can also have access to counterfeit locks that are extremely difficult to detect.

That hole was as dark as the security safe in a bank. But it was as hot as hell and as humid as a steam bath. But none of that scared me. I was preoccupied with what was waiting for us once we arrived in Colombia. All the terrible stories I heard from other bills flooded my mind.

The next day my worries were confirmed when we heard the crane engine start. We felt the container lift, move, and then drop gently. Shortly after this, amid a lot of noise and voices, we heard a siren announced the ship's departure. Soon we felt the rise and fall of a ship underway. Outside we heard some men talking and learned we were travelling on *El Conquistador*. Our destination was Colombia.

## 8
# New York to Cartagena

We sailed down the east coast of United States and made a short stop in Miami, which is what we heard people talk about outside. After four long, hot days the ship reached the Colombian coasts and docked in Cartagena.

A temperature above 40 degrees welcomed us to the tropics. Inside that metal container the humidity rose as the minutes passed, and in Cartagena you could feel the water in the air. Humidity is our worst enemy. It was probably noon when I felt the container lift then felt it move around and descend.

"We're back on solid ground," the General announced.

"That means we're now in Colombia?" I asked timidly.

"Where else?" he replied. "And you'll soon know why we're here."

"*Este contenedor se inspecciona mañana,*" a loud male voice said firmly––"no inspection today," he insisted.

"I see nothing has changed in this Colombian port," the general said. "Customs won't inspect this container until tomorrow, so the cartel's people have time at night to get us out of here. That man giving the orders outside is probably the customs inspector. It will be his men coming tonight. Be prepared, Benjamin."

As the hours slowly passed fewer people milled around our container. By midnight all was silent, which began to scare me.

"It won't be long, now." the General muttered.

Thirty long minutes later we heard the security locks silently release. "*Rapido, rapido,*" we heard from outside. The plate screws came out one by one, and within seconds a big black man wearing a green coverall pulled us out. A second man standing behind stacked the bags. It took them all of fifteen minutes to retrieve the six bags and a minute to put the plate and locks back in place.

The tropical air was a combination of humidity, salt and dust. I could hear the sound of soft ocean waves slapping lightly against the dock, and the distant smell of fish in the breeze reminded me where I was.

"Let's go." one of the men said. "Let's get this money to the boss."

They each grabbed three bags and walked to a small old Ford parked few yards from the container. They tossed us into the back seat and drove away, slowing down at the port exit. The port gates opened wide, giving the car time to disappear in the streets of Cartagena.

"Check and make sure the second vehicle is escorting us," the driver said.

The passenger glanced back. "*Si*, it is two cars behind us."

"Contact them and tell them we are going to the building on the beach side, not to the downtown house as planned."

I looked questioningly at the General. "They always change routes at the last minute in case there is an ambush planned," he said. This was the General's second voyage to Colombia in the hands of drug dealers and I guessed he was reliving his previous trip.

The driver was driving carefully if seemingly erratically. At the last moment he swung hard down one street, then turned into another then another. When they were satisfied that they weren't being followed by police or any other car, he began to drive with more purpose. We soon pulled up to the back door of a building where three men, each holding a rifle, waited.

"*Cómo estás?* Do you bring the bags?" one of them asked. The other two stepped behind pointing their rifles straight into the car.

"*Si, si,*" replied the driver, smiling.

"Take the money out and come with us. The Yankee is waiting for you guys."

The men lowered their guns, smiling a little. No problems here.

They took an elevator, and we stopped on the twentieth floor. The doors opened to what I think was the penthouse. The men walked down a bright marble hall down to a white double-door entrance, where a young man stood guard with a rifle leaning next to him.

"Who are you?" he asked, his eyes fixed on the bags of money.

"We are here to see the Yankee."

"Wait here," the man ordered, as he opened the apartment door quietly and escorted the two men into a large entrance, opulently decorated. The floor was polished like a mirror, and two bronze statues rose like pillars, each inset in the walls either side of the door. Busts and paintings from renowned artists displayed the owner's wealth. Beyond the hall, to the left, I glimpsed a big glass-topped table with four men playing cards. They all wore colourful shirts, half open to show off their chests. Each had a pistol sitting beside him on the table.

"Take a look at this place," I said. "It's a showroom for what money can buy—though a bit tasteless."

"Yeah, this man buys all this because he believes if something is unique and expensive it must be good. But he doesn't have a clue about the historical and artistic value of the objects he owns."

"Who is he, anyway?"

The General smiled and eyed a sofa next to the balcony. "That, Benjamin, is the Yankee."

The Yankee? There was a tough-looking man, well built, with thick brows and one blue eye, the other green. His skin was acne scarred. He was dressed in pointed leather boots, dark jeans and a yellow shirt that matched the colour of his golden Rolex. He sat on a shiny red sofa with one white blond girl on his right and a dark skinned girl on his left. Both were beautiful, and young enough to pass as his daughters, although I'm sure that they were not. He lifted his big body from the depths of the sofa. He was tall, at least six-three. His rough voice filled the room.

"Come in guys," he said. The Yankee shook hands with the two men. "Are these the six bags from the New York container?"

"*Si señor,*" one of the men replied.

"Follow me," said the Yankee, as he walked out to the penthouse terrace and made his way to a bar next to a medium-size circular pool. He poured himself a whiskey.

"This was a good job," he said as he drained his glass. "Please serve yourself," he added, politely.

"*No, gracias señor*. We have to leave fast. Remember, three containers are also arriving tonight from your people in Los Angeles."

The Yankee smiled with satisfaction then gave a low whistle. In seconds, a young man was standing by his side.

"Do you need me *señor*?"

"Yes, take those six bags and count the money." The young man took us inside and laid us on top of a beautiful old antique desk.

Lying there I was able to take in more of the apartment. It was glass-walled in all the rooms I could see. The living room and dining area had a view of the Caribbean ocean. The exterior glass walls looked thicker than usual, maybe bulletproof, and

I guessed that the closets were loaded with the latest fashions. I'd seen my share of wealth, but I'd never seen a thug with this much wealth.

I also noticed this big display cabinet on one wall. "What's with the Star Wars stuff?" I asked the General.

"You must understand, Benjamin, the life span of a drug dealer is so short they spend their money on things that are meaningless to most people. Most of them went through poor childhoods, maybe even were homeless and grew up on the streets. They jump into this business as a way to make a fortune and have what they were deprived of as kids. The story on the street is this Yankee is a big Star Wars fan. I've heard his collection is worth several million dollars. For every guy like this one there are at least two who died trying to reach that dream, and a third in jail. Only a very few become drug lords; and even they only stay in power for about five years before they are killed by rivals or sentenced to life in prison."

*This is no easy money,* I thought. "You say he's called the Yankee?"

"Yeah," he replied, "but some also call him 'The Doctor'. This man is one of the bosses of the Colombian North Atlantic coast cartel, and has strong ties to paramilitary groups."

"But why's he called the Yankee?"

"No one really knows how he got the nickname. Some say it's because of his Caucasian features; others say because he is a New York Yankees fan. I do know he was born in New York. His parents were Spanish immigrants and lived there for part of his childhood until the family moved to Colombia."

"This means he is a US citizen?"

"Yes. And that has allowed him to travel back and forth between the two countries––that is, until he became one of the most wanted men by Interpol and the DEA." The General started to get his impatient look. Suddenly he blurted out, "When is this dog cleaner going to finish counting us?" He looked darkly at the young man patiently but quickly counting the money by hand.

"Why'd you call him a dog cleaner?"

"That is what Colombians call the people who do small jobs for drug lords. They have a really low place in the hierarchy in the cartel and they're usually the ones who end up in jail or dead. They pretend to be important, driving their boss's cars and carrying their guns. They own nothing, but they love doing what they do. They're common within Colombian cartels."

Dollar by dollar the dog cleaner's dirty, rough hands counted until he confirmed it was the same amount Whirlpool said he would deliver.

"*El dinero es correcto señor*," the dog cleaner announced.

"*Guardalos bien*," replied the Yankee.

We were rewrapped with new plastic and marked with a "W."

"The Yankee's an organized man and keeps careful records of the source of every dollar he receives. He's not an easy man to cheat, but if you do and get caught, he would show no mercy. One day he's going to catch Whirlpool and Half Lip and I hope we won't be around when that happens," the general said.

Looking satisfied, the Yankee picked up his phone and walked on to the balcony. As he admired his view of the Caribbean, he phoned Whirlpool.

"*Hola* Whirlpool. *Como estas*?" The Yankee sounded serious. "I received the cargo and it is complete. Does this money come from Hilario's sales … Next month I will ask Hilario to get more money for you. I can see you are fast in delivery."

With that he ended the call. He swirled the ice inside his glass of whiskey and said, looking at his men, "Never build up friendship with the people who work for you. That way you don't have to hesitate killing them when they deserve it."

The room crackled with tension but everyone just gave an exaggerated nod of agreement.

"Take that money to the room and stack it in the P section," he ordered the dog cleaner. The young man took a last sip of his whiskey, grabbed us, and left.

The dog cleaner took us down a hall off the entrance and stopped in of a door. He punched in a security code, and the doors opened on to one of the biggest amounts of foreign money I had ever seen in my life, and believe me I have seen a lot of money. There was money from all over the world: British pounds, Japanese yens, Euros, francs and Canadian dollars. But not a single U.S. note. It was almost impossible to walk through the narrow aisles in that room; the piles of money were piled above the dog cleaner's waist. Boxes of money to the left, boxes of money to the right. The dog cleaner hesitated a moment, looked around and walked out of the room, carefully checking the lock when the door closed. He stood in front of the next door and punched in a code. I could smell the American dollars in this room. And this was the room where the Yankee kept his U.S. dollars. It felt like being back at home. This was my family. There was as much money in that room as there was in the safes in the largest banks in New York.

The stacks of U.S. dollars were piled by sections, and each section was marked depending on where that money was going. There were sections that said Guerrilla, other sections said Paramilitary, and others had people's names––important Colombian politicians, according to the General. The cartels financed all these groups and individuals so they could freely grow and sell their drugs.

*There's enough money here to corrupt any good government,* I thought.

The dog cleaner put us in the section marked Paramilitary. "I don't like this," barked the General. "Those groups have inflicted appalling atrocities on ordinary Colombians."

I calculated there was probably close to three hundred million dollars stored in that room, mostly in Benjamins like me. It was hard to believe all this money was owned by one man; it was harder to believe that we were hidden in an apartment in the middle of a city where, the General had told me, more than half the people lived in poverty and went to bed hungry every night.

The General said, "We're U.S. dollars here. We'll move through the hands of drug dealers and gangsters. This won't be the first place we will see this much money. We'll see many places loaded with money made from selling drugs in the U.S.—well, pretty much around the Western world, really. This is why we're here. Prepare to be stained with the blood of innocent human beings, Benjamin. These people will kill for us. They will burn entire town and villages for us. Innocent boys and girls are going to die because of us."

I was surprised by his speech. I'd never seen the use of drugs from that perspective. Ever since I had rolled off the press as a crisp hundred-dollar bill, I had thought we were made to bring happiness and joy to whoever carried us. I never thought we could cause so much suffering. I thought of Robert and those guys who went to the bank and used me to purchase the cocaine. If Robert had known what I now know, maybe he would have had the strength to say "No" when Tony offered him the coke.

But the General hadn't finished. "I was in this country before. Drugs brought me here that time, too. Believe me, nothing good will come out of this trip."

The General paused and then slowly began to speak again, but quietly this time.

"On my first trip to Colombia I met a beautiful Colombian ten thousand peso bill. Her picture was on both sides of the note. She was thin with long black hair, and she was known as Catalina, the Indian. We spent time more than a year inside the wallet of a paramilitary commandant who controlled an area known as Magdalena medio. We lived in the jungles, participated in attacks, and saw innocent people die. Soon I could distinguish what type of arm was being fired just from the sound of it. I saw the paramilitary destroy towns and villages. Many times the commandant's bloody hands touched my paper. I despised him, but we bills don't decide who we stay with. He always kept us together and I came to believe my destiny was to stay in Colombia forever. That destiny changed one rainy October day when the paramilitary went to town to visit his wife and kids. He played with his children all afternoon. We knew he only saw them for about three hours per year but he still sent a cheque every month.

"At five he told the kids to stay in the yard, then he and his wife went upstairs and made love for thirty minutes. After that, his time with his family was over. He gave a hug to each child, a last kiss to his wife, and walked to the truck he had parked in front of his house. As he opened the truck door, he noticed a black jeep with tinted windows and four men inside, watching him. He knew something was wrong and reached for his pistol. But it was too late. The drums of three AK-47 assault rifles emptied bullets into his body. We could hear the bullets pierce his flesh. After seeing him fall lifeless in the street, three of the men walked over to be sure he was dead, their rifles still smoking. One of them put two more shots in his head.

His kids and wife had run into the house at the first round of shots and watched through the window how the husband and father they never really knew was murdered by criminals like him. That day I was separated from Catalina. One of his killers checked his wallet, looking for information that could lead them to the rest of his group. But he just found us. He kept me and gave Catalina to his partner. We had no time to say goodbye, and the last thing I remember is seeing her being rolled in the hands of that criminal.

"I never heard from Catalina again. A few months later the biggest bank robbery in the history of Colombia took place.

Alex Barr

All the millions robbed were in ten thousand-pesos notes. After that, the Colombia government took the ten thousand pesos out of circulation so the thieves couldn't use them. They replaced the beautiful Catalina for a different woman. She was a white blond Spanish patriot named Policarpa. This is the ten thousand pesos that circulates today. They say that she's also a beautiful and attractive woman, but I haven't had the pleasure of meeting one yet.

"The killer who took me went straight to a bank and exchanged me for pesos. The next week I was sent back to the U.S. in the wallet of a young tourist. But with drug consumption increasing in America, it didn't take me long to start a new voyage to Colombia."

He sighed deeply. "Here I am again. The more drugs people use the more we will travel to countries like Colombia. At the moment, this country is the world's biggest producer of cocaine. That's the reason we've ended up here."

We were all listening closely to the General when Ulysses abruptly interrupted him.

"So Colombian currency has women on their notes?"

"Yeah," the general replied. "Other countries have them too."

"Not us U.S. dollars," Ulysses replied indignantly. "I don't understand why our government goes around the world preaching about women's rights and gender equality, but they don't put women on their bills. Are they saying there haven't been any important women in the history of United States? A women who deserves to be perpetuated in a note?"

The General smiled. "I don't know what goes in the minds of the people inside the department of treasury, Ulysses. Maybe the bosses there are gay.

"Just because the treasury bosses decide to keep men on the U.S. bills doesn't make them gay. I think you talk too much, General."

The General was silent for a while, then, "Well if that is not the case, there must be a reason why they don't like girls"

The General then looked at me smiling. I just nodded.

Unfortunately, I had to listen to a whole bunch of other opinions; but eventually we came back to the simple reality: we were owned by a drug lord called the Yankee, and we were packed in a stack of dollars inside an apartment in Cartagena, Colombia, ready to be delivered to the paramilitary groups.

"Going to the paramilitaries is not a good sign," the General said. "We could be sent to the combat zone."

"Who are these paramilitaries?" I'd never heard of them before.

"They are criminal organizations formed some years ago by drug dealers and rich farmers to combat the growing guerrilla groups. Politically, they're the extreme right and the guerrillas are the extreme left. But in reality, both groups fight for control of all areas of production and transportation of cocaine and heroin, which are their major source of income. Now there's all-out war between them, which means hundreds of thousands of Colombians have been killed, more than three million others forced from their homes and off their land, and the country's infrastructure is in ruins."

"But the Colombian government's got an army. I mean, they're the government. Why don't they get tough?"

"The Colombian government tries to combat them, but both groups are better equipped than the country's armed forces. They have to fight two armies on constantly shifting fronts. The paramilitaries and guerrillas have way more sophisticated equipment than the army. They've got way more money––look around this room––with the billions of dollars they make from selling drugs to kids like Robert they can easily buy the best. Drug dealers like the Yankee also give a quota of money to both these groups as a form of protection."

Alex Barr

"Be quiet, be quiet!" Ulysses yelled. "Check out that light shining beneath the door. Someone's outside." The door slowly opened and the Yankee, backlit by the corridor light, stood staring at his piles of money, staring the section labelled paramilitary. Staring at us. That unsettling sensation came back to me.

"What's he here for?" I was scared.

"He's coming for money, for you and for me," the General said.

The Yankee yawned, and then began moving twenty stacks of $100,000 each at a time. Our stack was the second one moved into a leather bag. When he was finished he took us down to the underground parking lot where a brown 4 x 4 Toyota with two men inside waited for him. Again, there were no formalities as he passed the bag to the passenger. "It is two million dollars divided in stacks of $100,000," he told him.

The passenger opened the bag and looked inside, his eyes scanning the stacks.

"We'll give this money to 01 today," the passenger said. "He needs to buy more arms and ammunition. The war is escalating."

The Yankee smiled. "He can use this money for that. Next month I'll send some more."

The driver and the Yankee shook hands. "We don't have much time. We have to leave now. Thank you for your assistance, *señor*."

They placed the bag on the floor between the driver and the passenger. The 4x4 eased out of the building and after a few blocks turned into an empty street and moved quickly away from the city. The smell of the ocean gradually disappeared as we left the coastline behind.

I expected to hear the General or Ulysses, who had also been picked up in the stacks the Yankee grabbed, speculate on our final destination. But they said nothing. The landscape began to shift dramatically. We began driving over badly paved second-ary roads and jostling about in the bag like a bucking horse.

"This route's probably a shortcut to avoid the main roads. There're lots of police and army check points on the main highways. Hard on old bones," the General said. I could see this made sense.

We tumbled around in that bag for more than five hours over rougher and rougher roads, sometimes passing deserted areas. We could feel a change in the air temperature as we left the coastal zone, which was fairly humid. It began to feel warmer and damper and the light from the sun, which had risen as we travelled, dimmed as the truck entered deeper and deeper into a dark, at times, black jungle. We crossed two bridges. One sounded metallic, the other swayed as if it was a cable bridge.

"It's in these dense Colombian jungles that the criminal organizations hide their laboratories to process cocaine and other illegal drugs. They also use the heavy foliage to camou-flage their combatants and armaments," the General told us.

They must have had a lot of rain because the roads were slick, muddy trails. But those guys drove like rally drivers, and they managed to reach a security ring without wiping out.

"This guy, 01, where we're headed is a top dog in the para-militaries. Nobody can pass the first ring without being autho-rized by him, not even this car." the General said. "He's the law of the region, the most powerful man around."

"What's with the classy name?" I asked the General.

"Paramilitary commandants and drug lords use numbers to be identified. The lower the number the higher you are in the hierarchy. 01, what we might call 'Number 1' at home, is the lowest number so therefore the highest you can reach. As I say, he's top dog."

The driver slowed as he saw a wooden barricade in the centre of the road. Armed men surrounded the vehicle.

Alex Barr

"Who are you?" one asked, pointing his gun at the driver and not moving his finger from the trigger. Another man with a shaved head, shiny from sweat and sun, approached the passenger side. "Get out of the car," he ordered hitting the door with his hand, both eyes wide. These two seemed to know each other, but the stares didn't look friendly.

Both men slowly opened their doors and stood by the car. The driver, showing little emotion, stuck his hand in his pocket, took out a small plastic card and handed it over.

"I am one of 01's couriers, you can check my ID with the central station."

Both the guard and the driver smiled and the tension eased. But they still confirmed the driver and passenger's names by radio. The car was immediately authorized to continue. 01 was waiting for them. The General whispered this was the north Atlantic paramilitary group with an army of 6,000 men distributed along the Colombian northern coast. 01 was their leader.

We drove for another forty-five minutes before reaching the entrance to the farm, which was also the checkpoint for the second security ring. "At least another hundred armed men form this ring," the General said in a low voice.

The car stopped in front of a closed gate. A man dressed in a military vest approached.

"01 has been waiting for you guys all day." He smiled and ordered the gate opened.

The driver parked the mud-spattered 4x4 close to the entrance and walked with us into the house. Armed men standing at the main door and corners nodded as we walked through. At the end of an echoing corridor three men sat around a table talking. Two of them, wearing suits but loose ties and an open top button on their shirts, spoke Spanish but had strong German accents. The other man, wearing a military vest, looked Hispanic and spoke Spanish like a native speaker. I knew he was 01.

He was the opposite of the Yankee: short, dark skinned and he had a rather soft melodic voice that didn't match the ruthlessness we had heard about listening to the driver and passenger discussing him as they drove here.

"His enemies say that what life didn't give him in size he has in balls," the driver told the passenger. "Everyone, not just his enemies, fears him. Police. Army. Guerrilla. The man has never lost a battle because when he fights he fights to win. He is known as the boss of the bosses."

Alex Barr

# 9
## Aquí Voy

I COULD SEE, AS THE DRIVER STOOD HOLDING US, A WALL lined with pictures of all sizes. I could see 01 posing with Colombian army officials. There were pictures of him receiving honours of some kind. There was one of him giving a speech in what looked like a government chamber--maybe a congress or senate--I wasn't sure how the government worked here. Clearly he was no ordinary man.

The driver walked to the table and dropped the money in the centre. I looked again at the three men.

01 cleared his throat. "Gentlemen," he said politely, "we have been bargaining for more than two hours. It is time to close this deal. I have other things on my agenda today."

"Listen, Jurgen," he said, looking at the man on his right. "I like your equipment, but I find it high in price. Remember, you are not the only ones."

The two men tensed, looked at each other and had a quick conversation in German, the whole time their eyes were fixed on the money. 01 watched them, let them go back and forth with each other, and finally interrupted them in what sounded, to me, like fluent German. They looked at each other, startled and puzzled.

"Where did you learn Deutsch so fluently?" the one called Jurgen asked.

01 smiled. "My father sent me to multilingual schools where I learned English and German. I polished my German when I did my masters degree in Frankfurt. My father raised me with the idea that someday I would be the president of this nation."

He looked like he was trying for wisdom when he smiled but it came off as smug.

"Benjamin. Benjamin!" the General said. "Stop staring at the people at the table and take a look at the wall on your left." I drew my eyes to the wall. "See that hundred-dollar note encased inside that crystal frame?"

"The one yelling 'Newcomers! Newcomers!' and laughing?"

"Yeah. He's been eyeballing us and laughing that hideous laugh. I'm sure he's been on that wall for quite a few years. I think I have heard of him." The General raised his voice to be heard. "What're you doing that frame?" the General asked, trying to be polite.

The bill looked at us but didn't reply. He kept yelling, "newcomers," and laughing hysterically.

"What're you inside that frame?" the General asked again, this time upping the volume of his voice and adding a pretty impressive military stare.

The crazy Benjamin finally responded.

"Oh, hi guys."

"Why're you inside that frame," the General asked again. "It's like being caged. I don't get it."

"01 has kept me inside this crystal frame for years. I don't remember how many." His craziness melted away a little and now his tone was tinged with sadness.

"Why?" I asked.

"It all happened at Galeão Airport, you know in Rio de Janeiro," he said. "That day 01 saw the world's best soccer player, Pelé. He walked right up to him and asked him for his

Alex Barr

autograph. Pelé said okay and asked for some paper. 01 pulled out his wallet and took out a one hundred-dollar note––guess who?––and passed it to Pelé along with a pen. Pelé signed the bill, gave it back and shook 01's hand. Ever since, I've been hanging here. He thinks that having me inside this frame is the coolest thing ever. He's always showing me to everyone who comes to the farm."

"These sons of bitches are eccentric," Ulysses interrupted.

"This is not new for me, either." I said. "I also saw some weird stuff in Congress and the White House, believe me."

"Where're you all from?" the crazy Benjamin asked me.

"New York," I replied.

"No wonder you're here. Most bills come from New York, Miami, Chicago, L.A.––big cities like that. But the last few years more are coming from smaller urban areas. What's wrong with people?" He seemed calmer and more rational now.

"I don't know man, I really don't know."

What else could I say?

Even though I wanted to talk with the crazy dude, hear more about his story, I was more interested in 01's negotiations––and my future.

"What are these guys negotiations about?" I asked the General.

"Benjamin, don't tell me you don't know. Think about it. We're money obtained and transported illegally. These people are paramilitary groups. They don't do charity with money like us. When're you going to learn, boy?"

I hated it when he made me feel naïve and innocent about the world.

"I see some of you guys are fresh paper," the crazy Benjamin interrupted. "They're arms traders. *Arms Dealers!*" he screeched.

I looked at the General. "They're buying arms with us to kill people?"

The General nodded silently. I felt a wash of sadness mixed with fear. It was a horrible cocktail. The crazy Benjamin kept blabbering.

"They landed their private plane, their *private plane*, in the farm airstrip today at noon. Noon! I heard 01 call the radar control tower so their plane could move freely over Colombia."

"How can he do that?"

"01 can use money or other persuasive means to bribe any one or any institution in this country. His father didn't make him President, but he has more power than the President."

I turned back to the conversation at the table. Jurgen spoke perfect, if somewhat accented, Spanish. His partner, whose name turned out to be Hans, had trouble speaking Spanish; but Jurgen explained translated into German anything Hans didn't understand about the multimillion-dollar transaction they were about to make. Jurgen and Hans hunched closer to the table as 01 arranged twenty one million dollar stacks, one bundle on top of the other. He had already added the two million sent by the Yankee to the pile. We were in the last bundle added to the stack; so were sitting on top, which gave me a ringside seat to see the transaction. Jurgen and Hans couldn't stop looking at the money as they bargained with their client.

Negotiations restarted when 01 said firmly, "The most important thing for me is punctuality. If you do not deliver the arms on time, victory is at risk. Secrecy is also important for the success of any war." There was no doubt this was an arms deal.

As the negotiations continued, the crazy Benjamin resumed his hysterical yelling.

"You're face to face with Jurgen and Hans, arms traders extraordinaire. They sell the newest and the finest equipment made in Russia, China, USA, England, Egypt and India to this criminal organization. It murders innocent humans beings and destroys the dreams of boys and girls, mothers and fathers. They specialize in terrorist groups like the paramilitaries, or

Al Qaeda, or the Taliban. They sell arms to groups in Africa to murder people who have nothing to do with the conflict. Arms traders and the arms companies need these groups to keep their business alive. Long live tyranny!"

Oh boy that Benjamin could yell—and man, was he crazy.

Then the General added in a quieter voice, "Arm traders will sell their souls to the devil for money. These traders and the arms manufacturers benefit from the consumption of illegal drugs in countries like US, Canada, the UK, and the countries in Europe. They benefit from kids like Robert who use cocaine without knowing their money will ultimately be used to buy arms by a terrorist group in Colombia. The more drugs sold in North America, the more money there is for terrorists to buy arms."

01 looked impatient, anxious to close the deal.

"This will be my final offer," he said. "Fifty percent now and fifty percent when we received the arms." His military attitude gave him a sense of order and discipline.

The arm traders glanced at each other, talked briefly in German with 01 attentively following the conversation. Suddenly, the two Germans smiled and shook hands with 01.

"*Trato hecho.*" Jurgen said. Deal.

They went over the list of arms and equipment they would supply. Rifles and rockets interested 01 the most.

"I have suppliers from England for antipersonnel mines and anti-air equipment," he said.

The Germans carefully went through the list of equipment needed. They both replied, almost in unison, "No problem. We have all you need."

"Good to know," said 01 smiling. He then moved half the stack of money toward them. "Do you want to count the money?"

"No, it is okay," Jurgen replied.

We weren't in that pile of money, but we knew eventually we were probably going to end up with them.

01 then asked, "How long will it take to have the arms here?"

"At the moment," Jurgen replied, "we have a thirty thousand-ton boat loaded with arms in international waters, very close to the coasts of Colombia. We could deliver them next week."

"And how we will know the place of delivery?" 01 asked.

"We will give you a web address," Hans told him. "It is an animated webpage for children. Go to the link War Games. It will ask for a password, which we will provide. Once it opens you will see the list of arms you just gave me. You then hit the link War Location, and there you will see the exact coordinates and date of delivery. However, we can assure you it will be on a beach in the Colombian Pacific Ocean."

01 couldn't hide his satisfaction.

"I like that system and you are delivering in a very good time. I have never seen that before," he said.

Jurgen stepped close to him and said gravely, "You are dealing with the best. There are no intermediaries or middleman. We get the arms directly from the companies and our boats are always stocked to deliver to anyone who has the money to pay for them."

Hans took a sip of water and then picked up the conversation. "We are sitting here today with you and tomorrow we will have dinner with some managers from an arms company."

Criminals in tailored suits. I could see their smug faces. They had to know where their arms were going and even though they probably pretended otherwise, these manufacturers knew these arm traders were the link between them and the terrorists.

The Germans only counted the stacks then did a spot check of some individual notes to make sure they weren't counterfeit. Then they put the money in their bags and asked 01 to contact the control tower.

"We are going back to Panama," they told him.

"How can they walk through an airport with all that money?" I asked.

The General again gave me that professor look. *Wha'd I say wrong now?* I wondered.

"Benjamin, you've seen enough now to understand that arriving at an airport with this much money is no easy task. Basically impossible. But you also know the power money has to corrupt. These people will have good contacts inside customs. They will make sure they will not be searched. Believe me, every human has his, and sometimes her, price."

"I am not sure about that. I've seen many humans say no to bribes."

"Yeah, yeah, yeah," The General laughed. "The bribes you're used to seeing are drunk people offering twenty bucks to a cop to cancel a ticket. Obviously he'll say no. Bribes made to government officials, governors, judges and other people of influence in this country are in the millions of dollars. Believe me, there are still the people who say no to all that money. But is here when the bribes go higher. It's not just money offered but consequences are also put forward. If someone says no to an offer, they will be threatened with death. Or in some cases a close family member is threatened or a son or daughter will be kidnapped. Any relative or parent will say yes under that kind of pressure. Now you understand when I say that all humans have their price."

This was all going way too fast for me. It made my head spin. Could people really be this evil?

01 walked with the arms traders to the plane, shook hands again and ten minutes later the Super King 300 disappeared into the cloudy Colombian sky. He went back to his house bunker, calling to one of his men as he entered, "Go upstairs and try to make contact with front number 12. See what is wrong."

"*Si commandante.*"

"01's got a small control tower to help guide the planes that come in and out of the farm, usually loaded with cocaine or money. He also uses the tower to maintain constant communication with his men in the battlefronts. There're always one or two people receiving reports from the different front commandants, as they called themselves," the General told me.

The crazy benjamin weighed in again. "I know one of his fronts hasn't reported in the last forty-eight hours. In this business this is a long time. They usually report every four hours. 01'll find out what's wrong and one way or another he'll solve the problem. He's an analytical and experienced war lord."

Man, that guy was nuts. Now he sounded proud of the fucker who kept him behind glass.

We heard steps rushing down the stairs.

"*Commandante, Commandante*! We just received a brief message from front 12. It has been attacked by surprise by the guerrilla. Half of the front combatants are confirmed dead and a third of the remaining ones are badly injured."

"What are the damages to the front," 01 interrupted.

"The fight has ended but it is hard to measure the losses." The man looked nervously at 01 and rushed on. "The cocaine laboratory has been destroyed. The whole camp is on fire. Arms and ammunitions have been stolen."

01 looked angry and menacing but you could see his mind ticking over.

"The guerrillas think they have used all their power to make sure we don't recover easily or quickly. I will show them who runs this territory."

There was a silence that seemed to stretch into minutes. Finally, the General broke the silence among us.

"Paramilitary groups and guerrilla groups in Colombia fight for the areas used to plant the coca and transport drugs. They are prepared to protect those territories and routes with fire and blood. Nothing has changed since I was last here," he said quietly.

01 appeared to be trying to fight his anger. He walked to the window and gazed thoughtfully at the jungle for a moment then said, stepping away, "We have been betrayed by someone close. We will find who that was. He or they will regret being born." He turned to one of his men, "Organize the rest of this money. Pack it well. This will be the final payment when we receive the arms."

We were all put in a bag again and taken to the house basement.

# 10
## Royals and Republicans

WE ALL SAT IN THE BASEMENT, TOGETHER WITH OTHER money that had been languishing there for years. None of my colleagues said a word, me included. I contented myself by trying to convince myself this journey to Colombia would be over soon.

On one side of the bunker was a stack of large coloured bills—British sterling pounds notes, all in twenties. I knew from experience that British pounds aren't keen to interact with other nationalities, unless you have some kind of royal title. They rate highly against other currencies and are highly valued worldwide. Not in vain do they have Queen Elizabeth II on all their notes.

After awhile as a different distraction, I couldn't wait any more. I called out, "Hi Brits! How long you've been in this Colombian jungle?"

The Queen from one of the twenties on top replied, her British accent dripping with haughtiness.

"Thank you for asking," She paused, then continued, "Your accent, are you a farmer from America?" She made "farmer" sound like she thought I was some serf.

"Yes, mam, I am American, from a small village called New York, I use to farm in Manhattan."

Alex Barr

I hoped my tone conveyed my sarcasm. She was quiet for a moment then said, "It's a scandal! I have been here for more than a year and these people do not take me out. I know our Royal army will come to rescue us some day. They would never leave their queen in the hands of these wretched criminals."

"Mam, with all due respect," I said politely, "I don't think your army will come and rescue you from this jungle."

"You will die here," the General interrupted.

"Hey, General, don't be rude,. She's the Queen!"

He gave a quick nod, avoiding my eyes, then said loudly, "I don't believe in queens or kings."

She reacted immediately.

"Gentlemen, listen to me. Scotland Yard, SIS, our secret service, will soon have the exact location of this place. They will not abandon me. They will send British soldiers to rescue us from this miserable existence and teach these despicable people a lesson, as we have done in other countries."

I could tell she was convinced she was right.

"Keep dreaming," said the General.

"Please don't shatter her illusions," I pleaded.

"Your majesty. May I reply to what you just said?" he asked.

"If you must."

"You gotta bear in mind this is not the Falkland Islands, where you sent your atomic submarines and bombarded hungry Argentineans who were using obsolete equipment. If the British army comes to rescue you, they'll have to come to the densest jungle in the world, fight against paramilitary and guerrilla groups that know every inch of this jungle. They can smell the snakes."

"Smell snakes?" she said. "Don't be absurd."

"They're immune to local diseases. They have money to buy the most sophisticated arms and equipment available––probably the same or better than your soldiers' own equipment. You have your British and our American arms manufacturers to thank for this. They both sell arms to these paramilitary and guerrilla groups through the arms traders. So cut the complaining."

Suddenly we heard noise upstairs. That silenced us. It was 01 giving orders to his people in the room above us.

"I want every single person who gave information to the guerrilla to be exterminated," he yelled. "I want no mercy at all." He continued to rant until he ran out of steam.

When it was quiet upstairs, the General and the Queen restarted.

"Little do you know the British people," she said. "We have conquered the world and nothing will prevent my army from rescuing me. I'm certain the ship *Queen Elizabeth II* is being readied to send soldiers, as happened during the Falklands War, and like it or not we won that war."

*The Queen doesn't know who the General is*, I thought.

"I can't believe your innocence," the General continued. "Forget about being rescued. You're talking to someone who knows war. Your Majesty, if England were to send the *Queen Elizabeth II* full of soldiers to fight and rescue you, they had better send another ship full of body bags for the soldiers who'll die in this fight. They can contact the U.S. Defence Department. They've been buying them in quantity since Vietnam. They've got lots on hand since Iraq and Afghanistan when United States tried to follow the same steps of your lovely British empire. I don't want to destroy your illusions, but you'll never leave this place unless the paramilitaries decide to take you out. Otherwise you will die here. Listen to me, *you will die here*."

The General's words were devastating. The Queen responded angrily, "You are an arrogant and impudent American. I am here because of bad luck and it simply cannot be that I would die in this revolting place with its suffocating climate."

"I'm sorry your Majesty; you're here for the same reason as all of us. We're both here because our people are using drugs indiscriminately. You have any idea of the amount of money generated by the sale of drugs on the street? It's billions of dollars and pounds and that money makes it way to the hands of these people, who in turn finance private armies. It is your people and my people who are destroying this country, not this country destroying the world. Please try to remember the last transaction made with you before you started your voyage to Colombia. I bet it was buying heroin or cocaine."

Both the General and the Queen calmed down. Finally, they both were on the same page.

She gently closed her eyes, then responded softly, "Yes, it was a drug transaction; a man in London. He was in his mid-forties, and he kept me in his wallet for more than two weeks. I'm certain he did not use drugs. However, the last day, or I should say evening, we were together, he went to a big housing estate in the outskirts of London and knocked on the door of one of the flats. A thin, blond young woman, rather common looking, opened the door. He appeared nervous and asked, 'Are you Carol? A friend gave me your address.' This woman nodded yes and asked him to wait at the door. There were two children watching television in the lounge and she shooed them to what I assume was a bedroom and closed the door. It was all rather tawdry. Then she came and let the man inside and took him to her bedroom. She leaned closely and said matter-of-factly, 'The service costs a hundred pounds.' The man gave her five twenty pound notes from his wallet. I was one of them. The young woman tucked us into a pocket in her jeans, turned off the light, and well, need I say more."

I could see the Queen was really embarrassed, but then, I'd heard that the Brits are uptight about sex.

She sighed and continued, "After fifteen minutes all was over. The man put his clothes on, gave her an extra twenty pounds for…let us say, some additional service and left. Oddly enough, he did not look very happy. The young woman dressed quickly, told her children they could watch television again, and yelling above their squabble about what to watch, she told them, 'Right, I'm off down the corner. Don't open the door to anyone, yeah."

"We were inside the pocket of her jeans, which desperately needed washing. She walked about five blocks until she reached a dark back alley, so dark you could barely see anything. A man suddenly appeared from the shadows; his left hand was close to a gun he barely concealed at his waist."

"'Carol, you again. How many grams you want now?' He spoke to her as if he knew her, as if she were a regular costumer.

Carol handed him all of us and said, 'Give me all that I can buy with this.'"

The man took two small bags of white powder from his coat pocket and gave them to her. Not long after this, I was in this wretched jungle, held captive by these revolting drug barons."

I looked at the Queen. She seemed so naive.

"Your Majesty," I said, "I've known the General a long time, and I know he's kinda blunt, but I've learned a lot from him. This is my first time here and there's lots I don't know. But I do know the white powder you saw in those bags is cocaine and that they make it in laboratories here."

"Madam, they will protect these labs at any cost," the General interrupted. "Cocaine sales give the guerrilla and paramilitary groups money to buy arms and weapons, and they use them to kill innocent Colombians. That white powder and the money they make from it gives them more power than you have. They control of entire towns through fear and intimidation, backed up by killing. They force whole communities to grow drugs and send their children to fight with them."

Rather than becoming angry, the Queen became somewhat amused.

Alex Barr

"Well, our countries have to stop this," the Queen said. "I will do something when I return to England." Her eyes had a look of disappointment.

"You're finally getting it," barked the General. "But I still think you know nothing about what really happens outside Buckingham palace."

"What do you mean?" I'm sure she was shocked that anyone would speak to her like this.

"Don't you know that established companies in both our countries are the ones that supply many of the arms to these groups, through the arms traders?" The Queen looked at the General as if he was speaking Chinese. She had no clue. "Yes, your Majesty, our countries complain about the cocaine coming from Colombia and killing our people, but they don't do a damn thing about the arms these companies sell to these drug lords who produce cocaine and kill and displace millions of Colombians to maintain their power. Sure the cocaine they produce kills people, but the arms we make also kills, and faster. Your Majesty, you and I come from countries that have zero accountability but demand it from others. Madam, unfortunately drugs and arms trade are the two biggest businesses in the world."

I noticed a stack of Canadian dollars on the other side of the room. I smiled as I remembered that Canadians are known for being pacifists. The Canadians were listening attentively to our conversation. Seeing the General's attitude I bet they were intimidated.

"I have something to add," said a female voice coming from the Canadian stack. I was surprised it was a Queen from one of their twenty notes.

"They also have the Queen of England on their twenty notes?" I asked the General.

"Yeah, but that Queen has no British accent," he replied without much interest.

The Canadian Queen continued, "I am also the Queen of England, and I want to clarify what the General just said." The Queen from the British pound didn't let her finish.

"You are no Queen, you are just a clone. The real Queen reigns in Britain, not in Canada."

Before the Canadian Queen could reply, I jumped in to try to calm down the situation. "We're here in the middle of the jungle in one of the most humid places in the world, our skins are starting to feel the effect of the weather, and you're arguing about who should be the real Queen?" I could hear myself getting worked up. "Don't you get it? These guys out there don't care who you are. They only care how much value you have."

"Sorry, please continue." The British pound apologized to the Canadian dollar.

"We have been listening to your conversation and we are also here for the same reason as all of you. Canadians are consuming drugs indiscriminately and the only way for us to stop coming to this country is if our people stop using drugs."

All the bills nodded.

"But what can we do?" I asked.

"Nothing, we can do nothing that is in the hands of the humans."

Trust the General to shatter everyone's illusions. But, as usual, he was right. This whole mess was in the hands of humans.

I noticed the Queen from the British pound was sobbing. "Your Majesty," I said softly, "don't cry. You may still have an opportunity to go back to London and sit in Buckingham palace again. If you are lucky, the paramilitary will buy arms and war equipment made in Britain and it's possible they will pay the arms traders in pounds and then you will go back to your lovely island kingdom. My advice is don't lose hope and stay calm. Lots of Brits buy and use drugs and as long as they do, the guerrillas and the paramilitary will keep buying arms."

The Queen snapped back.

"How can you talk about patience when this heat and humidity are turning my edges yellow and wrinkling my ends? My numbers are losing colour, my crown is no longer shiny and you ask to be calm!" Her voice was rising in panic. "Soon no one will recognize I am the Queen of England! If my army, the British army, does not rescue me soon, they will lose one of their Queens."

After a while the Queen calmed down. I could hear some of the bills murmuring quietly about the conversation with the Queen, when suddenly we heard 01's voice in the room above. He turned up the volume.

"Don't worry," he said loudly, "we will send money so we can investigate who did this."

Shortly, we heard men coming downstairs. We heard them releasing the three locks on the door, and then the lights were turned on. One of the men was 01. He walked straight to the U.S. dollars and grabbed three stacks of one hundred thousand dollars each. My stack was one of the ones chosen. "He's changed his plans," said the General. "We're not going to be sent to the arms traders; we're going someplace else."

01 stuffed us in the outer pockets of his camouflage pants and walked away with us bouncing against his legs as he ran up the stairs. "We're probably going to the combat zone and we'll be used to pay for information leading to those who collaborated with the guerrillas," the General said. He seemed sure about this. "We're going to see for ourselves how these groups take revenge."

Unfortunately I wasn't able to say good-bye to any of the Queens. I only hope they made it back to England and Canada where they belong.

## 11
# Vengeance

01 WAS DEEP IN THOUGHT AS HE HEADED OUT OF THE HOUSE, five heavily armed escorts followed behind, their pistols and rifles at the ready. He climbed into his personal helicopter and shook hands with the pilot. "Fly this thing," he said, "Let's go to the farm *el Carmen*. My troops are waiting for me, and we don't have time to waste." I remembered the crazy Benjamin telling me the man had more than forty farms just in this area. 01 settled into his seat and watched in silence through the small round window as the helicopter gained altitude in the thin morning air.

This was my first helicopter trip, but believe me I was not happy. This flying machine was designed for war. The side doors were fully opened, and two machine guns hung from each side with a man pointing it outward, his index finger on the trigger at all times and eyes fixed to the ground. As the helicopter turned south toward the farm, 01's cell phone must have rung. It was hard to hear, but suddenly he was shouting into it.

"Tell all the commandants I'll be there soon." *This looks like a big meeting*, I thought.

The helicopter flew about seventy feet above ground, enough altitude to fly above trees and small hills.

Alex Barr

"Why are we flying so low? I asked the General. I knew that at this altitude we were vulnerable to accident or enemy artillery.

"Flying low is the only way to avoid detection by police radar," the General replied.

Clouds of dust and dead leaves swirled above the ground as we passed through small villages. Children on the ground tried to chase the helicopter, but soon disappeared in the clouds of dust left behind. During the whole flight no one said a word; the ear protection each person wore made it impossible. I didn't mind the noise; my concern was 01 who continually moved his legs nervously from side to side. This, and the helicopter swaying as it pushed against tropical winds, was making me feel dizzy.

Fortunately it was a short flight, and in less than thirty minutes the helicopter was turning, trying to land safely. The pilot landed in the middle of other helicopters. Men wearing military camouflage uniforms lined up, one next to the other, holding rifles as they awaited the arrival of their chief commandant, 01. He was watching every single movement through the window and was the first to jump down. He looked at everyone and gave a military salute to his commandants and combatants who opened a path as he walked to the house main entrance. Hundreds of men obediently lined up, which appeared to me more like an organized battalion formation than the group of bandits the General had called them. Every single person had a gun and held it as if they believed it was part of a man's adornment.

The commandants were dressed in green and the combatants in camouflage, something I deduced seeing that they were only the ones to approach 01. The combatants kept their distance. One by one, all the commandants obediently followed 01 into the farmhouse. Inside, all had been made ready for the meeting to discuss the response to the most recent guerrilla attacks. Computers were turned on, maps pinned to the walls, radios lined up, and beer was cooling. Each one took a seat at the rectangular table located in a large meeting room. There were twenty-four seats, one for each commandant. No one touched the middle seat. Clearly, it was reserved for 01.

A tough-looking man was the first one to greet 01.

"He's the commandant who lost half of his combatants when the guerrillas ambushed them," the General said. "He's known as *Commandant Guerra,* war. I know him from before." His clenched jaw and angry face showed his thirst for vengeance. "Probably Commandant Guerra wants a fast response from their side, but he knows only 01 will design the strategy. Only 01 will decide when to attack." the General explained.

"Let us get straight to the point," 01 said, as he sipped a cold beer.

The first to speak was Commandant Guerra. "You all know what those guerrilla sons of bitches did to my group," he said, his anger rising as he said the word guerrilla. "They want to take control of the Zone K so they can transport drugs through that corridor as we do. We can't let anyone take that from us. I have the names of those who gave them the exact location of our camps. We also know the guerrilla sent people to talk to peasants and farmers in the region before the attack, but those people will be difficult to identify. However, we are sure we were betrayed by the villagers around here."

"Do you have the names of some of these people?" 01 asked. "Do you know where they live? We cannot start killing people randomly. This time I want to kill the ones who did this."

Guerra looked at him and after a short pause replied, "I have some names, not all, but we can ask the villagers. I am sure they all know who the informants are. We just need to put pressure on them."

01 kept silent but nodded without conviction. I could see Guerra was searching desperately for something more credible to say.

"Even if we don't get any names, killing people randomly won't be a bad idea," he added. "It will bring fear to the region and that has always worked on our advantage." He smiled, looking at 01.

"You know something? You are probably right." 01 responded, looking down at his notes. "I don't care if people don't like us as long as they fear us." The rest of the commandants nodded in seeming agreement.

01 drank deeply from his bottle of beer and then slammed the half empty bottled on the table, insuring everyone's attention. "I want you guys to kill and disappear every single person who was involved in this treason. I want to leave an example in the region so no one will dare betray us again." He paused for another long sip, and continued coldly, "I want you to vanish all their descendents. The son of a traitor is a traitor. Finish them all off. Kill their children, grandparents, even their dogs and the cats. Do not leave a trace of them in this world."

We listened to this quietly inside 01's pockets. It has always scared me how humans can compress so much hate and violence into just a few sentences. I trembled more at the cruel, detached tone of 01's words than his explosive anger. I was sickened at the thought of the villagers, but I was to learn that the killing I imagined and the deaths I would witness would be unimaginable.

01 raised his body from the chair and went around pouring whiskey in everyone's glasses. "Listen carefully," he said, standing and resting his two palms on top of the table. "Send a contingent of your best men to support Commandant Guerra so he can reunite with his group and help him find the traitors." It chilled me when I heard 01 announce they would call their mission Operation Cleaning. He sat down defiantly and I could see a look of defiance and anger in the eyes of each man in the room. 01 leaned down and began pulling the bundles of cash from his pockets. He laid us in the middle of the table. Speaking

calmly and looking at Commandant Guerra he said, "Here is $300,000 American dollars you can use to start Operation Cleaning. Use it to pay for information in the villages. I will also send you more arms and ammunition that I will soon be receiving. You need to rebuild your group fast and restart the cocaine-processing laboratories.

Guerra smiled. "Don't worry, boss. I am going to make an example of what happens to traitors and collaborators in the region. No one will dare betray us again. I promise we will catch and kill all the people involved. "

Without bothering to count us, Guerra stuffed us inside an outer pocket of his camouflage pants. Just like the rest of him, his hands were cold and rough. His pants stank from sweat and gunpowder, unlike 01's pockets, which were impregnated with the scent of French perfume. Guerra stood up and quickly went around the table shaking the hand of the other commandants. He stopped in front of 01. "Thank you, boss, for your support. I am sorry this happened to my contingent."

01 smiled "Don't worry, Guerra. This is war and things like this happen. Just make sure it doesn't happen again."

They shook hands firmly; then Guerra took his radio and strode outside. Now I belonged to a paramilitary commandant. As we left I could hear 01 talking about other needs, something about how they could increase drug output in their laboratories.

It was time to roust my colleagues. I especially wanted the General's take on all this. He was sniffing like an old hunting dog, turning his nose up at the smell of the gunpowder inside Guerra's pants.

"I know this smell," he said, "and it always comes accompanied by blood." We all held our breath waiting, and with a long sigh he continued, "Soon we'll be separated and probably never see each other again. Many of you will never go home; others will pray to die so you don't have to keep seeing what these humans are capable of. And others will be stained with so much

Alex Barr

innocent blood and will live so long with criminals, like your owners you will forget you once had good feelings."

Most of us were shocked, unable to speak although one or two sniggered, reinforcing the General's point that it's possible to lose feelings of goodness.

Commandant Guerra left the house and boarded his helicopter, accompanied by some of his closest men. The pilot asked everyone to tighten their seatbelts, and in less than five minutes we were in the air again, this time flying to the combat zone. This helicopter had a pressurized cabin, which reduced the noise and made a normal conversation possible. Commandant Guerra immediately began to discuss his plans with his men. The first thing he did was to take us out of his pocket. He held one hundred thousand in his left hand and two stacks of one hundred thousand in his right hand. I was in that one.

"Listen closely," he told his men. "Go to towns and villages and offer money and rewards for information that can lead us to the people responsible for the attack. Once you have a list of names, organize a group to wipe them from this planet and make sure they suffer. We need this day to be remembered." He then gave one hundred thousand dollars to the man sitting next to him and gave the other two hundred thousand to two young men sitting in front of him. "Finish the task on time.," he ordered.

His men took the money and, as the General had predicted, we all ended in different hands. I went into the pocket of a young man who looked about twenty-five years old. He had dark hair, like most of the population in this country, and eyes that looked similar to counterfeit bills: they both have a dead soul and a dead spirit.

"I know this man," said a hundred-dollar note lying next to me. He said it with a touch of malice. "I never found out his real name, but I know he's called the Surgeon by his men and commandants."

"Oh, please, don't tell me what it sounds like you are going to tell me," I groaned. But the other Benjamin couldn't restrain himself.

"He's called this because of what he does to the bodies of his enemies. He's the cruellest and most evil human I've ever encountered. Not that the other commandants are angels, but he's definitely the worst of the worst." He paused for a second to let this sink in. "The Surgeon's the benchmark that other assassins' cruelty is measured against."

I tried to swallow my fear, but there was no getting around the fact that this Surgeon was my new owner. And if this wasn't depressing enough, I felt really alone because the General and Ulysses had ended up in the hands of the man sitting in front of Guerra. That guy's face said it all. Thick eyebrows, a scar that went from one side of his face to the other, and dead eyes the same as the Surgeon's.

"I know that one, too" the other Benjamin said. "He's called Hook, a nickname earned because they say no one escapes alive once he catches you."

"Okay, give it all to me. Who's the other one?"

"The other one sitting beside him is called *Sangre Negra*— Black Blood in English,"

"I know what it means. I'm not completely stupid, *amigo*." Nothing fazed this other Benjamin. He seemed to relish all this gory information. But I had to know.

"I don't know why they call him Sangre Negra," my new friend concluded, "but I am sure he didn't earn the name for being a humanitarian human being."

The Surgeon, my new owner, distributed the money Commandant Guerra gave him into different pockets. Like Commandant Guerra, the Surgeon's hands felt cold and his wallet also had a gunpowder smell, which I was starting to believe was these criminal's natural scent. He separated a small number of bills and put them in his shirt pocket. I was one of them and fortunately my new friend was also chosen. That shirt pocket was a perfect location to hear and observe but as I would learn was a terrible one for an innocent and naïve Yankee like me--someone who was always optimistic about humans.

"So where're we going?" I asked.

"We're heading to Zone K, where the paramilitary have one of the largest cocaine collection centres in Colombia. In Zone K they control their five biggest labs and each lab processes one ton of pure cocaine each week. The zone is a dense jungle in northeastern Colombia, and the paramilitary have total control of it. No one can go in or out without their authorization."

This guy was pretty knowledgeable—not as knowledgeable as the General, but he was easier to get along with. I decided to call him the Lieutenant.

From the air you could clearly see thousands of hectares of coca plants that supplied the laboratories. Seeing this it reminded me of something Ulysses had said: "Hundreds of thousands of hectares of tropical rain forest are devastated yearly by these groups to plant coca, and the rivers are contaminated with the chemicals and fertilizers used in the process. These people are destroying the world biggest lung."

At that time he told me this they were just words. Now I understood.

After twenty long minutes the pilot announced we were about to land. The helicopter made several turns, looking for the best approach for a safe landing but the threat of a storm wasn't helping and wind was picking up. On the ground, two men held torches to guide the pilot to a small opening in the middle of the jungle. The foliage was so thick I could barely make out people on the ground. I wondered how there could be more than five thousand combatants in this area if I couldn't see a soul. After three attempts the chopper finally descended, and then I understood why paramilitary and guerrilla groups wear camouflage. It really works! It was hard to see them, but as we got closer to the ground I could see the place was packed with combatants standing within the trees and bushes to avoid being seen by the Colombian air force that fly the area occasionally. On landing, Commandant Guerra was the first one to get off, followed by the Surgeon. The rest came behind.

A tractor pulled the helicopter inside a rudimentary hangar made of wood and camouflaged with leaves and dry bushes. It was already four in the afternoon, and in the tropics the sun sets at six and rises at six every day of the year. There were only two hours of daylight left. I heard the Surgeon say the plan was to go out that same night to the surrounding villages and gather information that could guide them to the people responsible for the attack. Operation Cleaning had started.

This primitive airport was surrounded by at least sixty camouflaged tents made with heavy military fabric stretched taut on steel frames. Surrounding the tents were small huts made of wood and dry hay; each had muddy footpaths leading to them. In the middle of the camp were two big structures with bare earthen floors, timber walls and zinc roofs covered with hay. They stored stacked drums of chemicals, microwaves and piles and piles of bales of compressed coca leaves. Not much infrastructure considering it's in places like this where the most lucrative business in the world begins.

The Surgeon walked quickly through the maze of footpaths till he reached a tent at the opposite end of the encampment. He didn't announce himself, just rushed in. "Where are my friends Machete and Slow Death?" he asked in an aggressive tone tinged with wariness. The tent was the size of a small house, and at least twenty men were resting on their cots.

"Hi Surgeon," said a man sitting in a small chair and calmly cleaning his rifle. "Machete is in Tent 6. He moved there last week. Slow Death was killed during the guerrilla attack." He said it as if death was as normal as buying bread.

Alex Barr

"Shit, they killed Slow Death," the Surgeon said with disbelief.

He immediately left the tent and looking at the sky he yelled, "*Hijos de puta.*" I could see he was wrestling with his anger. He walked fast, occasionally muttering, "They will pay for this," until he reached Tent 6. Inside were two shirtless young men playing dominos. The first thing I noticed was the scars on their shoulders left by the straps of the rifles they carry every day.

"*Hola* Machete, *cómo estás?*" the Surgeon asked, as he put his right hand on Machete's shoulder.

"The game is over," Machete announced and stood up and hugged his commandant. "*Hola* Boss," he said. "That face means war," Machete added, smiling.

"Things are getting hard these days and I need your help now." the Surgeon replied.

They exchanged recent combat experiences for a few minutes, then the Surgeon said, "I need a group of at least one hundred men to go with me to the village *La Esperanza*, and another hundred men to patrol the surrounding area. We are sure the villagers are the ones that have been giving information to the guerrillas."

Machete looked hard at him.

"What do we have to do once we are there?"

"We are going to hang some of the villagers until they talk," the Surgeon replied, without blinking an eye.

"Don't worry. I have well-qualified people that can do the job without any mistake or remorse."

"This is the type of job Machete likes," the Lieutenant said. "He loves ripping people into pieces, even if they are innocent. He'll see this as an opportunity."

Smiling, the surgeon walked out the tent and headed south, occasionally looking at three short men standing close to a warehouse entrance. The three were concentrated looking at the Surgeon. Each had a sack three times their size strapped to their backs and packed with leaves; coca leaves I assume. The heavy load bent their bodies forward. Their faces looked red and dry cracked.

"What the fuck you are looking at? Do I look like your mother?" the Surgeon cried out. "Keep working you peasant sons of bitches".

Two of the men lowered their heads and slowly walked away balancing their load as they went inside the warehouse but one stayed still and offered the surgeon a quick smile.

"*Señor un momento porfavor.*"

"What do you want?" the Surgeon yelled again.

"Can I please talk to you *Señor*?"

He timidly approached the surgeon and extended his trembling right hand. The surgeon avoided the hand.

The man drew a deep breath and with his eyes locked to the ground said, "*Señor* I'm very tired, I feel sick, please give me permission to go to the village and see a Doctor? It has been more than a year here."

"What is wrong with you? I see you can talk and walk, and you look healthy to me. So what is wrong? What the fuck is wrong this time?"

"Sorry *señor*, but I think the chemicals are harming my lungs. I can hardly breathe at night and sometimes I cough blood." I could hear his lungs whistling as he talked.

"You peasants and your stupid excuses to leave this place! You are here to work and pay what you owe to the paramilitary. Have you forgotten you didn't have the money to pay for the para-tax? We kindly gave you the option to pay through work. Don't come with all this bull shit now!"

The man looked thoroughly confused.

"*Señor* I think I have paid my debt already."

The Surgeon widened his eyes. It was clear he didn't like to hear that.

Alex Barr

"You know what?" he replied trying to sound compassion-ate. " I'm going to free you from all this pain." His hand went straight to the pistol.

"Oh no!" I yelled.

The peasant quickly grabbed the sack and walked away, repeatedly looking back at the Surgeon.

"Sorry *Señor*, I am very sorry," the man said as he speed up his pace; but the Surgeon was faster. He used his left hand to grab the man by the neck. His right hand held the gun. I heard that metal clink again. I knew this would soon get ugly.

"*Señor porfavor lo siento*, I am sorry!"

The Surgeon was silent. His cheeks trembled as the shiny gun touched his head.

"I won't do it again!" said the peasant as he knelt before him. "*Porfavor*, please I have a family waiting for me!"

Other peasants stopped and observed; none of them looked surprised.

"This is the only way you guys learn."

Then the inevitable happened. I heard three shots before the whole place went silent. The silence lasted only seconds.

"Leave the body in the floor for the rest of the day. I need everyone to see what happens when you have lung problems. And make sure the sack is taken to the lab." Now I was scared.

Before the sun had set, Machete had a battalion of two hundred heavily armed, angry men ready to fight. He had also organized his "manicure bag," as he called the box full of his implements of torture.

"Machete has taken out more fingernails during his tortures than anyone else, and he has cut into more human flesh than any doctor. Just by seeing the marks on a cadaver, people know if it was Machete's cruel work. Well, he comes from the Surgeon's school," a fifty thousand-pesos note inside the wallet said.

At the same time the other two commandants, Hook and Black Blood, were also organizing groups of men to go to other villages. My colleagues, the General and Ulysses were with them. I felt bereft at the thought that I might not ever see them again. I tried to console myself with the thought that at least they were lucky to be together. I wasn't alone in the Surgeon's pocket, either. Besides the Lieutenant, there were other dollars but they weren't really my kind of bill. It sounds funny, but many of them were the sort who think they are worth more than others, even if they worth less. I was also accompanied by a few fifty thousand-pesos notes. It sounds like a lot of money to be one single bill, but they are only equivalent to twenty dollars. I tried talking with those Colombian guys, but the pesos hate the dollars, or *gringos*, as they call us. We dollars have displaced the pesos from many areas of Colombia, because the people prefer to pay in dollars than in pesos. This has created friction between the two currencies

At 7 p.m., as agreed, Machete announced, "My men and the trucks are ready." Four trucks loaded with armed men stood waiting.

"*Vamos*," the Surgeon ordered, and the convoy of trucks pulled out, heading for the village of La Esperanza, "hope" in English, with Machete and the Surgeon escorting them in an armoured jeep. I was impressed how punctual they were in their departure; they had a strong sense of military discipline that surprised me, since everyone knows punctuality is quite rare in this part of the world. I suppose the paramilitary could be on time when they have an appointment with torture and death.

After about fifty minutes of steady, smooth driving, the Surgeon gave the order to stop. "Make the first ring," he shouted through his radio. One hundred men jumped off two trucks and fanned out, making the first ring of armed men, closing all the possible escape routes. No one could go in or out of the village.

We drove for another fifteen minutes and stopped at the village main entrance.

Alex Barr

"Do the second ring here," the surgeon ordered. Fifty men jumped down and fanned out, making the second ring around the village outskirts. "No one can escape now," he whispered.

The remaining fifty men accompanied the Surgeon and Machete inside the village. Like generals commanding a small army, both barked orders positioning the fighters across the village main entrance and strategically placing some on the village main routes. There wasn't a soul on the streets. Everyone had disappeared—although you could see a few peaked through their windows watching the Surgeon and his men as they approached the town centre. There was a frightening silence. The only sound came from the fifty pairs of boots hitting the paving stones of the narrow colonial streets.

They walked straight to a small house close to the village church. The Surgeon and Machete ordered the men to spread out. They knocked on the door of a poor-looking house marked with a number 12 on the upper part of the door. It told them this was the correct place. The door opened wide immediately, but only the Surgeon and Machete went in. The rest of the men stayed out spread around the entrance.

At the end of a small living room was a very fat old man sitting in a rocking chair. It looked as if he was expecting them.

"I've been waiting all day for you guys," the old man said, coughing and holding his chubby right hand on his chest. "Please sit down."

"We don't have much time," the Surgeon said. "Please give us the names you know and all the information you have related to the people that helped the guerrillas."

The old man looked anxious to speak and tell them what he knew, but he could not stop coughing. Eventually, he put his hand inside his shirt pocket and took out a yellow piece of paper with some pencilled writing on it.

"What is that?" Machete asked.

"This is what you guys are looking for," the old man said as he handed the paper to him.

Machete and the Surgeon smiled and glanced at the paper, which was a list of names and addresses. "Are you sure these are the people linked to the guerrillas in this town because these people will be murdered this same night," Machete said. The Surgeon, still reading the list, dismissed one person as a possible helper.

"Juan has been supporting us for years; I can't believe he took part of this," he said.

The old man tried to stand up but his knees weren't strong enough to hold three hundred pounds of human flesh. He remained sitting in his rocking chair and asked them to come close.

"The guerrillas kidnapped my son when he was only eleven years old and forced him to fight with them until he was killed. The names I am giving you are the people who arranged for my son to be forced into the guerrillas. They were also the same ones that gave information to the guerrillas about the paramilitary. Believe me, your friend Juan plays two hands. Everyone in this village knows who they are but are afraid to speak. I don't care if I die as long as I see those sons of bitches pay for what they did to my son."

Machete and the Surgeon looked at each other. The Surgeon looked hard at the old man and asked him coldly, "These names are the people that helped the guerrillas kidnap your son or the people that gave information about us? Because we are not here to take revenge on what happen to your son."

The Surgeon still looked hard at him, trying to gauge the depth of his sincerity. I could see that he had probably survived by learning to read people well.

The old man held the Surgeon's penetrating look, took his glasses off and said, "Believe me, they are the same ones."

This was what they wanted to hear. The Surgeon took twenty thousand dollars from one of his pockets and passed it to the old man. "Thank you very much for your information" He pressed the money into a chubby hand.

"I didn't tell you this for money. I think it is my duty. Just tell me if you are going to kill them all this same day. I've been waiting for this day for years."

Machete, looking coolly at the old man, said, "Don't worry. I assure you that this will happen tonight."

"Keep the money," the Surgeon told him. "There will be retaliations from the guerrillas and it will be better if you leave the village for at least two months until all has calmed down. This money can help you."

The old man put the money in his pocket.

Machete and the Surgeon left the house and joined the men waiting outside. Machete called four of them over and tore the list into four strips with names.

"Each paper has the names and addresses of the people that betrayed us. Each one of you make a group, and go find them. Bring them alive to the village plaza. I will do the rest."

The Surgeon was in constant radio communication with all his men, and now he asked the two security rings to move closer to the village. The hunt was starting. The Surgeon and Machete joined one group, and glancing at the first name on their list they silently approached a small white house a few streets away from the old man's. Once they made sure the house wasn't empty they prepared their men and arms for the attack. They ordered a truck to park at the end of the street the house was on, loaded their arms and took enough ammunition to bring down everyone and everything on that street. They covered their faces and moved in.

The plan was that the Surgeon and three of his men would knock on the door. If no one opened it, they would blow the door down. If by chance someone opened the door, they would be easy prey. The rest of the group would stay outside waiting for the Surgeon to give the order to go inside and start the shooting.

I tried to ignore my own terror as the Surgeon slowly approached the door, his ear cocked, trying to hear voices. He moved closer and put his eye up to a small crack between two boards in the upper part of the door. As he stared, a sudden noise came from inside the house. It sounded like slamming doors and the steps of someone running away. The Surgeon, fearing his prey was escaping, shot the wooden door twice and kicked it until he was inside. The shots passed through the knob and door like butter and his kicks blew the door down to the feet of two small, terrified kids standing in front of him. A boy who looked around seven and a girl not older than five stood across the room paralyzed, their little bodies shot full of adrenaline and fear. Behind the children, four mugs of steaming hot chocolate and a plate with pieces of bread sat on a wooden table slightly marked by years of use.

The boy tried to say something but his words were garbled from fear; his sister grabbed her brother's leg and stared up at the Surgeon with terrified eyes. Both started to cry uncontrollably. The scene unmoved the Surgeon and his men, and he strode across the room and roughly grabbed the boy's arm.

"Who else is here with you?" the Surgeon demanded, as he squeezed the child's thin arm. "Who else was going to eat here?" he yelled.

The trembling boy looked at the floor. "No one sir. We are just my sister and me."

The Surgeon locked an iron fist on the boy's chin. "Don't lie to me little rat, where are your parents?"

"I don't know, I don't know," the boy sobbed, tears running down his face.

"Come with me." The Surgeon barked and ordered the boy and girl to open one of the bedroom doors. He stood behind them, using them as human shields in case there were people with guns hiding in the rooms. He pushed the door open and listened. Silence. He stepped in but the room was empty. The Surgeon moved to the other bedroom door pushing his two small shields in front of him. This time he asked the girl to open the door. He stood behind, holding his pistol ready.

As the door began to open the girl child cried, "Papa, papa!" She slipped free, launching herself toward a man sitting on a chair, holding a gun to his head.

"What are you doing, you coward?"

The man kept the gun pointed at his head.

"I am not going to let you torture me for something I was obliged to do."

The Surgeon pointed his gun to the boy's head.

"You want to play? So then we are going to play. If you don't come with us alive to the plaza, I will kill your two kids in front of you. And then I will kill you if you don't blow your head off first. So decide right now. What you want, you son of a bitch?"

"No, no!" I yelled uselessly. I didn't want to see those two innocent kids murdered in front of me. If that was going to happen I preferred not to live any more. "Stop and give up!" I yelled desperately from inside that pocket when I saw that the man didn't reply as the Surgeon pointed his gun at the boy's head.

I knew the Surgeon wasn't going to wait all night for the man to make a decision. He called the rest of his men to come inside the house and placed them in front of the man.

"Don't let him move. We have to take him alive." He grabbed the two kids and looked at the man. "I won't take long. I will shoot them in the head and come back," he said as he dragged the two kids out the door.

"Papa, papa, please!" both cried, trying break way from the Surgeon's strong hands. The boy looked at his father, his eyes full of tears and a face that asked for mercy. The little girl cried but unaware she was on death row.

The Surgeon leaned next to boy and asked, "how do you want to die? With a shot in the head or a shot in the heart?"

The sobbing boy said, "In the head. But please don't kill my little sister. I don't want her to suffer. I love her too much."

Those were meaningless words to the Surgeon. He drew his gun. I clearly heard the metal clink as he pointed it at the boy's head and said looking at the man, "Say good bye to your children. This is the last time you will see them."

"Stand up, don't let these criminals murder your children," I kept yelling.

It was as if he had heard my words. The man put his gun on the floor, looked at the Surgeon and said, "Don't do it. I give up. Please release my children. You can do whatever you want to do with me." I felt a wave of relief.

The Surgeon grabbed the man's pistol from the floor and ordered two of his men to tie him up and take him to Machete at the plaza. They laid the father face down on the floor and tied his hands behind his back then yanked him up and marched him out the door. The Surgeon looked pleased. He'd found one of the men who apparently supported the guerrilla. But my relief again turned to agitation. What was going to happen to those two small kids? My answer came quickly.

The children were standing in the doorway watching the four paramilitary drag their father by his hair and jostle him as they marched him toward the main plaza. "That little girl is too young to understand what is happening. But the boy, he is old enough to realize his dad will be tortured in front the villagers as an example to them all. He knows this because he has seen the paramilitary and guerrilla do it before to others," the fifty thousand-pesos note next to me said.

"But the kids! What about the kids?" I asked. But the pesos would say no more.

Alex Barr

The boy leaned his head back, sobbing hysterically as the Surgeon came back inside the house smiling cynically. He pointed his black shiny gun at his little sister.

"What is this son of a bitch going to do?" All my senses were focused on the Surgeon.

The boy ran and knelt before the Surgeon, grabbing his legs as hard as he could, screaming, beseeching, "Please don't do it! Shoot me, shoot me! Please, not my sister!"

He held on to the Surgeon's pant legs, begging for mercy; but one swift toss of the killer's leg detached the boy. The Surgeon kicked the boy hard in his ribs to move him out of the way. Two shots were heard, accompanied by a small cry of pain from a small girl, dying from the shots to her chest, so powerful they made her little body fly over the table and land on the other side of the room. The dying child, blood pouring from her mouth, moved her head to see her brother, to give him the last good bye. He had covered his eyes trying not see his lovely sister's final moments, but at the last minute looked at her and saw her move her hands trying to call him. Without caring for his life he ran to the other side of the room to hold her hand but never made it. A third shot from the Surgeon's gun entered the little boy's fragile skull and went out his left eye. He fell only few inches from his sister whose heart had already stopped beating. That bullet killed him instantly. I was staggered, unable to believe what I had seen. I tried to find something else to look at, anything but those two lifeless bodies.

Two kids died and I couldn't do anything to save them. That day I hated them all—the drug users, the arms traders, the money launderers, the paramilitary and the drug dealers. They are the ones that make all this happen. I wanted to die that day. My life was meaningless. All I wanted was to leave that fucked up country, but I knew my journey in Colombia was far from over.

"Benjamin, try to stay calm. This is what happens in this country. You cannot allow yourself to get overwhelmed by what humans do. Remember, you are just paper," the fifty thousand-pesos note told me.

"How can I stay calm? Don't you see what just happened? Where the hell am I?" I yelled. "I just want to go home."

The Surgeon put away his gun and showing no sign of emotion said, "The son of a scorpion is a scorpion and you have to kill them."

I noticed one of his men with tears in his eyes looking at the small bodies of the two kids. He was unimpressed with what he'd just seen, but no doubt his fear of ending up the same way kept him from having the courage to stand up and stop the Surgeon. Apparently that's how it is down here.

The Surgeon walked outside, telling his men to leave the two kids inside the house and burn it to ashes. He stood outside watching as they obediently sprayed gasoline on the floors and walls and watched, smiling a light satisfied smile, for several minutes as the fire baked the wood and the bodies. The Surgeon had shown no hint of a conscience; he had smiled at the death of those two kids. It was the act of a sick human mind.

Still looking satisfied, he drove his armoured jeep to the main plaza where the rest of his men had rounded up the other people from the list. All were tied up, waiting the Surgeon's arrival. The smell of burning houses hung in the air over the whole town. It was then that I realized that in each of those homes something similar must've happened. *How many kids died here today?* I wondered. 01 had given the order not leave anyone alive, and I knew his men were good at following his orders.

In the main plaza, the Surgeon's men had eight people from the list laying face down with their hands tied behind their backs. "They all will be tortured," the Lieutenant told me.

Machete sidled up to the Surgeon. "How did it go for you?"

Alex Barr

"I had to kill two little rats of that son of a bitch lying there."
He pointed his gun at the man on the ground.

Machete looked at the father lying quietly, his face wet with
tears. "So let's start with him."

"Please no more blood," I kept yelling inside the Surgeon's
pocket. I couldn't understand how the other bills in there
didn't seem to mind. "Please," I asked some other Colombian
bills, "explain to me why the paramilitary do this." I desperately
needed to talk to someone, to understand. I needed a voice
of hope. But those bills wouldn't say a word. They adopted
an attitude similar to the villagers who were standing silently
watching. Could they be so used to seeing things like this that
all seems normal to them? How do you get used to this?

Machete walked over to the man and grabbed a fistful of hair
and lifted his head. "What is your name?" he asked roughly.

The man looked at him, puzzled and trembling, he replied,
"My name is Alfonso."

Machete knelt next to him. "Why did you give information
about us to the guerrilla?"

The man stayed quiet only blinking. Machete came closer
to him and said, "Open your mouth and show me the tongue
you used to talk about us to the guerrilla." The man closed his
mouth pressing his lips together as hard as he could. He knew
this was the preliminary to something they called the tie cut,
which consisted of opening a hole in the lower part of people's
throat and pulling their tongue out through it until it looked
like a long tie.

Alfonso kept pressing his two lips together but started
to open his mouth when he saw three men were bringing his
wife to the plaza. She was tied up and bleeding from her nose.
"We found her hiding in a neighbour's house. We recognised
her from a photo we found in the family's home," one of the
men said.

"Sit next to your husband," the Surgeon bellowed. Then, pointing his gun at her head, he said looking at Alfonso, "Show me your tongue and leave it out."

Alfonso opened his mouth and slowly put his tongue out, looking with wide-eyed fear at Machete who was taking out a pair of pliers from his manicure box. Machete sat next to him and said, "Show me all your tongue." He grabbed the man's tongue with the pliers and started to pull. Alfonso screamed wept with pain and horror.

His wife couldn't stand it anymore and screamed in anger, "Why you are killing us? Why you killed our children? They have nothing to do with this." Tears of anger streamed down her face as she continued. "The guerillas came here, raped me in front of my husband, and threatened to kill our kids if we do not tell them where the location of your camp was. Alfonso he had no choice than to tell them. Now you come and kill two innocent kids and torture us. Why you don't understand that villagers and peasants are in the middle of this war; we have nothing to do with this conflict. Please do not murder more people." The woman paused for a moment. "Do me a favour. *Por favor,* kill me––I cannot live without my children. You have taken my only reason to be alive." By now her face was red and wet with tears but she sagged with spent emotion.

Machete let go of Alfonso's tongue and put his pliers back inside the manicure box and said, "Your words do not convince me. You should have never talked. However I am going to give all of you a quick death." He took his pistol out and pulled the trigger twice, I heard two bullets split the air and hit the mother's head. Then he pointed his gun at Alfonso. "Put your pants down," he barked; the man didn't move "your pants, down!" he repeated. The man slowly lowered his pants. He, too, looked exhausted, dispirited. Machete pointed his gun at Alfonso's testicles. "If you had the balls to betray us, we have to get rid of those balls first." He emptied the whole magazine

Alex Barr

of his 9 mm pistol into Alfonso's testicles and abdomen, killing him relatively fast.

Machete then walked over to the other suspects, who asked for mercy and prayed as they saw him approaching and reloading his pistol magazine. "Do you guys think living in this part of Colombia is like hell?" he asked. No one said a thing. He then asked his men to bring him five gallons of gasoline and emptied the containers on the bodies of his victims. "Now you will know what real hell is, you sons of bitches," he said as he lit a match and let it drop.

I will never be able to erase the memory of the screams of those burning frightened people or the smell of human flesh burning like roasted meat or the terrified faces of those two innocent kids. They call it a drug war, but drugs are just a commodity. It's a money war. I didn't know it then, but I know now that anywhere there is a scarcity or a demand for scarce products, particularly an illegal demand, anywhere a black market exists, the sums of money involved in the production and support or the commodity far outweigh the real value of the commodity. It could just as easily be water, lentils, or rare books. It does not excuse the suppliers of the commodity who eventually gain control of all aspects of its production and will stop at nothing to protect their investment and marketplace. The profit margin is just too great not to protect their investment with weapons of war, torture and corruption. But consumers also have a responsibility. When they buy heroin, cocaine, crack, and other substances, they are supporting the arms trade, murder, torture, corruption, and the creation of generations of displaced people. They are destabilizing government institutions and the well being of societies.

Finally, the fifty thousand-pesos note had the courage to talk.

"In their short life, the two kids, Ignacio and Andrea, saw only suffering and injustice. They never had the opportunity to go to school because the Colombian government spends all the money that should go for education and health fighting these groups. Colombia has more than three million displaced people and more than one million refugees, people who had to abandon their farms and their homes, and move to other places inside the country or to other countries. From these three million, many have lost their children running away from these criminals. Many saw how these groups killed their parents. Many saw how the guerrilla and paramilitary raped their wives and daughters. And many are still looking for their children who were illegally recruited by these groups to fight for them."

He was starting to get quite worked up and his voice got louder as he spoke.

"Colombia is one of the countries with the most land mines in the world. Illegal groups lay antipersonnel mines along roads to get rid of the enemy, but it is mostly the children who step on them. These landmines are bought with money made from drugs and *you dollars are responsible for this!*" he yelled.

He looked particularly upset at me.

"Calm down, man. I have nothing to do with this," I said, looking at every single Colombian bill in that wallet. They were all listening closely to our exchange.

"Don't tell me you came here with a tourist?" another bill said.

I was getting frightened.

"No, I didn't. I came because people in New York bought drugs with me, but that's not my fault."

The pesos began to talk over each other, voices rising, until one voice cut above them all, "Until when you fuckers plan to come here and destroy our nation." This Colombian bill was more than furious.

*I should have kept my mouth shut*, I thought. Sometimes adding more to an argument make things worse. Or maybe sometimes you can't win an argument. I had another thought: *Am I partly responsible?*

Alex Barr

"Tell us who is sending all these dollars to fuel the conflict here?" another pesos asked.

"You dollars and your fucking drug addict gringos," another added for good measure.

I took a deep breath. "Listen guys, I finally understand that we dollars make our way here through drug trade. I also know that when one gram of cocaine is sold in US or Canada or anywhere else an Ignacio or Andrea is killed in Colombia. I never thought we could cause so much harm, but believe me, I'm with you guys." They didn't look too convinced, but tension eased a little.

Machete approached the Surgeon and after a brief discussion they decided it was time to leave. They ordered their men: "Shoot each burning body once in the head in case any are still alive."

I could see that some people still moved but didn't have the energy to scream anymore. The guns were fired and it was the end of it. The villagers who had been obliged to watch the executions were ordered to go back to their homes.

"Why didn't anyone say anything? Why do people stay quiet? I asked.

"Benjamin, death is always disturbing for humans, but these people have learned not to react to it. Showing anger is not a smart thing to do when you are dealing with criminals," the Lieutenant replied. "Many do feel anger, but many more are numb from hopelessness and seeing too much death."

"We finish for today. Time to go to sleep," the Surgeon said as he cleaned his hands with a paper towel. In less than ten minutes we were driving back to the Zone K. There wasn't much talk during the trip. But I found it hard to believe that someone can murder people that way and then fall asleep.

The fifty thousand-pesos bill looked at me and said in a friendlier way, "You know, Benjamin, tomorrow that entire village will become a ghost town. Everyone will fear the paramilitaries will come back. Everyone will leave behind their livelihoods and join the millions of displaced people in this country. They will walk hundreds of miles somewhere, anywhere else, many carrying their few possessions on their heads. Others will push wheelbarrows with their belongings and youngsters. Some will pause and look back at their lovely homes with hopelessness, knowing they will never be able to return. Most will end up in one of the big cities and become part of the rings of poverty."

Now that I had seen their faces, seen what they had seen, I felt really depressed at the thought of the bleak future these innocent people faced.

# 12
## The Horror Continues

WE ARRIVED BACK AT ZONE K ABOUT THE SAME TIME AS other groups sent by 01 were returning from other villages. I knew Ulysses and the General were inside the wallet of one of the commandants of one of these groups. Trucks and jeeps loaded with combatants arrived, all coming back from murdering innocent children like Ignacio and Andréa and their parents. According to the Lieutenant, probably more than three hundred people, including children and even the dogs and cats, were killed that night. They perished because the order given was to kill everything that moved.

One group came back with six men whose hands and feet were bound with chains. They stood in a grove of trees at the edge of Zone K. According to the group's commandant, they were guerrilla combatants who had tried to ambush the convoy and had killed two of the paramilitary men. They brought them back to be tortured for information about the guerrillas.

The captive men didn't say a word; they knew what awaited them. "It makes one wonder how someone can be part of these groups, how they can risk their lives for nothing and in the end be killed or tortured," I said to the Colombian peso.

"Benjamin, many Columbians end up in these groups because of lack of opportunity. These criminal organizations offer them dreams of fortune and wealth that never come true. But when you are hungry and desperate and have no choices, you will try anything. Other people are forced to become a guerrilla or work for the drug cartels because they were kidnapped when they were young and no longer know where their families are. Others become part of the guerrillas or paramilitaries to revenge what the paramilitary or guerrilla did to their family. Some want to escape and not be a part of either side but if they leave, their family members will pay the consequences so they have to stay. Here everything is solved with blood."

I was still inside the Surgeon's pocket. He looked with anxious anticipation at the six guerrillas lying in the middle of the camp. He never wasted an opportunity to torture a guerrilla combatant. For him this was a war to the death, and both sides knew it well. He walked over to the men and, as he approached them, heard a weak voice. It sounded like Ulysses. As the Surgeon walked closer, the voice got stronger.

"Where are you?" I asked. I could sense something was wrong.

"We're in big trouble, man," Ulysses said in a broken voice.

"What happened? Tell me what happened?"

"We're inside the pocket of one of the guerrillas and we just heard the paramilitary say they're going to burn them alive. We're going to die in the fire!" Ulysses cried.

"How did you guys end up in the pocket of a guerrilla? You left here inside the wallet of a paramilitary commandant!"

This time the General answered. "Yes, we left this place in the wallet of a paramilitary commandant known as Big Head who was in charge of one-hundred men. We went to a village named el Aquila. They had the names and addresses of some people involved in the attack. Both of us were in Big Head's wallet along with some beautiful Colombian ten thousand pesos girls. Suddenly Big Head asked the driver to stop the truck. He decided that he and five other of his men would get dropped off

Alex Barr

about a mile before the village. They wanted to enter it through the back so no one could see them. That way they would cut off any villagers who tried to escape. They planned to call in the rest of the group once they had located the houses of the people they were looking for."

"Big Head and his men started to walk downhill. He was confident it would go well, because he knew this area like the palm of his hand. He boasted to his men that he had grown up in the area and had been terrorizing these people ever since. A few yards from the back entrance to the village, a rain of bullets hit Big Head's body. We were jostled inside his wallet as his body jolted as bullets hit him from all sides. We could hear the shots whistling and breaking through flesh only a few inches from us. We were all still and scared and silent. Finally the silence was broken when a shot hit the lower part of the wallet, shaking all of us and injuring two of the ten thousand pesos girls in their upper corners. It didn't hit us because the Colombian pesos are bigger in size than dollars. I tried to calm Ulysses and the girls, but everyone was screaming at the same time. It's a wonder those screams weren't heard by the entire village."

The General paused for a moment and continued. "Finally, Big Head fell to the ground, still firing his new AK-47 in all directions. It was a successful ambush. Those six paramilitaries lay on the ground in an area no bigger than twenty-five square feet. Then there was a scary silence. No shots. No voices. It was complete silence but it didn't last long."

"Soon we heard the guerrilla talking and moving the bodies. *'Este es el cuerpo de* Big Head,' one yelled. He kicked Big Head's body over with the toe of his boot. Big Head was still alive! One of the guerrilla fighters lifted his head and said, *"Nadie es invencible."* And the guy took out his machete and chopped off his head. Then, with a smile, he held up the head by the hair, like a trophy, and said, 'No wonder why he was called Big Head. It weighs more than a sack of potatoes.' Then they all laughed.

He put the head to one side and began searching through Big Head's pockets until he found the wallet. He opened the wallet and grabbed Ulysses and me first and put us inside his wallet. He then gave the Colombian pesos to one of his men. 'Let's take the arms also,' he said as they turned to leave the area. So this is how we ended up in the hands of a guerrilla fighter," the General said.

"Shit, man, that's brutal. But how'd these guys fall into the paramilitaries hands?"

The General sighed. "What the guerrillas didn't know was that Big Head left most of his men close to the village, waiting for his command to go in. When they heard all the gunfire they immediately ran toward the sound of the shooting and surrounded the guerrillas. They outnumbered them by ten to one. In seconds Big Head's men had them pinned to the ground. Then the paramilitary picked up their dead and rounded up the guerrilla fighters to bring them to the camp for interrogation. Now, Benjamin, you know why we're inside the pocket of this guerrilla fighter."

There wasn't much we could do, only wait and see what the paramilitary planed to do with the guerrillas. The Surgeon came over to confer with his men and I could hear Ulysses sobbing. The General sounded calmer. The Surgeon looked at the chained men as if sizing them up. I was about to learn why he had that nickname. He opened his small bag and took out a new scalpel, opening it slowly in front of his victims. In a serious voice he asked them, "What did you have for lunch today?"

"Not–not much," one answered, confused by the question.

"It is better that way, because I hate when stomachs are full of shit. This is for killing Big Head," he said, and he raised the man's shirt. Then, giving credence to his nickname, he drew the scalpel down the center of the man's chest to a few inches below the belly button. The man tried to hold his breath, tried not to scream.

"Why are you in our area?" the Surgeon yelled at him.

Not a word came out of the man. Blood flowed from the incision as if valves on a pipe had been opened, pooling on the ground beneath the man. Not satisfied, the Surgeon stuck his hands inside the man's innards and began cutting his intestines into pieces and laying them beside the man on the dirt.

The man slowly died without saying a word. I wanted to yell, "No more. Please, no more!", but the word please doesn't exist in this situation. The odour of blood and human faeces began to penetrate the compound. I hoped that these guerrillas would die quickly. In this world you don't ask for a long life; you ask for a fast death. The other guerrillas were still lying on the ground waiting to die. "Bring me three gallons of ether," yelled the Surgeon.

"That is an extremely flammable chemical used to process cocaine. This place is packed with drums of it," the General said.

The Surgeon sprayed the chemical in the open wounds of another guerrilla. The man tried hard to ignore the pain and burning sensation of the chemical but, after a few minutes, all we could hear were heartbreaking screams.

The Surgeon walked over to the remaining guerrillas. "Tell me all you know about the guerrillas' plans around here and I promise I will kill you with a shot in the head." The best that could happen to you here was not to be tortured to death.

The men accepted his offer, and told the Surgeon the details of plans for an attack. They also gave important information about the guerrilla plans in the region. The Surgeon kept his word. Each man received a shot in the head.

"Wow. The Surgeon is acting with mercy," the Lieutenant said.

"You call this mercy?"

"*Si.* This is first time I see someone die by his hands without being tortured. The Surgeon is the Surgeon."

Ulysses and the General's only chance was if the Surgeon decided to search the dead men's pockets to find information that could lead them to more guerrilas. Once the Surgeon found the money he'd put them inside his wallet because who throws away one hundred bucks? But these thoughts faded fast. The Surgeon didn't bother searching them; he already had the information he needed. Instead he yelled, "Burn all those bodies right now and hang them tomorrow in the main road with a sign that says, 'This is what happens to the guerrillas.'"

When he heard the word "burn" the General lost his composure and started to cry like a little boy. I tried to calm him, but this was difficult when someone knows he will be in flames in minutes. The dead guerrillas were placed on top of dry wood and soaked with gasoline. The whole paramilitary camp was there to watch the bodies' burn.

This whole moment really pissed me off. I replayed in my mind how Robert bought drugs with us, and ever since then we've passed from hand to hand, each bloodier than the one before. We had seen so many people die in the short time we'd left New York. Now these good friends were doomed to die in this land. No one is safe in Colombia. Fucking Robert and kids like him--just couldn't say "no" the first time they were offered drugs. If they had known how many lives would have been saved? Ignacio and Andrea would be alive and at school because the government wouldn't have to combat illegal groups and could use its money for education, health and infrastructure. If they had only said "no", thousands of innocent people would be alive now and I'd probably be home in the good old USA.

Robert was already an addict indulging in the behaviour of an addict--he was stealing from his dad to buy coke. If he continued, as sure as God made little green apples, he'd drop out of engineering and begin a downward spiral of deceit that would ruin his health, his friendships and his relationship with his family. He might even manage to destroy his family.

Alex Barr

He might be luckier than most if his family could get him into rehab. But he'd never be safe again from his desires and it might take a stronger person than him to completely rebuild his life. Chances are, at best, he'd have only a small portion of the future he would have had as an engineer; at worst he would be a junkie––lonely, friendless, with a much-shortened life span.

The Surgeon lit the fire. "The heat is reaching the wallet; our edges are starting to fold and twist," I heard the General say. I knew the fire had reached them. Slowly the voices grew weaker and weaker until there was only silence. I was now alone in an unknown country, and in the hands of criminals.

They left the bodies to burn all night. Early the next morning, the remains were hanged from a tree in the main road so everyone in the area would learn the message.

# 13
## La Pausa

THE SURGEON FINALLY LOOKED TIRED AS HE SAT ON A narrow camp cot inside his tent. He took the money out of his shirt pocket, carefully lined us up inside his wallet and laid it next to his pistol on top of a rusted metal table. By now I was so numb that I didn't care if a gun was pointing at the wallet where I was lying. This was how much things had changed for me. I also was tired and hoped with all my heart that when I opened my eyes the next morning I would be back at home--I'd settle for any bank.

We slept until eight the next morning, when an incoming call on the Surgeon's radio woke us. The message instructed the Surgeon to go with a convoy to Camp R and deliver some new weapons that had just arrived. He picked up his gun and wallet, put on his camouflage clothes and left for Camp R in two trucks fully loaded with rifles and ammunition. A third truck with twenty heavily armed men in the back escorted the merchandise. The Surgeon rode in the cab of the third truck, along with the driver. The arrival time was estimated at two in the afternoon, but a stop along the way delayed the convoy-- and changed the course of my life.

We drove for more than three hours but covered only a short distance, since the trucks had to creep slowly over the steep, muddy roads. The roads didn't look well used since the dense surrounding jungle grew into them, reclaiming its land and keeping the roads narrow. Around noon, everyone looked dehydrated and hungry. As we passed through a small village, the Surgeon decided to stop and have something to eat and drink before continuing to Camp R. The trucks lined up beside one another in front of a small modest-looking shop on the out-skirts of the two-street village.

"Have a pop and a snack. We don't have time to waste," the Surgeon told his men. He was the first one to walk into the shop and the rest followed. "*Hola señor, Jorge*," he said, looking at the man behind an old wooden counter. "My men will have some snacks."

"*No hay problema*. They can have whatever they want," Jorge replied, avoiding the Surgeon's stare. In no time the paramili-tary finished most of what was eatable and drinkable inside that small shop––the few bags of chips, the few loafs of bread, the cookies, the coke, even the small stack of canned sardines disappeared. It didn't seem like to much of a shop by North American standards, but I knew peasants made a small living from little shops like that one.

Jorge tried to look busy, cleaning the counters and sweep-ing the floors. But his eyes periodically glanced at the visitors. While they ate and talked and laughed, a little girl, about four-years-old, was playing inside the shop with a ball that rolled between her father's legs. Her father kicked the ball away impa-tiently and it rolled straight to the Surgeon's shoes. He looked down at the ball and pressed it with his two feet. The little girl ran for her ball, stopping in front of the Surgeon, looking at the feet of this compact and powerful man who towered above her.

"Is this beautiful little girl your daughter?" the Surgeon asked, lifting her up under her arms, holding her suspended in front of him.

No!" I yelled.

"*Si señor*, she is my youngest," Jorge replied, his eyes widened in alarm.

The Surgeon's strong hands held the girl firmly. She just smiled and wiggled to be let down. I panicked. "What's he going to do?" I said out loud. But contrary to what I feared, he hugged her and began to play with her as if he were her father. He chased her and she chased him. They played together, kicking the ball around the small shop. I couldn't believe this was the same man who'd brutally killed two children the night before. The Surgeon laughed with her and enjoyed every minute. When it was time to leave, he carried her over to her father and sat her on top of the counter.

"I love playing with kids," he said. "I would give everything to see my kids alive again and play with them just for a few minutes, just for a few minutes." His eyes reddened.

"D'you know what happened to his family?" I asked the Lieutenant.

"Everyone knows what happen to them. The guerrillas killed his two kids and wife during an ambush. His hate for the guerrillas comes from there. This does not excuse him for what he is," he said, "but it makes you understand this war a little better." "Listen Benjamin," he continued. "It's true that many who are forced into this war become part of the spiral of killing and torture. Much is fuelled by personal loss. That is part of the cycle of the madness of war. Many criminals are themselves victims. But some others are psychopaths, pure and simple."

The General had told me that humans are capable of doing the unimaginable. I now thought it all depended on how far you push them.

It was time to pay. "How much do we owe you for the drinks and food?" the Surgeon asked politely. I was surprised because I'd heard some bills say these types of shop owners could get killed for trying to get paid.

The man replied nervously, "You do not owe me anything."

The Surgeon put his big hand on the counter and said, "No, no, Jorge, we were too many this time and we emptied the place. Give me the bill, please."

Jorge still nervous looked at the floor and said, "Whatever you want to give me will be okay."

The Surgeon took out his black leather wallet and took out four fifty thousand-pesos bills each. He handed them to Jorge, accompanied by a "thank you very much."

I still couldn't believe this was the same man I had been with these last days. Where was all this consideration and formality coming from?

Jorge took the money, saying politely, "Oh, this is more than enough. Thank you very much."

"Everyone to the trucks," the Surgeon shouted as he turned to the door. He stopped at the entrance and glanced back at the little girl and offered her a brief smile. She gently waved goodbye. He continued to look at her, not saying a word. I imagined he was trying to find an explanation for that feeling people have when they don't understand why life sometimes takes away what they love most. He pressed his lips together, his chin trembling. For a few minutes I was seeing the real human being he once had been and not the criminal beast this war made him. He stood still for a few moments more, looking at her, then slowly stepped back to the counter.

"Is there something more I can help you with?" Jorge asked.

The Surgeon shook his head as if suddenly awakened. "Please do me a favour. I am going to give you some money so you can buy your daughter some clothes and some dolls. She is a nice little girl but you don't dress her properly. You cannot imagine how I cared for my daughter when she was alive. She was always impeccably dressed and clean. She was a princess."

He opened his wallet again, looking through the bills for more Colombian pesos. But all he had were several hundred dollars. He stared us while I yelled, "Grab me, please, grab me!

I don't want to stay one more day with you!" His fingers came straight to me and to my neighbour. "Yes! Yes! We are leaving this wallet!" I said to the other bill as he handed us to Jorge.

"I hope to see her nicely dressed when I pass through town next month," the Surgeon told Jorge. They shook hands; then the Surgeon turned to the girl, hugged her and gave her a kiss on her cheek. Then he walked out of the shop, calling orders to his men as he left and they drove away. My only thought, besides being ecstatic at not being in his hands anymore, was my relief that I would never see him again.

I was relieved to be staying in that little village in the hands of Jorge. He put us inside an old cashier register next to several ten thousand-pesos bills. Finally I was away from criminals and in the hands of a humble family. I saw it as a promising moment that at last my future had changed for the good. But even though US dollars circulate in this part of Colombia the same way as pesos, I still felt like a foreigner. My only wish was to go back to the States.

In a bill's short life circumstances can change quickly. I was used to being changed from hand to hand most of the time, but here I had learned that one day I could be inside a church in the hands of priests and an hour later surrounded by criminals.

Money travels the world without passports or visas and the whole world wants to have us. People go to the university to be able to earn more like us. People work hard to have us, and they feel frustrated when they don't have enough. Some people even commit suicide when they lose us. Others kill just to have few of us in their pocket. But when all is said and done, we are just a simple piece of paper that weighs a fraction of an ounce.

We lay inside the cash register for the rest of the afternoon. Around six a young boy, about eleven, walked in the shop. He was thin with round black eyes with an intelligent glimmer.

"José! You are home at last," Jorge said.

"*Si, papa*. The bus was very slow today."

The boy looked tired and walked through the shop to the family living quarters in the back, where he hugged his mother and gave her a little bouquet of wild flowers. He lifted up his little sister and hugged her.

Over supper, José talked about going to a job on a nearby farm tomorrow. It sounded like he worked on a farm on the weekend and on Monday caught a bus to a village about four hours away. It sounded as though this was the nearest village with a school. He stayed in the village all week and travelled the long four hours home each Friday for the weekend and work. He told his father he needed to work some more to make a little more money.

"My little dreamer," his father said. "This is good, but you are so tired with all the travel and work."

"But papa, how else can I go to school and work to be a doctor?" the boy said.

"This is a conversation they have had before," a gorgeous 10,000 Colombian pesos woman lying next to me said. She startled me. I hadn't really paid any attention to her. But she continued, "It is rare to see kids from villages like this one going to school. The majority of them work in farms or coca plantations to bring some money home. José is the exception. He wants to be the first kid from the village to finish high school and go to the university."

I was flustered by this beautiful pesos talking to me and bit unsure why she was telling me this. So I just said, "Thanks." It sounded really awkward and I definitely didn't feel cool, so I added, "I can see how hard this boy has to work to just go to school. I hope he can persevere and that all his hard work pays off." And I really did mean this.

The father looked at José. "I have a surprise for you," he said.

"What is it?" the boy asked, still concentrating on his food.

"Do you still need money to pay your school registration?"

José stopped eating and looked at his father.

"Yes papa, I still need to pay it."

The father smiled. "How much do you need?"

José looked at his mother questioningly and said, "50,000 pesos."

The father stood up, walked into the shop and rang open the drawer of the old cashier register. He took out ten ten thousand-pesos bills and one hundred-dollar bill––me! He walked back to the living quarters and sat down at the table next to José.

"Take these 100,000 pesos and pay your school fees. I am also giving you this 100 dollar that some paramilitary gave me this morning. Use it when you have to pay your fees again."

José grabbed the money. "*Gracias*, papa, I promise I will use this money properly."

"I know, son, you have shown that already," his father replied, looking into his son's eyes.

José tucked us inside his nylon wallet where we were mixed with other pesos. Then he went into the small bedroom he shared with his young sister and sat on the edge of the bed, holding the wallet in his hand. He opened it and took out all of us one by one and put us on top of his bed. He started with the Colombian pesos. When he took out the last one, I noticed an attractive and interesting-looking woman. She was the same one who talked to me earlier, the ten thousand-pesos bill.

She was around my age, made in 2001, with long hair, brown eyes, and a smile that captivated me from the start. She knew she was attractive and flirted with everyone except me. I didn't really blame her since Benjamin Franklin is a pretty nerdy-looking guy. But I had learned from observing human behaviour how to fight for what you want. I looked at her but she appeared not to even notice. She wasn't interested in me; not even the fact that I was a foreigner caught her attention. But I thought she was the most attractive and interesting woman I had ever seen— although, honestly, I hadn't seen many, other than stodgy Queens on Commonwealth currency. Of course I'd

Alex Barr

heard from the General about of the Colombian female pesos, but this was the first one who'd ever spoken to me.

Finally José took me out of his wallet and coincidentally, or maybe it was fate, laid me next to her. He looked at all of us, but seemed more interested in me––a US 100 dollar bill––than in the pesos. He grabbed me and propped me up on top of a little wooden table next to a small statue of the Virgin Mary.

He came close to me and looked at my eyes as if he knew I was able to see him. He passed his finger over my face and sounded out my name under the engraving, whispering it in accented Spanish, "Benha-Min," the accent at the end. His innocent black eyes looked at me and made me feel there was a connection between us. Suddenly, he took out a black pen from his school bag and brought it near my face. "Whoa, little buddy," I said in an alarmed voice. "We hundred dollar Yankee bills are the most desired currency the world over. Don't ruin a good thing."

But it was in vain. José began to add some hair. Benjamin has a serious receding hairline, but when he had finished I didn't look that bad. He hadn't overdone it and had taken some years off me. José smiled and considered his handiwork.

"Okay kid, enough. Don't try anything else. Put your god damn pen away." I was getting really worked up. I needed to stop him before this became embarrassing.

Too late. He decided I needed glasses and drew two circles around my eyes. I considered the look. I thought it gave me an executive and professional touch. "Okay the glasses and the hair. That's it. Now stop." But José was on a roll. I was going to have a complete makeover. He added a thick beard all around my face. But thinking about this I realized Latin girls love a beard. I began to see José as my ally in my desire to win the heart of that beautiful Latina girl. José wasn't an artist, but he changed me the way I would've wanted. I'll always be grateful because that Colombian 10,000 pesos girl didn't take long in showing interest in the bearded, handsome gringo.

Finally satisfied, José put away his pen and put me next to her as if he knew that was what I wanted. The Colombian pesos girl looked closely at me for a moment then said, "You must be another type of 100 dollar note. First time I see one like you—only the Benjamins come down here."

I hated lying and I should've told her I was Benjamin Franklin, not another guy. But sometimes the throb of the heart makes us behave in sneaky ways. "Yeah," I replied, "we're only used for special transactions." I was trying to sound professional; but honestly, I thought I sounded pompous. "We rarely leave the US. We move in the highest spheres of government so that's why you haven't seen guys like me before." Man, I was in! In a few minutes we had a conversation going. I remembered the General's words: "When a Latin woman likes you, she will find a way to talk to you." I was in heaven. I had her attention. *Her* attention!

She looked at me with her beautiful dark eyes. "What is your name?"

My thoughts raced. *Why did she have to ask me that question? If I say Benjamin, she will realize I am a Benjamin Franklin. If I give her a different name, I might forget it and that'll be worse.* I stayed quiet, thinking, and then replied, "My name is Benjamin Walker."

She smiled and said, "Oh, they kept the first name and only changed the last name but fortunately you both look so different." She looked at me thoughtfully. "Why Walker?"

I laughed. "Because humans walk with us all over," I replied.

"Oh that makes sense," she said, "humans are always walking."

I hurried on. "What's your name?" I asked.

"My name is Policarpa, but I don't like it. My friends call me Jenny."

"I like that," I told her. It sure was easier to pronounce than the first one! "I hope we'll stay together for awhile. I think we could be good friends."

"I wish also, but you never know how long you will be inside a wallet. Remember, any time a human walks there is a chance we will be used."

"Yeah, I know," I sighed. "Even though we're important to people, we have no control over our destiny and never will have."

José put us back into his wallet, and luckily Jenny and I were beside each other. Feeling her soft paper grazing the left side of my body and the sweetness of her gorgeous Colombian words and delicate Spanish accent gave me the courage I needed to stay awake on this journey. In less than forty-eight hours I had lost the only two real friends I had ever had and met an attractive and interesting woman. Heh, it could have been worse, as I now knew well.

José left his wallet on the table and went to bed early. That was the best night of my life. Jenny and I laughed a lot and told each other about our lives. The other pesos were unhappy to see a gringo entertaining one of their ladies and tried to ruin our fun with comments and threats, but eventually they gave up and ignored us.

## 14
# La Travesía

THE NEXT DAY JOSÉ DECIDED TO TAKE HIS MONEY OUT OF the wallet and hide us inside a black jacket hanging inside a yellow wooden wardrobe. He left us there until the next day, Monday, when he had to go back to school. Early that morning, his father called him so he wouldn't miss the only bus that goes during the week to the village where the school is. José sprang from his bed, opened the closet and put us inside his wallet. We were lucky again. José put Jenny and me together in the left compartment and the jealous Colombian pesos in the right compartment.

José said goodbye to his parents and little sister, thanked his father twice for the money, and went out to catch the bus. We got a decent seat, although it sure filled up fast as we picked up more people along the way. Jenny and I were happy to know we were still together and I relaxed a little, feeling that finally life was treating me well. I was in the hands of a decent boy and accompanied by an interesting and lively woman. What more could I ask? My only worry was that sooner or later Jenny was going to learn I'd lied to her. She'd know I wasn't the person she thought I was. Only the fear of losing her friendship stopped me from telling her the truth. Since I'd gotten to know her better, I'd realized her flirty ways covered a kind heart and that she liked honesty. I knew she would feel betrayed, and I was pretty sure she wasn't the forgiving type, so I stupidly continued with my lies. I didn't want to lose another friend.

After picking up and dropping off people in at least ten villages, we reached a bridge that crossed a small river connecting two small towns. The bridge was old and there was only room for one vehicle at a time to cross so the bus driver pulled over on the right to wait for an oncoming car to cross. As it slowly passed the bus, the car driver called frantically out his open car window, "Don't continue through this route. The guerrillas are stopping all the vehicles just twenty kilometres from here." The man looked scared.

"We have entered the guerrilla zone of influence," Jenny said animatedly. "In Colombia, guerrilla groups and paramilitary groups have their own areas of control and these zones, these areas, usually bump up against each other. The government has no power in these zones and the laws of these groups are the ones people have to follow."

People inside the bus tensed and began to talk among themselves. None of the passengers wanted to leave the route because other roads were in worse condition than the one we had been travelling on and could also be dangerous. Some were unhappy about the delay if we took another route. But it was the only way to avoid the guerrillas—unless we turned around and went back.

The bus driver stood up and asked the passengers, "Do you want to go back or take another route?" Almost everyone replied, "Take the other route." José was quiet but I knew he was worried about being late for classes.

Jenny had told me more about her life. Because she was a ten thousand-pesos note, the equivalent to five dollars US, she moved from hand to hand faster than bills with higher value. She had lived with prostitutes and beggars; she had seen armed robberies, seen her owners killed; she had cried and dreamed.

Low-value currencies like her suffer premature aging because they are touched more often. Some call them the sluts because everyone touches them but no one keeps them. They fade faster, get more wrinkles; and if they get lost people aren't desperate to find them, as they are with me. Some end their days forgotten in closets and drawers. Jenny wanted to be a traveller like me, but no one takes a ten thousand-pesos note for a trip abroad. It's just too small a denomination.

Jenny was quiet for a while and I thought about her story. Then she said, "This also happens when people travel. Colombians have a lot of trouble travelling because they carry the stigma of the drug trade and countries are unwilling to give them tourist visas. What the world does not understand is that ordinary Colombians are putting up with the death, blood, and destruction so that the people in other countries can get high."

Beautiful though I thought Jenny was and even though we were the same age, I could see her skin had lost the shine and the radiance of youth. Her eyes, once like black pearls, looked grey because of a fold that crossed through the upper part of her face. Her hair was wilted from stains left by dirty fingers and greasy wallets. She looked older than she was. She was beautiful because she had a beautiful personality. She was honest, loyal and made me laugh. She brought happiness to my life and in the end this was all that mattered. Ultimately, we bills don't care for the physical aspect of our friends. We don't lose our value no matter how old or wrinkled we become.

The bus had turned around and we were now travelling a different route. We all knew we'd reach our destination late and would be travelling on real poor roads, which we noticed when the bus started to jump like a wild colt. Bags and luggage fell from the upper compartments, and none of this was helped by the driver who didn't reduce speed on the curves or potholes. He was rushing to stay on time.

Alex Barr

Finally we reached a road in better condition and the trip became more comfortable for everyone. We travelled like this for more than an hour, when suddenly we heard screams coming from the front row: "A guerrilla checkpoint!"

José had been dozing; he woke with a start. He looked out the window and then looked at the passengers. He walked down the aisle and asked a man sitting a few seats forward, "What is going on?"

The man was staring out the front window and pointed ahead saying, "There is a guerrilla checkpoint just there."

"Why we don't stop and go back?" José asked still confused.

"It is too late. They have already seen us."

José, still feeling sleepy, rubbed his eyes and looked again. In the distance he saw a group of armed men behind a barricade of logs and wire in the middle of the road. No car was allowed to pass. Small vehicles were parked on the left side, buses and trucks on the right.

The man looked at José again. "Don't worry, boy, they do this constantly. They will check our documents and let us go. Just try not to be nervous and hide any money you bring."

I was immediately alert. "Wake up, wake up!" I called Jenny, who had also been dozing. "Something is not good." I had seen enough in Colombia to know that things can quickly get ugly with these groups.

José went back to his seat. All the passengers were focused on the road ahead and taking advantage of the moment, he took out his wallet, stacked the bills one on top of the other, and slowly rolled us tightly with his fingers until we became a thin roll of bills. He looked around and in a single, quick motion unfastened his jeans belt and unzipped his fly. He rapidly stuck his hand down the back of his pants and stuffed the roll between his buttocks. He quietly sat and waited.

The bus slowed as rolled slowly to the check point and came to a stop in front of a guerrilla fighter, pointing an R15 assault rifle straight at the driver. Five guerrillas came up to the bus.

"Open the door," they ordered, banging it with their rifle stocks. In less than ten seconds there were five armed guerrilla men inside the bus and more than twenty surrounding the bus outside waving and pointing their guns, frightening and intimidating everyone on the bus.

"Good morning," said a tall, dark guerrilla wearing an army beret and holding a pistol in his right hand.

Everybody on the bus obediently replied, "*Buenos días, señor.*"

The man moved his beret to one side, ordered two of his men to move to the back of the bus and said politely, "I need every single one of you to get off the bus and leave all your belongings inside. Just bring your identification. We have been tipped there are some paramilitary informants in this bus. So if you have nothing to do with the paramilitary, then you have nothing to worry." He sounded sarcastic.

The passengers slowly filed off the bus one by one. José didn't move from his seat. I could feel his gluteus muscles pressing us. The guerrilla parked in the front door looked at José with suspicion. "Hey, boy, you also have to go down."

"*Si señor.*" José stood, pressed his buttocks tightly and walked with shuffling short steps to the front door. The man didn't take his eyes off José's legs.

"Are you sick? What is wrong with you?" he asked gruffly.

"I don't feel well," José replied quietly.

The man pushed José down the steps. "*Rapido, rapido,*" he screamed, and then looked at his partner. "This boy walks like girl." They all laughed.

José was the last one off the bus. One of the guerrillas ordered everyone to form a line facing the bus. The tall, dark guerrilla started interrogating people, checking their wallets and confirming their identification documents. Four guerrillas stayed inside the bus opening passengers' bags and seizing what was useful to them. The interrogation began with the first person on the right-hand side of the line. The guerrilla commandant came close to the man and looked straight into his eyes. "What is your name?"

The man was nervous and tried to compensate for his fear by standing erect and breathing slowly. "Rodrigo Rivera."

"Give me all your documents, Rodrigo. I want to check them," the commandant ordered, extending his hand. The man took out his wallet, but before he could remove his ID the commandant grabbed the wallet from his hand. "I notice you've been nervous from the start. Are you hiding something?" he asked while he went through the wallet.

Rodrigo was fast to reply. "No, not at all. Is probably the trip." He tried to smile. But the commandant kept a blank face. He finished searching the wallet, took out all the money available and despite finding no link with the paramilitary he announced, "I still have my doubts about you."

The interrogation of the passengers continued. José was standing stiffly at the opposite end of the row. It looked as if he was going to be the last one questioned. The commandant and two others checked at least five people when they came to a man in his mid-forties. "Why you don't have your wallet in your hand?"

The man coughed nervously. "I lost it."

"Where did you lose it?" the commandant yelled, his face inches from the man's.

The man attempted to stay calm but the constant movement of his hands gave him away. "I don't know where," he faltered.

The guerrilla didn't look convinced. His eyes narrow with suspicion. "Comrade Snake," he yelled, "there is a passenger who says his wallet got lost."

Snake was a thin, bald, scary-looking dude. His arms were heavily tattooed with snakes and dragons and a cobra was tattooed on the back of his bald head. Snake came and stood beside the man, took off his black sunglasses and stared at him. "This must be the son of a bitch we are looking for." Then firmly grabbing his upper arm asked, "What is your name?"

"Vicente," replied the man.

"Tell me your last name," Snake ordered, pointing his gun in Vicente's face.

Before Vicente could speak, a guerrilla yelled from inside the bus, "I just found a wallet." He waved a brown wallet through an open window.

"Bring it here," Snake ordered and looked at Vicente. Snake held up the wallet and asked loudly, "Who is the owner of this wallet?" No one replied. He looked at Vicente. "Is this the wallet you lost by chance?"

Vicente didn't say a word. Sweat poured down his face. Snake opened the wallet carefully so all the documents stayed in place. The first thing he found was a piece of paper folded in half. His eyes rapidly scanned the document.

"I recognize these names," Snake said in an oily voice. "Paramilitary scum," he spat, snarling like a rabid dog.

Snake put the paper back in the same place he had found it then took out an identification card with a picture on it. Snake looked closely at the photo. He turned his angry face to Vicente. "Is this person here you by chance?"

Vicente lowered his head knowing his enemies had caught him. Snake said in nasty tone, "Now I know your last name is Rodriguez."

Snake called the rest of his men together and asked a couple of them to tie Vicente's hands and feet. Then pointed his rifle at his head and asked," Who else is coming with you in this bus?"

"No one," Vicente replied.

Snake pushed him to the ground and helped by another guerrilla, they dragged him by his feet to an open spot close to the road. Once there, Snake loaded his gun and said, "I am going to kill you the same way the paramilitary killed some of my men days back. And I am also going to hang you in the middle of the road."

Vicente laughed and said, "Do whatever you want to do. In the end you are all a bunch of cowards and sons of bitches."

"This is a tactic most prisoners use to annoy their captors, hoping to get them angry enough to shoot them in the head and avoid torture," Jenny said.

But Snake was an experienced fighter and replied smiling, "That old trick won't work with us my friend. I am going to burn you as the paramilitary did with the people in that town."

Snake decided all the passengers had to witness what he was going to do to Vicente so they would know what happens to paramilitary supporters. I couldn't believe just a few hours ago we were in paramilitary domains and now we were in the middle of the guerrilla-control zone, getting prepared for another round of blood.

We were still rolled tightly, hidden in the crease of José's buttocks. He periodically pressed us to make sure we were still in the right position. Snake called one of his men and asked him to bring "the black knife." He ordered the bus passengers to make a circle around Vicente. The terrorized people had no choice but to do it and watch. Snake, helped by four guerrillas, ripped Vicente's clothes and left him half naked in the center of the circle. Vicente turned violent and kicked and insulted his captors but as quickly as it came his violent display disappeared when he saw each of the four guerrillas sharpening a small, curved knife by rubbing it against a small rock. Vicente saw with wide eyes how they tested the knife by slowly passing their index finger over the sharp edge.

"It is good to remove tissue," they each finally announced.

"Perfect," Snake replied.

He looked at the frightened passengers then walked to the middle of the circle. "We are going to see how brave the paramilitary are," he said pressing one of the knives to Vicente's forehead, just enough to cut the epidermal layer. He drew the knife in a circle around the crown of his head. Vicente didn't say a word. He struggled to escape but two men held his head and four kept him pinned to the ground. Snake took out four small hooks and inserted them in opposite points of his head in the skin below the incision. He called four of his men "each one of you hold a hook and pull down when I give the order, you have to pull hard so the skin can separate" he said with a smile. The men, pleased that it was now their turn, came close and each one grabbed a hook. Snake looked at Vicente and said, "Sorry, this is war," then yelled, "pull, pull!"

The four men pulled until the skin separated from the muscle and peeled down his forehead like a flexible mask. I had never seen anything like it in my life. They pulled the skin down to his chin. His eyes were two cavities surrounded by face muscles that moved as Vicente screamed in pain. This was the most grotesque scene a human, or a bill, could ever have the misfortune to see. He was now a man with no skin on his face and still alive. *How far humans can go?* I wondered. *Are there any limits to their cruelty?*

Snake looked at the terrorized passengers, "If he hides his identity that means he doesn't need his face."

He took out a small plastic bottle containing a white liquid, probably a mixture of acids and sprayed it on Vincente's skin-less face. Vicente screamed so loud that José tightened his gluteal muscles so hard I thought we might melt together. The guerrillas were thirsty for blood, and like hungry wolves they continued peeling the skin from the rest of his face and part of his body. After an hour of blood, screams and panic, finally and thankfully Snake gave the order to kill Vicente. *How ironic this life is*, I thought. I never saw myself being happy because someone was going to be murdered, but that day I felt only relief seeing that bullet hit his skull and finish that man's suffering.

Alex Barr

Two shots ended Vicente's life. After that his body was burned and hanged on the roadside with a note written with his own blood saying, *"Este es una zona de guerrillas."* This is a guerrilla zone.

"What do you think about what you just saw?" Snake asked the frightened passengers in his sinister voice. "This is what happens to anyone that deals with the paramilitary," he repeated, almost lazily.

No one said a word. They could only watch, agree with nods, but there were no words to describe the horror they had all witnessed. Snake sniggered, walked to the bus door and ordered, "Start filing into the bus and I will say who stays and who can go. We need combatants and some of you will have to stay." This was not what people were expecting and they all became agitated, verging on panic.

The first ones to climb the steps onto the bus were an old couple, and Snake barely glanced at them. They were followed by two women. Snake lowered his rifle, stopping them at the door.

"How old are you?" he asked eying them from the hip down.

One answered, "Fifty-two years."

"Forty-nine," said the other.

He allowed the fifty-two-year-old on to and stopped the forty-nine-year-old.

"You want to stay or you want to go?" he asked.

"Please, I want to go, *señor*," she said trying to control her fear.

He came close to her and whispered in her ear. "Raise your skirt, so I can see if it is worth you staying. If not you can go."

She lifted her skirt, slowly, fearfully, in front of the guerrilla fighters. She raised it to her hips, but they all yelled, "Higher, higher." She was forced stand with her skirt up for more than a minute, until Snake said, "You can go."

It was a relief for her and for me. The woman went into the bus and sat next to her friend trying to control her shame. However, she was unable to hold back the tears that ran uncontrollably down her face. I never knew if those tears were caused by the humiliation or by the happiness of not being forced to stay.

Next came a couple in their early forties and a woman carrying a baby. They were all allowed to board the bus, but not before Snake checked inside the baby's blankets to confirm there was really a baby inside. Snake suddenly changed his tactics and said, "To save everyone time and to let the bus go sooner, I need all the people between ten and thirty years of age to take one step forward.

I couldn't believe José's misfortune. If they took José to fight with them, what would happen to his education? He wouldn't become a doctor like he dreamed. He'd probably become a child soldier and die before his sixteenth birthday. I tried to talk to Jenny about what was happening, but what with being tightly rolled and the ruckus of the rest of the bills jabbering and giving opinions all at the same time, I was having trouble making myself heard.

Jenny was also dealing with a little sexist problem of her own. A fifty thousand-pesos note was taking advantage of his location to hit on her. He was behind her and rubbing her back every time José squeezed us with his muscles. He was also whispering to her, soft enough so I couldn't hear.

I needed to tell everyone what was going to happen so I yelled, "If the guerrillas take José with them, let's get prepared for a journey of blood."

I was a bit surprised at myself. I was talking like an expert, like the General had; and even though I hadn't been with the guerrilla I had seen enough in Colombia to know that both were the same thing, just with different names.

We all knew José was nervous. In our hiding place, we could hear his accelerating pulse and his digestion moving faster due to his stress. He was probably thinking he would never see his family again.

Three people stepped forward: a young man and a young woman both in their twenties and, sadly, José. Snake came close to the three of them and immediately looked at José and said, "You stay with us; I know you will like it."

He turned to the young man. He looked about twenty-five, was well dressed and wore glasses. He looked well educated to me. "What is your complete name?" Snake shouted.

"Mario Martinez," the man answered tensely.

"Have you ever shot a gun?"

"*No señor,*" he replied, avoiding Snake's eyes.

Snake smiled. "Don't worry. Soon you will be tired of shooting them."

Snake moved his eyes to the nervous young woman. "Do you have a husband or a lover?" he asked her in a quiet, menacing way. I had a feeling she was sweet and gentle.

She opened her eyes wide and shook her head slowly, softly replying, "No, I am single."

Snake rubbed a length of her long hair between his thumb and forefinger. "Then you are talking to the man who's going to be your lover from now on."

The young woman began to cry hysterically and ran to the bus yelling, "*Por favor me ayuden.* Please help me, please help me. *Por favor, por favor.*" But she was stopped by three guerrillas. She now belonged to Snake and nothing was going to change that.

There was still a group of passengers waiting for Snake to allow them inside the bus. He came close to them and said with a maniacal smile, "I hope you never forget what you saw today."

"No we won't," replied the passengers, barely hiding their contempt and impatience.

"Now get on the bus," he ordered.

Jose tried to board the bus. He was trying to control the adrenaline rushing through his veins. "I see you are a school-boy," Snake said snidely.

*Si señor,*" José whispered.

"You do not need school," he told the boy. "You will come with us and you will have an exciting life. And we will also give you a good education."

José looked crushed. "Can I go inside the bus and get my bag? I will need more clothes."

"Boy, don't worry for clothes. From now on you will only wear military camouflage that I will give to you once we arrive to the camp. We will take good care of you."

And with that, José was shoved rudely to one side.

The last person about to board the bus was a woman who was stopped in her tracks when Snake said, in his smiling, scary way, "*Hola, Señora Gonzales.* Don't tell me you thought I didn't recognize you."

"I know that woman," said Jenny. "She owns a supermarket in one of the towns and is well known by the guerrillas. All the bills around here have passed through her supermarket, me included. I know she hasn't paid the *vacuna,* vaccine. This is protection money paid by business owners and individuals to guerrillas or paramilitary. I am sure Snake knows who she was from the moment they stopped the bus, but he left her for last."

Standing directly in front of her, he drew his gun and pointed it at her forehead. "*Señora* Gonzales, we are tired of waiting for your payments. As of today you are a kidnapped person and the amount of money your family will have to pay us will be big."

The woman said nothing, but from the look on her face it was like her mind was bombarded by all those thoughts people have when they know it's too late to change anything. *Why did I come on this bus if I knew it was dangerous? Why didn't I spend the extra and fly? Why didn't I pay attention to my husband when he said it was too risky?* It was too late now.

The rest of the passengers were allowed on the bus. "Can we go now?" asked the bus driver.

"Go, go," replied Snake in a bored way. He was too busy to be bothered with the bus any longer. He was looking at his future woman. She was standing next to the other three captives, Mario, José, and Señora Gonzales. All four looked dispirited, unable to speak.

José didn't cry although I'm sure he wanted to. I mean, he was only eleven. But he was trying to be brave, even though the adrenaline flowing like a river through his body had lowered his body temperature, made his heart pound like a hammer, and made his legs tremble to the point where he could hardly walk. He moved closer to Señora Gonzales, maybe looking for some support. Maybe she reminded him of his mother. But she was so completely devastated and scared she barely noticed him. She was in serious trouble and she knew it.

"When the guerrillas kidnap you for not paying the *vacuna,* they normally ask for an astronomical amount of money, and then they kill you anyway as an example to others." Jenny told me. "La Señora Gonzales will be lucky to survive."

The bus departed. Snake ordered the road block lifted and instructed his men to return to Camp 7 where they had one of their many laboratories to process cocaine. The more things change the more they stay the same.

## 15
# Con los prisioneros

Snake ordered the four hostages to get into his personal vehicle; the rest of his men travelled in trucks and by foot. As expected, he told the young woman to sit beside him in passenger's seat. Mario, José, and Señora Gonzales sat in the back of the Toyota 4x4 Land Cruiser. None of the captives or the bills said a word; everybody knew we were lucky to still be alive.

Snake drove along the main road for only a few minutes, then veered hard to the left and took a small trail through the dense jungle. Every few seconds the jeep bounced into potholes that threatened to send the vehicle off the trail. The wheels spun in the puddles of mud and water but nothing made Snake ease up on the accelerator.

"This jungle is a web of small trails made by horses and peasants over the years. Now they are controlled by the guerrillas, and anyone who wants to walk through them needs a special permit," Jenny said.

Much is said of the differences between the guerrillas and the paramilitaries; but for me, they were only two groups, both financed by drug sales. The paramilitary guard their facilities in their areas same as the guerrilla guard their facilities in their areas.

Alex Barr

We drove for more than two hours, bouncing around like bucking horses and sweating like pigs. Finally, the long and brutal drive brought us to what they called Camp 7. It was a clearing in the middle of the jungle, large enough for wooden buildings the size of hangars.

"What is all this?" I asked Jenny.

"These wooden structures are the labs where they process and refine their cocaine," she said. "The area surrounding the camp is planted with thousands of hectares of coca plants, camouflaged by the jungle."

"Who're those people carrying stuff?"

"Those people you see carrying sacks in their backs and walking in and out those hangars are local peasants who are obliged to plant and harvest coca."

I thought about what I was seeing.

"So how much will these labs make a month?"

"Each laboratory can process around two thousand kilos of pure cocaine a week."

"*A week!*"

"*Si*, Benjamin, a week." I did the math fast and multiplied two thousand by thirty thousand dollars per kilogram, which is the average price of one kilo in the USA. That's sixty million dollars a week from just one of their labs.

A fifty thousand pesos bill was listening attentively to us. "Can I add something?" he asked, but just pushed on, anyway. "It is estimated that after bribing the police, paying intermediaries, paying for supplies and transport, thirty percent of that money will come back to the producers. That's twenty-four million dollars a week in just one of the many laboratories both the guerrilla and paramilitary operate in the Colombian jungles."

"Do you know how many labs are in Colombia?" I asked him.

"No one really knows. Thousands I would guess."

Snake stopped his vehicle in front of a green tent. He ordered the two men guarding the main door to drag the new prey inside the tent. "But don't touch the young lady––she deserves special treatment." He went around the car, opened the passenger door and holding her hand walked into the tent with her. She looked terrified. The other prisoners were roughly pushed through the door.

Inside a man was sitting behind a wooden desk in front of an open laptop powered by a small but noisy generator that also provided electricity to the single light bulb hanging from the tent ceiling. "He is a guerrilla leader known as Comrade Barbas," Jenny said. "Do you see his long beard? Most of the guerrilla leaders let their beards grow below their necks to have a revolutionary look similar to Fidel Castro or Che Guevara."

"Are they really politically left wing?" I asked.

"Let's say, yes," she replied. "They were once, but now they pay only lip service to a revolution. They changed their social ideology during the eighties when cocaine and kidnapping became their main source of income. They are drug dealers, same as the paramilitary."

"So where did they get funds before?"

"From Cuba, or let's say the former Soviet Union."

Barbas politely directed the captives to four chairs arranged on the opposite side of his desk. "Bring some water and something to eat for these people," he barked. This formality made it hard to guess what was in store for these captives. They sipped the murky water and nibbled a bit of bread.

Barbas looked at José and turned to Snake, "Where did you get this little fighter from?"

Snake put his hand on José's head and said, "He was on the same bus as these others."

Barbas turned to José and said in a friendly manner, "Don't be scared boy. What is your name?"

The boy was so gripped in fear could hardly say his own name. Barbas continued in the same friendly way, "Don't worry,

Alex Barr

tomorrow you will start an intensive military training and in two weeks you will be fighting for the revolution."

Jenny didn't let him finish. "Don't believe those stories," she shrieked. "This is what the guerrillas tell the peasants and people to make them fight on their side. There is no revolution. Only the fight for the control of the cocaine trade." Nearly sobbing with frustration she took a couple of breaths and spoke a little more calmly. "Colombia has one of the highest rates of child combatants in the world. Around ten thousand boys and girls around José's age are in the battlefield fighting for the paramilitaries and the guerrillas. Benjamin, what can we do?" she asked. But she didn't really expect an answer.

She continued sadly, "Many will die in the hour it takes for a young North American banker or student to visit with friends over a beer in New York."

Comrade Barbas then yelled, "Commandante Ernesto."

Almost immediately a short man with a thick moustache came inside the tent. Barbas pointed at José with the thumb of his left hand; his right hand held a lit Cuban cigar.

Ernesto smiled as he looked at José. "You will like this place. I will be your trainer." A second smile played across his face.

*Why does this have to happen to me?* I wondered. Why did those fucking kids in New York have to buy drugs and send me down here to see all this? What's going to happen to José? All were unanswered questions except for the last one: I knew the answer to this one all too well.

The sweat, the movement and nerves by now had created a blister on José's left buttock. He urgently needed a place where he could rest and remove us. "I am sure José will come out of this one," I assured Jenny, thinking this would calm her. But I had forgotten that she was Colombian and knew better than me that this was just the beginning of a long and probably last journey.

Barbas looked at the young lady and noticed the stains on her face left by the tears of desperation. "Who is she?" he asked Snake. He looked at him with suspicion.

"She is a young lady from the same bus."

"Why she is here?" Barbas asked.

"She is the right age to become a good combatant. And she can also attend me," he added with a knowing wink of his left eye. "She will stay with me," he said draping his left arm over her shoulder. Barbas smiled and winked his right eye.

Barbas then looked at the last captive, Mario. "I know who can be a good combatant and this one looks like a city boy. They all lack balls." Despite this assessment he told him, "Tomorrow you will fight for the revolution."

Then he called Snake to one side and quietly whispered, "Put this young man in the front line and make sure he never comes back. He will try to escape whenever he has the chance."

Finally, Barbas addressed Señora Gonzales. "I know you are the owner of the Miramar supermarket and we have dealt with you before. *Señora Gonzales, usted tiene un gran problema.* We will ask your husband for one million US dollars for your ransom."

*Can this be the same man who offered us bread and water?* I wondered.

With tears in her eyes Señora Gonzales replied, "We don't have that kind of money, not even if we sold the supermarket could we raise that much. We have many debts."

Barbas pulled thoughtfully on the lower part of his ashen-coloured beard. "We will let you make a phone call so your family can start looking for the money. Otherwise you know what will happen to you. And please don't push me to repeat it; I have already said it to several other hostages today."

Jenny and I were both concerned about Señora Gonzales's situation. Picking up the phone handed to her, the woman dialled home. Her son answered the call. Barbas immediately put the phone on speaker mode.

"*Hola mi Niño*," she said holding her tears, "can I speak to your papa."

We heard the exchange of the phone, and a male voice came on the line.

"*Hola amor*, why haven't you come back yet? We are waiting for you."

Her voice trembling, she replied. "I have just been kidnapped by the guerrillas and they are asking for one million dollars to let me go." Her husband was silent, probably thinking about all the times he had told her not to stretch her luck, how she was too confident, and now it was too late and not the moment to bring up blame.

Tears streaming down her face, Señora Gonzales looked at Barbas. "Please let me go. I promise I'll pay you the money you are asking." She was confused and scared.

"*Lo siento Señora Gonzales*. You have to stay here until your husband pays. I promise you will be okay." He was trying to be reasonable.

"My children need me. Please let me go."

"No, no, you are staying, and going right now to the captive zone."

"*Por favor, por favor*," she begged, but Barbas was cold and rigid like ice.

He shouted a name, and in seconds a middle-aged short man with a scar across his throat from ear to ear came in the tent and stood beside José'. Barbas made some signs with his hand and pointed his index finger to Señora Gonzales. The man nodded. It was clear he couldn't speak. Barbas stood up and whispered to the man, so low we could barely hear him: "*Mata esta perra.*" *Kill this bitch.*

I looked at Jenny, pretending to be calm and trying to ignore my fears. But she'd also heard Barbas whisper. "Why they do this? Why?" she screamed.

Señora Gonzales was hustled out and, from the way she said goodbye to the other captives, I was sure she was not aware she was now on death row. That was probably for the best, I decided. We never saw Señora Gonzales again.

That day I began to understand that in countries like Colombia, freedom is not free, and never will be.

# 16
## Guerrilla Camp

José's story is typical of what happens to thousands of boys and girls in Colombia. He was now in the hands of Commandant Ernesto, the person in charge of training minors. He took José to a primitive hut, built with four beams at the corners, supporting a straw and banana-leaf roof. The floor was packed clay so that water could run off. There were no beds, just hammocks hanging from the roof.

At first Ernesto appeared to be a considerate person, but this turned out to be a tactic to win José's confidence. Soon Ernesto would let José know who he really was. For now, he was all smiles. Ernesto pointed out a hammock to José. "Here is where you will be when you are not in combat or training," he said. José pressed his buttocks twice to confirm we were still in position as he listened to Ernesto's instructions. Ernesto handed him a small-size set of military camouflage clothing. "Wear this at all times so we can identify you as one of us, in case of an attack."

In this part of the world the afternoons are always fresh, cooled by a wind that blows from the mountains. That day was windier than usual and blew so hard you could hear the leaves rustling in the trees. José looked around, took off his clothes and put on the camouflage clothing, keeping us pressed in case we slipped out. He wanted to use his hand to move us to one of his pockets but Ernesto didn't take his eyes off him.

"*Rápido, rápido.* I have lots to show you," he said. José finished putting on his uniform.

"This is probably recovered from the dead body of one of their child combatants. They know that soon they would be removing it from José's and be passed on to another kid. No point in giving them new uniforms." Jenny said.

"Don't say that, Jenny. Please don't say that again. I just know this boy will survive." We were as desperate as José to get out of that place. But right at that moment, we all needed fresh air and that rubbed sore needed us gone if it was to heal.

"I need a bathroom, urgent," José told Ernesto.

Ernesto looked at him. " Don't expect something like a toilet here in the jungle," he said, smiling.

He walked José over to a small structure enclosed with zinc sheets and with a deep hole in the centre. The hole was loaded with faeces and urine, but it had the privacy that José needed. José walked in and looked through a narrow crack between the zinc sheets to make sure Ernesto wasn't somehow watching him. He lowered his pants and grabbed us tightly in his hand. This was a relief for him and for us, a little happiness in a sea of doubt and fear. He carefully unrolled us, making sure we didn't fall inside the smelly hole.

When he opened the roll, in front of me was the face of an eleven-year-old innocent boy who should be dressed for school, not for combat. Soon he was going to be carrying a rifle and not notebooks like kids his age should do. His education was not going to be focused on giving him knowledge or teaching him to think; he was only going learn to shoot first so he wouldn't get killed. He rolled us again and put us in the pocket of his camouflage pants. He probably hoped he'd find a way to escape, and that if he did he was going to need us. He had a pee and walked more comfortably out of the latrine than he had walked

Alex Barr

in. Even though I had protested to Jenny that I knew José would survive, deep down I had my doubts, the kind of doubts you don't like to think about because deep inside you already know the answer. He was an innocent boy with dreams and he was never going to get away from this place. But I hoped with all my might that we all were underestimating him.

José looked exhausted. His eyes closed as he listened to Ernesto's training plans for the next weeks. "I am tired. Can I rest?" he asked timidly.

Ernesto looked at him hard but could probably see that the kid was falling asleep on his feet and with a wave of his hand just said, "*si,*" and walked away as José fell into his hammock.

Early the next morning Ernesto showed up with a smile on his face. "*¿Cómo estás José?*" he asked. "I hope you are you rested today because today you start training."

Ernesto woke up the rest of the kids and took them all through a winding path in the jungle towards an open spot where the guerrilla had four men handcuffed and tied to a tree. All had their heads covered with a black cloth. I groaned inwardly when I saw them.

"I don't like the look of this," I said. "Who're these guys? What now?"

"They are probably peasants from a nearby village brought by the guerrillas to be punished for helping the Colombian army," Jenny told me. They were tied one next to the other and each had a crude handmade bull's-eye hanging from their chests. A commandant was standing to one side and was giving the orders.

"He is called Comrade Boris," A fifty thousand-pesos note told us. "He is the guerrilla version of the Surgeon. He is a cruel son of a bitch."

Boris was an average height but had a big chucky frame and carried a lot of weight, quite heavy to live in the jungle. He looked at José first. Jenny and I were nervous, not knowing what to expect. "Come here, boy." he said, sounding like a drill sergeant. José walked over to him. As he came closer I saw in Boris had those same empty eyes all these criminals have, whether they're guerrilla or paramilitary. They are empty inside. With beads of sweat forming in the hot sun on his forehead, he looked at José.

"You must be new. First time I see you."

The boy nodded.

"Do you see this?" Boris asked, showing José a pistol on his right palm.

"*Si, se trata de una pistola.*"

"Have you ever shot one?"

"*No señor.*"

Boris smiled and stepped closer. He put the pistol in José's hand.

"Listen to me," he said. "Hold the gun with your two hands and use your right index finger to squeeze the trigger."

He explained how to aim at a target. José was a fast learner and despite this being the first time he had fired a weapon, he hit a small tree. Boris asked him to aim at with precision. Boris smiled.

"Okay, José, let's see if you have balls." He placed José right in front of the four prisoners.

"You see these four people?" Boris asked roughly. "They like to give information to the army and the paramilitary. We have to get rid of them. I am going to give you the honour of killing these rats yourself."

"José is a peasant like them," Jenny said. "He knows better than anyone they are just victims of the war. He knows peasants in Colombia are not part of any group but sometimes they have to take a side just to save their lives. That's life here."

José, still holding the gun in his hand, turned to Boris and said fearfully, "I cannot do this. They have done nothing to me."

Boris's mood did a complete turnaround.

"Shoot or I kill you," he growled.

José's eyes widened but he still didn't raise the gun. The rest of the kids looked terrified. "Do it. Do it!" they yelled. "He will kill you. We have seen him do it!"

But José just stood stiffly with the gun at his side. Boris slapped José's face. He took his gun out and pointed at José.

"At the end of three, shoot. Otherwise I will blow off your head. One, two…"

"José, please do it, please do it," implored Jenny.

"What are you saying?" I exclaimed. I was disgusted. "How can you want that boy to kill someone? What is wrong with you, Jenny?"

Jenny looked at me, her eyes clouded with tears. "Benjamin, this is the way things are here. It is José or the prisoners. Both are victims, but if José does not shoot to kill, Boris will kill him and then kill the prisoners, too, simple as that. Benjamin, you have to learn that death is no stranger for us here." And just when Boris was about to say three, José, blood running from his nose, closed his eyes, lifted his gun, pulled the trigger and we all heard one shot.

"Did he do it?" asked Jenny, with her eyes closed.

Before I could reply, Boris yelled at him. "You need precision. You have one last chance."

I heard a familiar 'Klink' come from Boris's gun.

"Aim to kill, José," I heard myself scream. I couldn't believe I said this!

José raised his gun again, wiped his tears and aimed at the target a bit unsteadily. "Shoot, shoot!" I yelled as I saw Boris aiming at José with his gun. Then came a BANG followed by a short silence. "What happen?" asked Jenny *"What happen?"* she cried frantically.

"Don't worry, José shot to kill," I replied. I felt sad for those people, sad for me, and, most of all, sad for José. But what else could he have done?"

Boris, with a nonchalant gesture, lowered his gun.

"Well done. The second person you shoot will not be so hard."

He told the rest of the kids to finish off the other prisoners. They all jumped like hungry piranhas and began shooting indiscriminately until they had finished off the other three men.

During the next few weeks José became an expert at firing the AK-47 he was issued. Early in the morning he had target practice and in the afternoon the young combatants were taught some revolutionary theory. Eventually, José and about forty other kids were given the job of protecting the cocaine laboratories, the guerrillas' most valued commodity.

José's days went by fast and sometimes I thought he had forgotten about us.

Early one morning, José's Commandant Ernesto rushed into the dormitory, yelling loudly to rouse the dorm. "I need you to come with me," he told the sleepy kids. "We are going to Camp 37. You will escort me." José grabbed his rifle and they all jumped into the jeep, the driver revving the motor loudly.

Camp 37 was only about forty-five minutes away, but it was unsafe to travel there. The paramilitaries had been ambushing guerrilla convoys in recent months, and when these two sides clashed there were always fatalities. The driver didn't seem to know there was a brake pedal, and he slammed the jeep into the pools if water left by overnight rain. Some were level; others were deep enough to make the car chassis bend as it bounced through them. I hoped that I would just survive the trip. But I also had another worry. I figured we were probably going to some kind of meeting, and had learned the hard way that when guerrilla and paramilitary have urgent meetings, it is not usually to find a solution to a problem. More often it was to find ways to pour more fire and blood into the problem.

Alex Barr

This camp was bigger than the camp where José was living. This one had an air strip long enough to land and park turbo propelled planes.

"Guerrilla use them to transport their drugs out and bring in their supplies," Jenny said.

As the Jeep parked beside some others, I could see Commandant Barbas walking with two men up some narrow stone steps to a huge tent standing in the middle of the camp. Barbas was the first to enter, followed by the two men and the rest of the comrades who had come for the meeting. José was ordered to guard the entrance and to make sure only the invited could go in. After an hour of deliberations, Commandant Ernesto came to the tent door and smiling broadly told José, "Go to the jeep and bring me my personal agenda. Knock on the door twice when you are back."

José hustled there and back quickly and knocked twice on the door. A voice from inside said, "*José, siga.*"

He opened the door quietly and walked over to Commandant Ernesto and handed him the agenda. When he turned to leave I heard the voices of two foreigners speaking in heavily accented Spanish.

"I've heard those voices before," I told Jenny, but she wasn't interested. '*Please don't leave,*' I mentally implored José. I needed to see who those voices belonged to. As José stepped a little to one side to duck around someone, I found myself face to face with Jurgen and Hans, the German arms dealers who had closed the multi-million dollar arms deal with 01, the paramilitary leader. Now they were doing business with the guerrilla. They were the last people I had expected to see that day.

José stood, transfixed, his eyes wide at the sight of more than thirty million dollars stacked on top of three tables. For sure, he'd never seen so much money in one place and undoubtedly had no idea how much one could buy with all that.

I was told by some dollars lying on the table that the Germans had arrived from Panama. They moved in the higher echelons of social and government circles, they reported, and were interested in the war in this country since it was an ongoing market for their deadly products. Apparently the guerrillas were buying thirty million dollars worth of military equipment, arms, and ammunition, and planned to pay another fifteen million for anti-air missiles to combat the Colombian air force, which had been bombing their laboratories and training camps. They had incurred heavy causalities and had been obliged to relocate in other areas of the jungle.

Everyone inside that tent listened attentively to the Germans; no one noticed that José was standing quietly inside the door. I listened with fascinated horror to the negotiations and heard the Germans promise the guerrilla the best anti-air missiles available.

"The same ones the United States used in Iraq," Jurgen told them, looking at the money.

"We can find you any weapon you need, as long as you are willing to pay the price," Hans added.

The Germans counted the money, agreed on a time of delivery, shook hands with their customers and left in their private plane to return to the sanctuary of Panama City. This time they were taking thirty million dollars. I now understood how arms dealers get obscenely wealthy off the drug users addictions and the blood of innocent people. But they don't care. Money is their god. No one except me knew the Germans were playing two hands, but that didn't mean much. There were hundreds just like them doing it. They're like bad weeds––when one dies ten flourish.

José and Commandant Ernesto left minutes after the meeting ended. Ernesto couldn't hide the joy from his sweaty face, already beet red in the forty-degree heat."Soon we will get new arms and sophisticated artillery," he told José as they all got inside the Jeep. "Time to get back," he said cheerfully, and the rodeo started again as we bucked and tossed our way back to camp.

# 17
## El Escape

Saturday, exactly a week after the meeting, was a beautiful day: deep blue sky, no clouds, all seemed calmed. That was the day I chose to confess the truth about my real identity to Jenny. José was lying in his hammock and Jenny was calm--the perfect moment. Frankly, I needed to come clean. I felt like a prisoner of my own lies and I wanted to tell her before she heard it from other sources. I knew it was a gamble. She would either forgive me or would end whatever we had built up. Still I hesitated, the more I thought about it, the more doubts appeared in my mind. *If I tell her I lied about who I am, she's going to think that everything I told her were lies*, I thought. But in the end I stuck to the first rule of friendship: honesty. Today was going to be the day.

Around four in the afternoon as I was preoccupied with polishing my explanation, Jenny noticed a roaring sound. "Why airplanes coming close to this place? They sound like fighters," she said.

The wooden structures trembled as the sound got closer and closer. Anxiety swirled through me. People began to come out of their tents, looking in all directions trying to locate the source. The sound grew louder as suddenly the fuselages of two bombers flying low came into view on the southern horizon. It was too late to react; the first bombs had been dropped on the camp. I felt the ground shake as José leapt out of his hammock looking for refuge. Roofs were falling around us. The explosion lifted a cloud of dust and fire that covered one side of the camp. That first bomb found its target, dropping precisely on the camp communication centre. The second bomb hit the kitchen and the west dormitories. Vibrations from the blasts ripped through José's body. All was chaos. Two more bombers appeared from the north. They were attacking from all sides.

"Don't they know there are kidnapped people down here?" Jenny was confused.

They dropped their deadly cargo over the rest of the camp. It looked like the guerrilla didn't have a plan for an attack of this magnitude. I could see that the explosions had killed many, and that others were caught in the fires that began to spread with the help of the wind and the combustion of hundreds of drums of chemicals used to process cocaine.

"This is the Colombian army, Jenny called to me. They have identified this guerrilla camp and are displaying their military might. They also have to show progress to the Colombian public with aerial attacks like this one."

As soon as the attack began, the guerrilla had turned on sirens and brought out their anti-air artillery, no doubt recently bought from some arms dealers. Even though they were able to fire some missiles, they had no impact. There was almost no visibility because of the smoke from the burning tents and the ignited chemicals. The ether, gasoline, potassium permanganate, and acetone were all catalysts spreading the flames.

Fire was everywhere. The acrid odour of burning chemicals stung eyes and nose, lungs gasped for air in the heavy, black smoke. Those still alive and fearful of dying panicked and ran in all directions looking for shelter. Between the smoke and their panic they couldn't see Barbas standing on the only untouched side waving his hands, attempting to calm his troops.

The anti-air artillery was destroyed when it was hit by one of the bombs. The four guard towers, built to protect the camp from intruders, were blown apart away with the guards inside. Within minutes, little was left standing in the camp except for the northeastern part where Barbas was trying, without much success, to reorganize his people. Most were dead or were looking for refuge.

As quickly as they had come, the bombers left and a calm silence settled over camp. Then came a deep silence, no more explosions, no more shots, no yelling, no whine of bomber engines, not even wind. It was as if the jungle had died. But it lasted just seconds.

It was just the first round. Within moments we heard then saw six more fighters coming straight at us. Their target was the untouched part of the camp, where most of the survivors were seeking refuge.

The first bomb hit the shelter where Barbas and other commandants were trying to make telephone contact with other guerrilla groups for support. A single bomb hit the heart of that shelter, instantly killing Barbas and three others, and badly injuring the rest.

I'd had the feeling that José had given up any hope of escaping. He'd been in the camp long enough to have heard stories of failed attempts, and he seemed resigned and intent on keeping his head down and staying out of trouble as much as that was possible. Now he had the opportunity of his life. For a few precious minutes he was out of sight, hidden in the smoke and everyone's distraction. He glanced around and saw he was nearly alone and nobody was looking after anybody.

"Don't think. Just start running!" I said.

"It's now or never," Jenny agreed.

José looked around again at the devastation, grabbed his rifle, felt for a compass in one of his pants pockets and for his money in the other pocket. I was scared but also happy to see

José had this chance. Jenny was still shaking from the explosions. I felt pretty shaken myself but I tried to look strong for her and for José, even though he didn't know it. I knew that if José died in the jungle, we would too. Deep inside I knew that running or staying were both bad choices but running trumped staying captive with the guerrillas.

"Anything is better than this place," Jenny muttered.

There are moments in life when you cannot think too much. This was one of them. "Move, boy, move," I yelled as I heard voices approaching. To my relief José gasped for some air and ran to the kitchen and began looking desperately for food. But the bombing had destroyed the kitchen. There was nothing edible to take. Exploded tuna tins and rice scattered on the ground was all you could see.

I didn't know it then, but I learned over the next few days just how hard it is to survive in the jungle. It's a wonder José even thought to look for food. His heart was in overdrive and he began muttering to himself, probably out of extreme anxiety.

"No one survives the jungle without food," I heard him say to himself.

"This is a good sign," Jenny said. "José, he is a village boy living on the edge of the jungle. He has probably many times heard stories about surviving in the jungle. That sounds like something maybe his father has told him."

Looking disappointed he turned, watching survivors run to the black mountain, as it was called because of its light, or rather lack of light. By day it was like night because of the thick foliage and the dense canopy of the trees that stopped the sunlight from reaching the ground. I could see the attraction of this as a hiding place, a place to wait until the attack was completely over and maybe make a break for freedom.

"What is he thinking?" I asked Jenny. "Please, don't follow those guys. Run away from them," I yelled.

José kept looking at the black mountain, eyes concentrated, hands shaking. He put his cold and trembling hand inside his pocket. I could sense the fear and doubt. Suddenly, he pulled his rifle strap over his shoulder so his rifle was to his back and started running in opposite direction. He jumped over decapitated bodies, ran over and round hands, legs, and burning uniforms. He tripped over a mountain of crushed cans, fabric and debris and kept running. I saw the remains of Snake and his new girl, lying on the ground. José glanced at the dead body of his captor, smiled, then jumped, dodged and ran some more until his thin body quickly disappeared in the shadowy, dense jungle. He ran as hard as he could without looking back and without caring if anyone was looking.

## 18
## The Long Run

José ran non-stop for the first thirty minutes, until the jungle became too dense for him sprint without tripping over tree trunks. His heart was pounding hard enough for us to hear it. He was fuelled by anxiety and adrenalin. My sense of direction got completely turned around––all the trees around looked the same, north looked like south and east was no different than west. It was impossible to have a reference point and I worried that José was running in circles. He gulped for breath but we could hear him talking to himself in breathy gasps from time to time, "Lost in the jungle, find a small ravine …small ravine to bigger one … bigger one to river … rivers … fisherman … help." As he ran deeper into the jungle, trees got denser and denser.

José made good use of his first hours of freedom. I figured the guerrilla would need at least twenty-four hours to reorganize and maybe another day to figure out who had died during the bombing. I wondered how many others had used this situation to escape. I reckoned José had forty-eight hours before the hunt started.

Jenny was now feeling calmer. She turned to me and said, "I have been in other bombardments before, but it is hard to get used to it. Normally the Colombian army attacks by air because it is not easy to fight the guerrilla on the ground. The jungle is their habitat. They've been here for decades and they don't need compasses to keep direction. They know the location of trees by memory, and they have very sophisticated ground-fighting weapons. Also, they are immune to some of the tropical diseases."

"Do they launch air strikes like this one, often?" I asked.

"Like today the air strikes don't last long. The army only wants to destroy the cocaine laboratories, kill some guerrilla and have something to show on the evening news. On the other hand, the guerrilla will change their camp and laboratory locations, illegally recruit more young combatants to replace their dead, then in revenge for the attack, destroy a village with their famous cylinder bombs and further increase the number of displaced people and refugees. When the army finds a new location, they bomb again. I think you call this cat and mouse."

"So who is winning this war?"

"I don't know who is winning but I can tell you who is losing. The thousands of kids illegally recruited that die like ants on the battlefield. Also, the thousands of innocent Colombians killed, and the heartbroken millions whose homes and livelihoods are destroyed and have fled to live as dispossessed people in cities far from their ancestral homes, families and lands."

I could hear the sadness in Jenny's voice. I felt bad that she had seen so much and knew all this. But at least she was helping me make sense of all the craziness. José kept running, avoiding the small tracks in the middle of the jungle. He knew they all had anti-personal mines under the soil to keep away intruders and stop their combatants, like him, from escaping.

"Only the high-ranking commandants know the exact location of each land mine." Jenny added.

José's lungs cried out for him to stop but he knew he wasn't safe. For starters, he was badly dressed for this escape. His heavy, oversized boots got stuck in the wet mud, slowing him and tiring him; his wet uniform chaffed; a heavy AK-47 rifle pulled at his shoulder and hit his back as he jumped over logs and bushes and further sapped his energy.

After two long hours, José stopped to take a good breath and to think what he had just done.

"No one makes it through the jungle with no food or water and carrying a rifle that is not going to help if they find me," he said aloud.

"That's my boy; he's thinking," I said to Jenny. "Make yourself lighter and keep running."

As if he could hear me, he laid the rifle under two big logs, out of sight of any guerrillas passing by. He finally looked closely at a wound on his left arm where he had been hit by a flying piece of rusty metal roofing during the first raid. I remembered he had raised his hand to cover his face and the sharp edge of the metal had cut through his uniform sleeve and penetrated his arm like a hot knife in butter. It hadn't bled much but he had to find medical attention soon, before it got infected.

I've been in many wallets and have seen humans make heroic moves and unimaginably difficult decisions. I've also seen many lose their enthusiasm halfway through difficulties and give up when they are on the verge of achieving what they set out to do. I knew that if José gave up, it would be the end for him and us. But I kept my thoughts to myself because Jenny had become convinced we were going to make it. Destroying her illusions was the last thing I wanted to do. But I knew that José's hunger, his thirst, his solitude, and his fear of dying were telling him to go back to the camp.

The boy, hovering with indecision, sat on a log. Sweat dripped from the end of his nose and neck. Don't stop; don't think; just run, I silently willed him. He put his two hands around his neck and started to cry like the frightened little boy he was. He cried with grief; he yelled, "Mamá, mamá, papa." He stood up then sat down, over and over again.

"Cry and cry; get rid of all that fear but please start moving. Think of your sister. Think of your mother. Stand up, stand up," I said between gritted teeth, "we're wasting precious time." Every bit of my concentration was with him.

Jenny looked at me. "What is happening? Why he is not moving?" she asked.

"Don't worry. He's just resting," I told her, hoping it would reassure her. But I knew José was seriously thinking about going back. If that happened he would be executed. He was probably thinking he could go back and tell the guerrilla he ran through the jungle afraid and got lost. But I had been told that these groups have a set of internal rules they strongly enforce and one of them is that any attempt to escape is punishable by death.

Seconds later, José stood up. He looked to the left at the path that would take him back to the camp. Then he looked to the right at the path that would take him to freedom. This decision was going to change the course of a life forever.

"Please go to the right," I begged. But José didn't move, and his lack of decision was killing me and was going to get him killed. He tied his boots and then, without warning, he began moving, his legs jogging at a steady pace away from the camp. His wish for freedom and perhaps the hope of seeing his family again gave him the strength he needed to keep going. He was getting a second wind.

"Atta boy. This is the José I want to see," I said to Jenny. "If he can persevere maybe he'll get back to school one day, get that education he wants so badly. Y'know, I once heard someone say, 'wherever there is love there is hope,'" I told Jenny, as my own spirits rose.

Later, the sun disappeared and the night brought a cool and humid breeze. The loud noise made by the tropical birds was replaced in seconds by millions of bugs whistling and flying through every inch of breathing space. Sitting and resting was probably the logical thing to do, but the majority of the animals hunt at night, and you can easily become disoriented and end up running in circles or returning to your the starting point. But now José was a decision maker and wanted to take advantage of the hours he had ahead.

He slowed his pace and took out his compass. "I am so tired," he said, "but guerrillas they are good trackers, and my papa say they can move three times faster through the jungle than a normal person," he murmured. It was hard walking through the jungle at night, there was hardly any light, but José slowly kept heading north. Deep down I worried José could not endure the jungle night--the cold, the dark, the animals lurking, his own disorientation.

"I wonder what's happening back at the guerrilla camp," I said to Jenny.

"You ask me as if I were an expert on the topic!" Sheesh, what now?

"Heh, I'm sorry, but you kinda are. This is all new to me. You've been through bombardments before. At least you know more than this New Yorker."

She smiled. "In the guerrilla camp things are probably calming down. The bombardments for sure have ceased. There is probably nothing left. Even if something has been left standing it is meaningless because the Colombian army has now the coordinates of that camp and will strike again."

"So they'll have to move?"

"The guerrillas will move this camp to another location. Not a difficult task in an endless jungle."

"What about all the injured?"

"Many combatants will be reported dead, and if they have time they might bury them. The survivors will regroup. Reinforcements will come from other guerrilla fronts in the area to restart their laboratories."

"So when do you think they will notice José isn't around?"

"José's name will not show in the list of the dead. He will come to be the only one missing and the only one who escaped."

"You think he will be the only one escaping?"

"Benjamin, no one in the guerrillas will try to run away. They will fear the guerrillas would take revenge on their families. José didn't think about that, but he knew it very well. It was the first thing they told him during his training. Deserting is severely punished by the guerrillas and the paramilitaries. The hunt for José will start soon and will not stop until they find him dead or alive and made an example of him that would frighten the rest. They will commission their best hunters. I am sure they will call a commando called Sleuth."

Through the night, José made ten- to twenty-minute stops to rest then pushed himself onward. One complete day and one night had already passed. His feet were raw from blisters that formed when his skin rubbed the stiff wet leather of his boots. Mosquitoes and other bugs bit most of his uncovered skin, leaving hot, itchy rashes. He desperately needed to find fresh running water to drink. He was almost completely dehydrated from the heat and humidity and the exertion. He was beginning to weaken and was losing hope, which is a symptom of extreme dehydration. I knew that if José fell asleep he would never wake up.

"Hang in there, little fella," I willed him. Dig deep for just a little more energy. But the only water on the jungle floor was muddy and impossible to drink.

We could tell that José felt that every pound of his body weighed four times more. He was starting to stumble and his leg muscles began to give out. He could hardly move forward. He no longer resembled the boy kidnapped by the guerrilla three months ago. His eyes were dull, his body had used all his fat reserves and his skin was hanging from his bones. He sat against the trunk of a big tree, took two deep breaths and his eyes closed, simple as that.

Alex Barr

"Stand up, stand up," I yelled, but he was in a deep sleep. I could hear his heart pumping but for how long, I wondered. I turned to Jenny and with my heavy heart I said sadly, "I don't think José can make it. He's too dehydrated. Soon this humidity will start rotting our fibres. I don't think he's going to stand up again." I, too, had given up hope.

José slept and we tried to do the same. I woke few hours later and decided I was going to tell Jenny the truth now. *Why keep being a liar*, I thought. So I turned my head to her, "Jenny I have something to confess."

"Tell me what this gringo needs to confess," she said joking.

"No, I'm serious." I replied.

Suddenly we heard the ripping sound of bombs striking very close to us. The whole ground moved.

"Benjamin, Benjamin, the airplanes are back," Jenny said, frightened.

I couldn't believe the army was striking again. "We can't be that close to the camp," I said. I listened closely to the sound and suddenly knew what we were hearing. "Those aren't bombs. That's the rumble of thunder. Soon we'll have rain!" My spirits rose by the moment. "Rain is water and José needs water! We might survive," I yelled.

Jenny giggled with relief. The thought of rain lifted her spirits, too. I was so relieved that I forgot about my second attempted confession. "I'll tell her later," I thought when I remembered afterward.

The sky opened and huge drops of water began to fall. First just a few, then after several rows of lightning and loud thunder crashes the sky opened and it turned into a thundershower. José needed only a few drops on his face to wake up. He looked at the sky, held his hand out to feel the water and said quietly, "*gracias a Dios,*" and crossed himself as he realized he had been given a second chance. Still weak and tired, he slowly moved his hands to his face and rubbed the water over his mouth. He tried to direct the water that ran from his forehead down to his chin but there wasn't enough. His body needed more than drops. A shudder ran through his body as he saw huge amounts of water falling but he wasn't able to collect enough to drink. He stood up and stumbled toward a small tree with broad leaves. Shaking, he folded one of the leaves upwards and started to catch the rainwater diverting it to his mouth.

"I love this boy," I told Jenny. "Drink all you can and start walking," I tried to urge him.

He paused while drinking and looked at the ground. The falling water formed small streams that moved in the same direction. He followed them several feet and stopped. He held his breath and heard the sound of water running over rocks. "*Un río,*" he whispered. He ran in that direction and found a spring bubbling pure water. This was what he needed. He took off his boots, rinsed the sand and dirt from his feet, drank some more water and cleaned his wound.

I began to get nervous. Time was passing, and the hunters had probably already found his tracks in the jungle. "If José doesn't start moving we're all going to be recaptured."

He kept in mind his father's advice and rapidly jumped over stones and logs and followed the running water. It didn't take him long to find a small ravine that connected to a shallow river. Just as his spirits rose he encountered a problem. The other side of the river was flat and open and would be much easier to run on. But on this side it was muddy and covered in bushes. He stopped and with dull, discouraged eyes looked across the riverbank. He decided he had no choice; he had to cross it. He moved slowly to the edge. It was shallow.

"Why's he stopping?" I asked Jenny.

"Calm down, calm down. He knows anacondas, piranhas, and alligators lie in places like this, always ready for an easy meal. Give the boy a break, Benjamin."

Alex Barr

I could sense José's heart racing. He removed his pants and boots and carried them each in one hand. Jenny and I gasped as he raised his hands, firmly holding us above his head as he headed into the water. He didn't want to lose the boots or us. Taking small hesitant steps he began moving toward the other side, keeping his legs opened wide to resist the current. We had reached almost the other side when suddenly everywhere was water.

Jenny began yelling desperately, "*Me estoy ahogando*, I am drowning."

I wasn't sure what was happening. Water soaked into my paper like I was a sponge. "Calm down," I urged her. "He probably slipped and we hit the water. Stay calm."

I tried to see what was happening but the water was too muddy to see anything. I could feel the water beginning to soak deeply into my fibres. I felt heavy. The current passed over us with great speed, forming a vacuum inside the pocket that started suctioning us out. Struggling with the current I yelled, "Jenny! Jenny are you still here?" I called her again and again but got no response. The water kept entering and the vacuum was pulling me out. Visibility got better and I realized I was the only one left inside that pocket. Jenny and the other pesos were gone, probably floating near the riverbank.

*What happened?* I wondered. At first I thought José had tripped on a stone but then I realized he wasn't moving. His body was under water except for his head, and he was breathing slowly, trying to control his pounding heart. Why aren't we moving? Please move and reach the edge and look for Jenny, I said, willing him to hear me.

But José was more scared than us. He was staring at a dark, long shadow swimming slowly under the water. It was definitely moving toward José. "*Es un caiman*," he said quietly and with fright. What in hell is caiman? I wished Jenny were here.

José began to slowly lower himself under water, rising every minute or so slowly to gulp air, then slowly descended below the surface to keep the water calm. As the shadow came closer it made a stop almost in front of the frozen boy. José slowly gulped air and stopped breathing. All I could see was a long head with a mouth loaded with sharp teeth. This animal is probably preparing for the attack; this is it. I thought my days in Colombia––hell, anywhere––were over.

José was able to control his body movements and breathing but not his pounding heart. After a few seconds, the shadow slowly moved downstream pushing its body with its massive tail. In seconds it disappeared in the muddy river.

There was only silence inside the pocket. I felt Jenny was close but couldn't hear a reply when I called. Gradually, José's heart slowed down, and he began moving carefully, still watching for other predators, until he reached the other shore. He was still gripping his pants and boots in each hand. Slowly we made it to shore.

José took off his wet shirt, squeezed out the excess water, and draped it over the rocks. He reached into the pocket and realized it was only me inside. I was soaked through. He laid me on top of a rock facing the sun and put a smaller stone over me in case the wind picked up.

"Look for Jenny. Look for Jenny," I yelled helplessly. On the other hand I knew we had lost a lot of time and I worried that the guerrilla hunters would be closing in. The distance and time between them and us was shortening.

José turned to look back and his eyes widened when he notice a bill lying flat on the beach. He ran and saw it was one of his ten thousand pesos. As he approached I knew it was Jenny. She had survived! The current had brought her to the surface and pushed her to a small beach ten feet downstream. He grabbed her and laid her next to me. She was soaked but in one piece. I couldn't believe it!

Alex Barr

"Jenny! You survived. I thought I'd lost another friend forever!" I was elated and convinced our destiny was to be together. She didn't reply. "Are you okay?" I looked at her wondering what was wrong. All was silence. "Jenny, it's me, Benjamin." Now I was confused.

She rolled her black wet eyes and said smiling, "Benjamin, your beard is gone, your glasses are also gone, but you still look good!"

"Jenny, I'm so sorry. I know I should have told you before that José was the one who drew all that on me. Really, I'm just a very ordinary one hundred bucks."

She laughed. "Benjamin, you can't be so naïve to think I believed your story. I know there are not any special U.S. notes. I thought you were just joking and followed along. That is what I found attractive in you, not those horrible glasses and beard drawn with cheap ink and no art. Honestly, I am glad all that is gone."

I felt incredibly stupid. The General was right. I am naïve.

With José on the other side of the river his energy returned and with it his resolve not to go back to the guerrillas. He set a fast pace along the riverbank. Rivers are wide open spots where it was easy to be detected when you are hunted, but he had no other choice and time was of the essence.

"I'll bet that torrential rain washed away José's tracks and the guerrilla Sleuth you mentioned will lose his trail. I hope he decides to go back to camp without him. Because José's young, they might think he's wandering in circles or might be dead . . . or they might head out again tomorrow," I added soberly. "But this might buy him some time."

"Even though they think he is going to die, the guerrilla commandant will order his men to take custody of his family's house in case he makes it through the jungle and goes home. He belongs to the guerrillas and has to stay with them. That is the law here." Jenny said.

Man, are they harsh. But I knew she was right. I thought about José's parents and sister and how much harder their life would become, probably when they thought it couldn't get worse.

José walked on but he hadn't eaten in over twenty-four hours and he didn't have a lot of fat reserves to draw on. We could see he was losing strength from hunger. He began the muttering thing again, "eat what monkeys eat . . . no bird food."

"This boy has paid attention to the stories in his village," Jenny said. "They say you should never eat what birds eat because their digestive system is very short and poison fruits don't affect them."

But he had seen no monkeys in the area. He kept walking but began to slow down as time passed. He stumbled along the beach until he reached a bigger river. This is what he was looking for. *Finally a big river where some fisherman can help him,* I thought. But through all his travels he had not seen another human. The beaches on this large river began to disappear and the riverbanks became completely covered by dense jungle. It was impossible to keep walking. This is the part his father never told him about. He could do one of two things: he could swim in the river, risking his life with piranhas, snakes and alligators or he could walk through the jungle. He didn't have the energy for either.

His body started to move awkwardly as pain exploded in his muscles. His legs trembled and his mind became disoriented. He slowed, stopped and slowly his light body fell to his knees. He tried to will a return of strength but he had nothing left. My hope of leaving that jungle fell with him. He tried to stay on his knees but exhaustion, hunger and the disappointment of not seeing humans on the river finished him. He fell forward on top of the rocks. His heart was still beating but his mind and body were disconnected from this world.

Alex Barr

As we all lay I tried to regain hope and find a way to get José to stand up walk a little more. But there was no communication, of course. If he kept lying there he was going to be an easy target for animals or even the guerrillas. My last hope was that he would rest for a few hours, then wake up and continue his walk to freedom. But that never happened either, because three hours after he dropped, several men wearing military vests surrounded his body.

Two of them pointed guns at his head while two more came close to see if he was dead. They approached him and nudged his small body with their boots but José didn't move.

"The boy is dead," one of them said.

"He is wearing a guerrilla uniform," the other replied. "The rest must be around and he must be the bait, be careful."

One of them pushed him face up with his boot. He gave José a closer look, then said to the others excitedly, "He is not dead. The son of a bitch is breathing."

José opened his eyes painfully and saw four rifles pointing at him. The sun was shining straight into his eyes and he could hardly hold them open. He and I thought the guerrillas had recaptured him. Scared, he rolled his body into a foetal position and covered his head with his hands.

"Stand up, you little son of a bitch," shouted one of the armed men, still pointing his gun at him.

That shout was like an uncontrollable stroke of adrenaline that rushed through José's body. He began to cry and yell for mercy.

"I am sorry. I didn't mean to escape. Please don't kill me," he begged.

"Who are you? What is your name?" asked one of the armed men.

José uncoiled and sat up. Without the sun shining in his eyes we could see they were wearing military vests different than the guerrilla. It could easily be another criminal group or the paramilitary again.

"Who are you?" the man asked again. "Are you a guerrilla fighter?" He grabbed José by the head and dragged him into the bush.

"What's going on?" I yelled. "Tell them you were kidnapped by the guerrillas, you are not a guerrilla. You're the victim here! Wearing a guerrilla uniform was not your fault!"

The man took a pistol and pointed it at José's head. "I will count to three and if you don't tell me where are the rest of your people I will shoot you in the head now."

José took a breath and said trembling, "I am not a guerrilla fighter. I was kidnapped by them and escaped several days ago after a military bombardment."

The man look unconvinced, but replied. "We are from the Colombian army and if what you just said is true you are saved. If you are a guerrilla telling lies, you are fucked."

Unconvinced he turned to his men and said, "You guys know if we did bombardments around this area recently?"

"*Si señor*, that is true."

This time the soldier looked at José with pity. "So where do you live?"

José was crying. "I live in the town of Robles and my father's name is Roberto. He is also the owner of the shop named PAZ. You can call him; he must be looking for me." All the soldiers nodded.

The oldest of the soldiers gave him water and some bread. "We will take you to the battalion and help you find your family. You made it, boy. You made it."

## 19
## With the Army

"WE MADE IT! WE MADE IT!" I SAID EXCITEDLY TO JENNY "This is a miracle!" I tried hard to not let my tears fall––my tears of joy.

We were now in the hands of the Colombian army. What more could we want? I was impressed with José's perseverance, his will to stay alive. If you'd asked me in the beginning if he could walk as far as he had, I'm not sure I would have said yes. And now he had been found by an army patrol on a routine inspection of the area.

One of the soldiers was on his radio. "We need a helicopter. Now. We have just captured a guerrilla fighter during a long combat with one of their fronts."

I was amazed. "Long combat? What's he talking about?"

"They are getting ready to make themselves into heroes," Jenny said. "Just wait and see."

"But none of this is true! How can they say these things about José? He's just a little boy!"

It didn't take long before we heard a helicopter spinning on top of us. José was handcuffed and roughly pushed inside. Four men were needed to escort this inoffensive kid. When would this nightmare finish for this kid? All questions with no answers. Now I wasn't sure what was waiting for us in the hands of the Colombian army.

I don't recall how long the ride was, but I sure remember the reception they'd prepared when we arrived at the battalion base. There was a huge crowd waiting for us on the airstrip. The helicopter landed and waited. No one was allowed to get off. José occasionally looked out the window at the crowd of people surrounding the aircraft––cameramen, women holding microphones and reporters––all pushing to be at the front when the doors opened.

"They are all ready to blow out the news about the boy captured in a 'long' combat with the guerrilla," said Jenny sarcastically. "José does not understand very well the magnitude of this setup, but I still believe it is better for him to be with the army, even if the story will have a different outcome."

"I don't think he cares much either. José wanted freedom and he got it." I told her.

A few minutes before the helicopter doors opened, a man dressed in dark green from head to toe came and sat next to José. He took off the handcuffs "Don't say a word to the press when they approach you, just let me talk," he said in an intimidating way.

"*No hay problema señor*. I will do what you say," José replied. He seemed frightened.

"Who's the dude in green? I asked Jenny.

"The stars and insignias on his shoulders make him a colonel," she told me.

Finally the doors opened. I could hear media people outside. "Where is he?" "How old…?" "Hey! Watch where you're stepping…"

"Come with me," the colonel said as he grabbed José's shoulder. "Remember not to say a fucking word," he repeated as they both stepped outside. The wind was hot and humid, everyone looked at José with sympathy as the colonel marched him to a shed not far from the helicopter. The crowd clambered after them.

In the shed was a pile of AK 47 assault rifles, ammunition, grenades and military uniforms, all perfectly stacked. José looked at all this, looking like he was wondering what all this was about. I wasn't too sure either. The colonel held a microphone and addressed the crowd.

"Today has been a hard day for the guerrillas. We have captured one of their fighters, killed many of them and confiscated great amounts of arms and ammunition. We are committed to finish with these bandits."

"What will happen to the boy?" reporters asked.

"The boy will be given treatment and will re-enter into civil society." Cameras clicked and whirled as photographers and cameramen took pictures of José standing next to all the armaments. Reporters stood with little recorders held at arms length to capture the colonel's final words: "Soon the guerrilla and paramilitary groups will be eliminated from this country."

"Are they going to use this boy to show results?" I asked Jenny.

"All this is about that," she told me.

After the pictures, José was taken inside a building on the base to a small interview room on the second floor. One man dressed as a civilian and another wearing a military vest were sitting at a round table.

"Have a seat, boy. Have a seat," they both said when they saw José nervously enter the room.

"My name is Augusto," said the civilian, "and his name is Rafael." José sat timidly, looking puzzled.

"Listen to me José," said Augusto, "we have two options. One is sending you to prison for rebellion and the other is sending you back home. You have to tell us right now which one you prefer." He didn't take his eyes from José.

"I want to go home," José told them beginning to cry.

The men look at each other and smiled. "If you want to go home you just have to sign these two documents, which say that you accept you were part of a guerrilla group. The second document explains the circumstances how you were captured. Sign and you go. If you do not sign we cannot help you and tomorrow you will be sent to prison facing a thirty-year term."

José's eyes widened at this information.

"Yes, thirty years is what you will get," Rafael said.

At this point, I was sure José knew what was going on. He looked at the two men in front of him, probably thinking there was no point in insisting he wasn't a guerrilla.

"How do I have to sign?" José asked. His eyes looked sad, depressed.

"Listen, José, if you do not know how to sign you print your name and put your fingerprint beside." Rafael pushed the papers closer to José.

"What is this, Jenny? Why're they doing this? He's just a victim and shouldn't be treated like this." I was starting to get indignant.

"*Si*, I know. But is better for him to say yes to all these requests. If not he might never leave this place alive."

"What are you saying?" I was almost shouting but I could hardly believe what she had just told me.

"*Si*, Benjamin. It would not be hard for them to kill him and say he tried to escape. José has to sign those papers now, no matter what is written in there, and leave this place. They fear what can happen if the press gets to know all this was a set-up. Heads would roll and they know it. They need to protect themselves with José's statements in case someday the truth comes out, which I hope never happens."

"Jenny, how can you say that? Don't you think it would be good for the public to know the truth?"

"Yes, Benjamin, I do. But right now José is the only one that can deny their version. That puts his life in big risk, in very big risk."

José printed his name and Rafael inked his finger and he pressed it on both documents. "*Gracias señores,*" José said in a thin voice, trying hard to look happy.

"This was a good decision," Rafael told him, forcing a smile on his face.

José was assigned to a soldier who handed him some worn-looking kid's clothes told to follow him. They left the building and walked a few blocks down a base street to another where he was escorted to a room and told to shower and change into the clothes he'd been given. José walked slowly to the changing room and tried to stall before undressing, hoping to have a chance to take us out of his pocket. But the soldier didn't take his eyes off him.

"Move, boy. We don't have much time," he said.

"Please, José, don't leave us inside here." I begged.

The soldier moved close to him and told him in no uncertain terms, " I have to send that guerrilla uniform to the incinerator in the basement. We do not have all day."

"They are going to burn the uniform," I whispered in a horrified voice. "What'll we do?" Jenny was silent.

The soldier held out his hand and José had no choice but to quickly undress and give his uniform to the soldier, with us still inside. Many times I'd thought I'd die on this journey, but hadn't. This time I held out no hope. I could only think of the General and Ulysses.

José took a quick shower and dressed fast. Then was told he was going to be taken to have something to eat and then would go for a medical checkup. The soldier had folded the uniform and as they left the room, he asked a soldier passing by to throw it in the incinerator.

That moment was the last time I saw José. Against all odds, he had succeeded in escaping the guerrillas, and I now think he made the only decision he could when he signed the documents. I hoped life wouldn't prove me wrong.

As I was contemplating José's future, Jenny weighed in. "José life from now is not going to be easy. He will have many psychological and medical tests until he is approved to go back to the outer world."

"Then he really will be free," I said optimistically.

"Yes, Benjamin. But that freedom will come at a very high cost."

"What'd you mean?"

"Very soon his family will start receiving threats from paramilitary thinking that José was part of the guerrillas. His mama, papa and his little sister will have to flee their small town and move to the city. They will become part of the more than three million displaced people that are currently in Colombia."

"What about their small business and little farm?"

"They will not have time to sell anything. They will leave behind their animals, their small shop and the whole way they make a living. They probably move to the capital, Bogotá. This city already has more than seven million people. It is not easy for a peasant family to establish with no money and only farming skills. Many like them are discriminated against and pushed to live in the periphery slums. They will not be the exception."

"So what will happen to them? How will they survive?"

"Eventually they will end up in the streets begging for food."

I didn't want to believe her. I refused to believe her. "José is a good student, very motivated as we have both seen. I don't see why he can't pick up his schooling, maybe even become a doctor, like he dreams."

"Benjamin, José now has two powerful enemies, the paramilitary and the guerrilla. If he does not leave this area, he is dead."

"Why are they his enemies? He's done nothing to them. They're the ones who have treated him badly. Jenny, I don't understand what happens here. This country… Please Jenny, tell me that José's dreams of being a doctor someday can be real."

"Benjamin, all his dreams of studying died the day the guerrilla kidnapped him from that bus."

I didn't want to believe in Jenny's reality. But I know now that there are thousands of boys and girls who are prisoners of the guerrillas and the paramilitary. Many are dying as you read. Thousands of kids don't have a mother and a father to look after them because this war took away what they loved the most. I'll never forget José and his bravery and what I lived through with him.

At the moment we were still inside the uniform pocket and the soldier was getting closer to the incinerator with every passing second. I was ready to die; I knew my hours had been counted. Then, suddenly, there was a bump, and I fell, face-first. I could see nothing. We had fallen from the pants pocket as the soldier jogged down the stairs. Call it luck or call it misfortune, it happened.

I heard a woman coming up the stairs stop and say, "I think something fell from the clothes you are holding."

The soldier looked back, stepped up two steps and picked us up from off the floor. He quickly took out his wallet and slid us next to some other Colombian notes. When he reached the basement, he made a quick turn through a door into the men's washroom. He searched José's clothes pocket by pocket hoping to find more bills like us, but he found nothing. Looking disappointed, he grabbed the uniform and walked down a long hall and through a door marked *Incinerador*. He opened the hatch of the furnace and threw the clothes in.

Inside his wallet, Jenny and I soon learned from some Colombian bills that the soldier's name was Rodrigo. He was part of an anti-guerrilla squadron operating in that part of the country. Apart from participating in combats, Rodrigo, along with a few others, also gathered military intelligence from the surrounding villages, to detect guerrilla supporters. You'd think that being with the army life might change for the better, but according to those bills, life for us was going to get worse. "You will never imagine the type of alliances the Colombian army do to combat their enemies," a senior Colombian bill told us.

On his way out of the building, Rodrigo met a soldier who took him to aside and whispered, "The colonel is frantically looking for you. You better see what he needs."

Rodrigo smiled. So did the old Colombian bill sitting next to me. "The battalion colonel trusts him more than anyone else, especially if it is regarding dirty jobs," he told us.

"*Oh no, otra vez no!* Not again!" exclaimed Jenny. "What do you mean with dirty jobs?" she asked the old bill, furious. The old bill said nothing, but had an annoying 'you'll see' look on his face.

Rodrigo retraced his steps down the street to the colonel's office. The door was half open, but he didn't knock; he just walked in. "He is the only one that has permission to go in and out without announcing," the Colombian bill said.

The colonel was sitting at his desk, talking intently to someone in the phone. It was the same colonel from the helicopter. I'd guess he was in his fifties. Even though he was a big, heavy man, he looked in good shape. He looked up at Rodrigo and brought his index finger to his lips, warning him to stay silent. Rodrigo stood waiting while the colonel finished his conversation. After the conversation ended, the colonel hung up the phone and turned to face Rodrigo.

"Sorry, Rodrigo, I was talking to General Mondragon." The colonel looked excited. "Rodrigo, I have been looking for you all day. I need you to go today to the village of Robles, same time, same place, and talk to a friend of mine there. You know who I am talking about," he said, winking. "He is going to give you key information about those bandits. Apparently they have identified several of them and they need our permission to do the job."

The colonel sipped some water from a glass on top his desk and continued. "Make sure you also talk about the agreement we have. That is also an important point."

The colonel stood up and offered his hand to Rodrigo. "Make sure to be punctual and go unnoticed."

"Don't worry colonel. I'll be there on time," Rodrigo told him as he shook the colonel's hand.

He hustled over to his dorm, changed into civilian clothes, walked quickly to a parking lot, and drove off in a small red sedan. We were on our way back to Robles, José's village, to have a meeting with the colonel's friend.

Driving into the village, we passed PAZ, abandoned, the once-flourishing garden overgrown.

"*Lamentable*," he muttered to himself. "These villages get more depressing by the day."

He parked on a quiet street close to the main plaza. It was clear he didn't want anyone to recognize him as 'army.' He walked to the main plaza, to a restaurant beside a small bank. He took a seat at a table at the rear of the restaurant and sat with his back to the wall so he could watch who came in and out.

"Also to avoid being attacked from behind," Jenny added.

All the bills inside the wallet looked nervous, including Jenny. Me, I was calm. Why worrying? I was with the army and they're the ones who look after our safety, don't they? But what happen next caught me completely off-guard.

"Good afternoon, Rodrigo," a quiet voice said. "Thanks for coming."

A man moved a chair to sit. I knew I'd heard that voice before. I'd know it anywhere. You could've knocked me over with a feather. *The Surgeon.* I thought I was never going to hear that paramilitary criminal's voice again in my entire life.

And now here he was, a man I'd watched torture and murder villagers and kill two small kids like they were flies, ordering a beer and talking with the army. "Tell the colonel we have the addresses and locations of some guerrilla supporters. Our people are ready to attack and kill all those *sapos*."

*Frogs, people who talk too much. He's still at it. Why is the army talking to a man like that?* I wondered. *Isn't the army supposed to fight them? Why they don't use this opportunity to take him into custody?* I didn't know whether to laugh or cry.

It looked as if the Surgeon knew Rodrigo well, and before continuing their business, they spent a few minutes talking about their soccer teams, arguing about which one was going to be that year's champion. Rodrigo joked about his team and the Surgeon tried to find arguments to justify his team's chances to win. They carried on like great old buddies. After several minutes of deliberations they decided neither of the teams were going to the finals. Now came the moment to talk about serious stuff. It was the Surgeon who began as he took a sip of his beer.

"Rodrigo, tell the colonel we have everything ready to attack the town of Andalucía tomorrow night and hang those sons of bitches. Tell him not to send any military troops close to the area. Around 10 pm we will enter, and probably at midnight we will execute ten frogs."

The Surgeon, who was sitting sideway to Rodrigo, kept checking the front door to be sure his four body guards were still standing outside. "Also inform the colonel that on Friday at fourteen hundred hours we will send several planes loaded with cocaine to the Mexican coasts and we have to make sure the radars are off for at least two hours. Tell the colonel to do the proper arrangements. Tell him that if they keep helping us, we will continue with the extermination of guerrilla collaborators and help the army win this war."

Okay, now I was boiling mad. "You're the sons of bitches," I yelled. "You call anyone collaborator just to have something to show to the army and that way receive their favours. Thousands of innocent people are killed under the name of 'collaborator.'"

Finally some of my questions were being answered. But it was more complicated and ruthless than I had ever imagined.

Rodrigo listening carefully to the Surgeon made some coded notes in a small notebook. After his second cup of coffee, Rodrigo asked the Surgeon, "The colonel wants you to tell your boss, 01, that he is still waiting for the monthly payment for the radar operators."

"I know, I know. He, himself, is still waiting. He knows about the debt, but the Yankee and 01 had a problem with some counterfeit money laundered by Whirlpool, one of their money launderers. But don't worry, that problem also is already solved. This week we will send the money." I couldn't believe they'd caught Whirlpool. *Why do people do things they'll regret later?*" I wondered––yet again.

"Okay, I will inform the colonel about that." Rodrigo paused, then asked quietly, "How did you guys solve the counter-feit problem?"

The Surgeon lit a cigarette, glancing again at the main entrance.

"Whirlpool and his partner, Half Lip, had been changing the good money for counterfeit for a long time. We got notice when one of our arms dealers phoned and told us some of the stacks were not good. It took us a long time to notice because most of that money is kept hidden for years. It seems the Yankee and 01 were poisoned by anger because it coincided with a phone call made by Whirlpool's ex-wife alerting them of what her ex was doing."

By now Rodrigo was anxious to hear the whole story. "So what did you do then?"

"The Yankee immediately contacted Whirlpool and asked him in a friendly way to come to Colombia to negotiate the cleaning of a hundred million dollars. The greed blinded

Whirlpool, and he did not think that it could be a trap. Very early the next day he and Half Lip were flying first class to Cartagena." The Surgeon looked at his watch then checked the main entrance again. "I was the one who picked them up in the airport." He said this with the same smile he had when he killed Ignacio and Andrea. I knew if he picked them up then both were tortured to death. I tuned out; I was tired of blood.

Shortly after the Surgeon arrived the restaurant had spontaneously begun to empty. Suddenly, there wasn't a soul in the place. It didn't take long for villagers to notice the Surgeon's presence. Four vehicles loaded with armed men outside the restaurant alerted the villagers there was a high rank paramilitary inside and one glance told them who. They knew how dangerous it was to be close to him. They also knew he didn't like to be looked directly in the eye. They knew many had died just because of that.

The sun was beginning to set and the fresh afternoon air started to pick up. The two men had finished their business and it was time to leave. The Surgeon asked the restaurant owner for the bill. "You owe nothing," the owner said. The Surgeon didn't insist. He shared a handshake with his soldier friend, and both left. The Surgeon got into one of the cars waiting outside and disappeared in the plume of dust left by the spinning wheels of the convoy of criminals. Calm settled over the village again and the villagers dared to shed their fear of raising their heads.

I still couldn't believe there was an alliance between the army and the paramilitary. I couldn't believe the Colombian army supported criminals like the Surgeon. But at the same time, I was impressed how the reach of the drug lords had penetrated the highest spheres of the Colombian army and involved them in their activities. "Drug dealers earn billions of dollars," Jenny reminded me. "How hard do you think it is for them to bribe a policeman that earns a minimum monthly salary equivalent to three like you?"

Alex Barr

All I had ever overheard from other bills about the "drug tour" was nothing compared to all I had seen. Maybe they didn't have the words to describe it. Even I felt that in some ways you had to do the tour to understand it. Only now was it becoming clear that when you buy drugs you start a chain reaction of events impossible to imagine if you don't see them for yourself.

Rodrigo waited until the Surgeon and his assassins disappeared. Then he strolled like a normal villager back to his car and left. It was dark by now and since nobody leaves their home after dark the roads were empty. But I was sure Rodrigo felt safe because the ones that terrorize the zone were his friends.

When we arrived at the battalion base he immediately reported to the colonel, who was still in his office waiting for news. He didn't give Rodrigo time to sit.

"Tell me what happened," he asked anxiously. Rodrigo took out his notebook and went through the conversation in detail, telling him what the Surgeon had told him. Rodrigo emphasized the colonel should stop an army troop from going close to the village Andalucía. The paramilitary were going to do a "cleanup." He also told the colonel of the importance of contacting the radar personnel before Friday so the paramilitary could ship their cocaine with no interference. "No one wants last-minute surprises," he said.

The colonel stood up and walked over and sat next to Rodrigo. The office lights above his head made the medals hanging from his chest gleam. I wondered how someone like him could earn a dogcatcher award. Did the person who bestowed these medals on him know him well?

"Don't worry Rodrigo; I will contact the radar personnel right now," the colonel said, smiling. "But what about the money?" he asked.

"01 and the Yankee had some trouble but it is over now. Money is now available," Rodrigo replied, smiling.

"That is good. That is good. Nothing moves without money," he laughed. "Come Rodrigo, let us call it a day. Meet me at 0700 hours when the troops depart for daily inspection. I have much for you to do tomorrow."

# 20

# Bogotá

EARLY THE NEXT MORNING PLANS FOR THE CONTINGENT OF soldiers assigned to patrol Andalucía were changed. A last-minute memo from battalion colonel ordered them to stay on the base. The soldiers didn't know the reason, but Rodrigo and I knew the Surgeon was planning to visit Andalucía that day.

The same old knowledgeable Colombian pesos told us, "The villagers from Andalucía had asked the army to patrol the area because there were rumours the paramilitary are planning an attack on the civil population. The petition was authorized by the army. But now the colonel has put in his criminal hand and those poor people are now exposed."

I wanted to leave Rodrigo's wallet and run to Andalucía and tell everyone to escape, but the only thing I could do was to wait with dread and try not to think about the carnage I had seen at the small village of *La Esperanza*, where I first saw the Surgeon apply his skills.

It had rained all morning, but in Colombia this is not a refreshing event. Here the sun raises the temperature of the soil so high that when water falls on it, it warm vapour, similar to steam, rises from the earth and turns the place into a giant sauna.

Sweating in the rain, Rodrigo and the colonel stood outside the battalion entrance to be sure that all the patrols left in the opposite direction to that of Andalucía. Then, surprise, surprise, the telephone lines to the battalion stopped working. No calls in, no calls out. And the people who repair the phones had been sent early in that morning by the colonel to another battalion––in case they needed some repairs. No one from Andalucía was going to be able to call for help when the massacre started and the paramilitary, like lions, began devouring their prey. The colonel also had the perfect excuse when the government and the press asked questions. "Unfortunately the telephone lines were not working when the villagers called for help."

All I could think was, does anyone who asked these questions believe this stuff?

Pleased by how smoothly everything was going, the colonel asked Rodrigo to follow him to his office.

"Is very possible you have to fly to Bogotá today," the colonel said as he opened the door.

"Bogotá? Why Bogotá?" Rodrigo seemed confused, probably because he was only in charge of business inside the battalion area.

"You have to pick up two million dollars the cartel and the paramilitary are sending us to pay the radar personnel and some is also for us," he said smiling. "The son of a well-known politician will be waiting for you at the airport. Don't ask names. His father is the link between the cartel and the army. He will drive you to one of 01's offices. You will receive the money from them; make sure is the exact amount. Then put it inside this double-layer bag." The colonel took out a bag from a metal cabinet and handed it to him. "Once you have the money hidden inside the bag that same man will drive you to the military airbase on the outskirts of Bogotá where Colonel Rodriguez will be waiting for you. He won't let anyone check your belongings. Trust him. He is also on the cartel payroll. He will put you on the first helicopter that comes to our battalion. I will be there waiting for you."

Rodrigo looked happy. This was a huge demonstration of trust to a low-ranking soldier. "Don't worry boss. You will have your money here today."

The colonel accompanied Rodrigo to the base airport where he boarded a small twin-engine otter. I was going to Bogotá, the capital city. It's always nice to travel and see new things but, on the other hand, I was depressed at the thought that we were going to pick up more Benjamins that were used to buy drugs and were now coming to support this marathon of blood.

The one-hour flight was tranquil except for a few hard shakes crossing the Andes Mountains. When the pilot announced the arrival at El Dorado International Airport, Rodrigo pulled out his wallet to check that we were there and fastened his seatbelt. He had never been to Bogotá and on top of that he didn't know the person who was waiting for him. He seemed a bit nervous, a bit out of his element. An elegant young man in his mid-twenties approached him as he reached the arrival area. He was wearing tinted glasses and a black Armani suit. Don't ask how I knew it was Armani; I just knew, the way you do when you've spent time in the cash registers in some of the most elegant boutiques in New York. You need to have many like me in your wallet to be able to buy an Armani.

"*Hola* Rodrigo, *Como estas? Yo soy* Orlando." Rodrigo looked a little unnerved to be recognized. And he probably felt a little shabby beside this guy. "I am going to take you to the boss's office and give you the package." Orlando tried to keep his distance. They crossed the street to a parking lot, where the man clicked open the trunk of a black Mercedes Benz W-211. "Leave your bag here," he told Rodrigo who dropped it onto the trunk floor. They got into the car, took the North exit and entered the traffic on El Dorado highway, heading toward downtown Bogotá, shimmering in the distance.

I looked at the old Colombian pesos. "So this is Bogotá."

"*Si*. Bogotá is enormous city. Here you find luxuries of the developed world right next to the needs of the third world. Is in this city where the big drug lords as the Yankee and 01 can hide, mixing themselves within the good people of the society."

"So they walk up and down the streets like nothing?" I asked.

"Many of them have found their place in the society as big executives and owners of recognized businesses they made to distract the attention. Many of them went to prestigious universities in and outside of Colombia. They dine in the same restaurants ambassadors go to, play golf with the high class, and some end up in politics. This is the power of money."

It was hard to believe I was in the same country were those two little kids, Ignacio and Andrea, were brutally murdered. "What does your average normal Colombian think?"

"Benjamin, the citizens here live as if nothing was happening around them. They walk up and down, showing no interest about what is going on in the jungles and in the remote areas of this country."

Jenny needed to add her two cents worth. "Is in this city where decisions are taken and the politicians and citizens don't hear the screams of suffering of their countrymen that die in towns and villages in the hands of criminals. Probably they don't yell enough to be heard, or maybe their blood doesn't splash enough to stain their Armani suits."

After driving for a good hour, the car slowed down at an intersection and turned into the basement-level parking garage of an office tower. Orlando told Rodrigo to follow him, and they took an elevator to the eleventh floor.

The doors opened in an elegant and exquisitely decorated reception area. The back wall displayed a tasteful logo; 'First Investments Consulting' shone in brass letters beside it. There was an air of calmness and serenity about the place. The atmosphere was cool, fresh and clean, and, if the receptionist behind the desk was anything to go by, I'd bet that everyone working there was elegantly dressed to match the decor of their elegant offices.

"We are here to see Señor Daniel," Orlando told the receptionist.

"I will let his assistant know you are here," she replied. "May I tell him who you are?"

The young man hesitated, then, flashing a smile said, "Tell him we are the two he is expecting."

Rodrigo really looked like a fish out of water now. "What is this?" I wondered aloud. I couldn't believe these offices were linked to the Surgeon's boss. No gold chains or pistols. Like Whirlpool's business, this was the legal side of the drug business, where nobody would even think of dressing like a drug heavy.

"In Bogotá, 01 is a prominent businessman. He moves in all the spheres of society and politics," the friendly old pesos said. "His name is known for honesty and hard work. This office is a façade to cover blood and corruption. But I have an idea that many of the people who work here deny the truth from themselves. They believe the elegance and think they work in a legitimate business––and some of it is legitimate. But clean money and dirty money are hard to separate; and even if it comes in clean it leaves stained with blood."

A few minutes later, another , elegant, sparkling Colombian woman approached the two men.

"Señor Daniel is going to take two more hours before he can come to the office," she told them in a delicate voice.

"Daniel is 01's real name," the old pesos said. "Many people in Bogotá have heard about 01 but no one links him to Daniel. He plays golf in Bogotá's country club with influential politicians while his men assassinate innocent villagers and ship drugs out of the country and import roomfuls of money to support the drug production and support several national economies with their arms purchases." The old pesos sounded sad and bitter.

"We will go and get some lunch and come back," Orlando told the assistant. And with that, we were in the elevator and back in the Mercedes.

"I am going to take you to Unicentro shopping mall," the young man told Rodrigo as he slipped into the Bogotá traffic.

Unicentro was a big mall and the place was packed. As the two men approached a small restaurant Rodrigo stuck his hand inside his pocket and took out a ten thousand pesos note, not enough to buy supper in a mall like that. Any sandwich could be worth three times that note. "Can we go to a currency exchange office? I want to change one hundred dollars."

"Exchange! What? Woohoo, that's me!" I said with surprise, even pleasure. At last, at last! He was going to drop me in Bogotá. Finally I was going to be away from these rotten people. That was the good news in the middle of all the sadness and hard-earned knowledge I'd acquired. There was a good chance I'd eventually get back to the States. And just as suddenly, it felt a little like bad news. I would be leaving my Colombian friends behind.

"What about you?" I asked Jenny.

"I might stay here in Bogotá," she said hopefully.

Rodrigo found the currency exchange and asked the lady sitting at the counter behind a bulletproof Plexiglas security window. "How much is the US dollar to the peso today?" He was holding his wallet in his right hand.

"1900 pesos per one US dollar."

Rodrigo opened his wallet and withdrew me and pushed me under the security glass.

The lady checked all my sides, put me under a fluorescent light and confirmed I was the real deal.

"I will give you 190,000 pesos. If you have 10,000 pesos, I can give you back 200,000; I only have fifty thousand-pesos bills."

"*Si*," Rodrigo replied. He opened his wallet again and took out the only 10,000 pesos he had––Jenny.

He pushed Jenny under the security glass, and the lady gave him back four fifty thousand-pesos bills. That was the last I saw of Rodrigo as he walked away and vanished in the crowds.

The woman put Jenny on the counter and placed a stack of fifty thousand-pesos bills in between. I knew we would be separated soon. Currency exchange offices constantly circulate money, mostly US dollars. But I also knew that luck had been on our side and anything could happen. Jenny and I waited quietly.

I was thinking about this when a middle-aged man approached the counter and said, "Do you have US dollars for sale?

"*Si*, we sell them for 2200 per one dollar. How many do you want?" the cashier asked, looking at me and some other dollars she had over the counter.

I turned to Jenny "These people are scammers. They make a lot of money off us. They buy us for 1900 and sell us for 2200! This isn't fair to the people."

"I need 400 dollars. How much will that be in pesos?"

The cashier took out her calculator and said, "880,000 pesos plus 10,000 tax. All will be 890,000 pesos."

The man opened his wallet and took out eighteen fifty thousand-pesos bills and passed them under the security glass. The cashier counted them as fast as any bank teller or money launderer and said, "900,000 pesos." The man nodded.

The cashier grabbed me and three more benjamins then looked at Jenny and picked her up. "Here is your money, sir, and she counted one hundred, two hundred, three hundred, four hundred. Then she pushed Jenny toward the window and asked, "Do you want your 10,000 pesos change in dollars or pesos?"

The man thought for a moment and said, "Give me pesos."

"Yes! Yes! Yes!" I yelled. Jenny was coming with us!

The lady pushed Jenny under the security glass. "Thank you for doing business with us."

The man slid all of us inside his wallet and walked away.

"This can't be true! We're still together!" I said to Jenny, smiling.

She nodded and said, "I told you our destiny is to be together."

*But for how long?* I wondered.

# 21

# Back to USA

THE MAN WALKED TO THE ESCALATORS ON HIS LEFT AND went down to the food court on the first floor. He passed several fast food restaurants and stopped in front of an outlet called *Lena y Carbon*. He looked around and spotted a man sitting next to a middle-aged lady, four tables away. The man stood up and waved. He looked at them and offered a tentative smile.

"Andrés" the lady mouthed at a distance. He nodded and walked to the table.

"*Hola* Andrés. I was having trouble recognizing you" the lady said.

"*Hola Señora* Patricia, I wasn't sure it was you either since we have only seen each other once," Andrés replied.

"What are you having?" she asked.

"Just a Coke, *gracias*. You know I should not eat anything." "So how is everything?" the lady asked, lifting her eyebrows.

Andrés leaned into the table, closer to her. "All is going well señora. I am now ready to travel to Miami."

"Yoo-hoo. I'm going home and you're coming too," I told to Jenny.

"Calm down, hurricane," Jenny said. "He still can use me before travelling."

"Ah, shit, I hope not," I said.

The lady, whose Spanish accent sounded strange to me, kept asking Andrés questions. "What time is your flight departing tonight?"

Andrés took a swig of his Coke. "It leaves Bogotá at seven tonight then stops in Panama City for thirty minutes. I expect to land at eleven in Miami." She nodded as he continued. "I just bought a few dollars in case I need to buy something. It is always good to carry some cash."

"She doesn't sound Colombian to me," I told Jenny.

"Your ear it has really gotten better," she told me. "She has a Portuguese accent. She must be Brazilian."

The lady asked Andrés to come closer to her. He leaned in even further. "Listen, Andrés, the boss asked me to give this to you." She opened her purse and pulled out a small notebook and passed him a card. "This is the phone number you have to call once you arrive in Miami. Before calling make sure you don't have a tail. You understand?"

Andrés smiled. "Yes I understand."

Jenny looked disappointed "Even if we travel together to the USA we will never be together. I am useless there. Andrés will probably pay for something with you once he arrives in Miami and keep me for his return to Colombia. I don't think all this is going to be good. At least if we both stayed in Colombia, there are more chances to meet again."

I didn't know what to say. She was right. But staying in Colombia was not going to make things better for us, and I didn't want to go back to the cartel. We were talking like we had control over our fate, but the fact is we can't decide where we go or stay.

Andrés finished his Coke. "Good bye," he said to the couple. "I will call you as soon as I have sorted all out after I arrive."

Andrés shook hands with both and walked to the elevator that took us down to the basement parking. He walked to his small grey Mazda drove for nearly an hour to an outlying suburb.

Alex Barr

Andrés parked in front of a modest house, locked his car, and walked up the walk to the front door. Halfway there he was greeted by two pretty little girls calling, "Papa, papa," as they came running to hug him. They had to be twins; I'd guess about eight years old. Andrés walked into the house carrying a girl in each arm, calling out as he entered the house, "*Mi amor,* I'm home."

He put the girls down and gave his wife a passionate kiss. "Isabel, I have to go out of town," he told her "This new job will require a lot of travel."

His wife looked happy. "I'll only be gone for three days," he told her as he packed. I won't need much and can travel light."

He put a pair of pants, several shirts, and some underwear into a small bag. Then he and his wife and daughters sat in the kitchen. "So where are you going?" asked his wife timidly.

"To Miami. The company wants me to contact some new clients in there."

"Have something to eat before you go," his wife insisted. "I prepare the empanadas that you love."

"*No mi amor.* I am not hungry, *gracias.*" His wife kept looking at him as silence fell between them.

"You know what?" she said brightly after a while. "I am so happy you got this new job. It has been almost three years since you were laid off from the brewer plant and finally you got this job. I remember your sending resumes and knocking doors ever day."

Andrés smiled, "Yeah, finally I got a job." Then it was time to go to the airport.

He hugged his two daughters and we could see tears in his eyes as he told them, "I love you my girls." Then he turned to his wife. "*Lucero, mi amor.* Life would have never be the same without you." He hugged her.

"What is wrong?" she asked breaking the hug and taking a deep breath. "Why you act like if you were going forever. You are only going a few days?"

He smiled, affectionately. "*Triste mi amor*, I am just anxious about flying, I hate airplanes and fear the worst."

The taxi he'd arranged to take him to the airport was outside waiting and honking. He looked through the window. "*Mi amor*, time to leave." He grabbed his bag and walked away. He didn't look back.

The taxi dropped us at the airport departure level and Andrés went directly to the American Airlines counter. The line was still short—only two people ahead, and then it was our turn.

"Good evening, sir. Are you going to Panama or Miami?" said a young blond woman.

"Miami."

"Please give me your passport with the US visa and your ticket."

He handed her everything. "Two things are difficult in this country," a young hundred-dollar bill said. "One is to live without fear, and the other is to get a visa to United States. The visa officers believe all Colombians are all drug dealers, which is a big mistake, considering only a very small percentage of the population have anything to do with drugs. Unfortunately, the whole country shoulders the reputation of the few."

"Many Americans use drugs but Colombians don't believe all Americans are drug junkies," Jenny pointed out in an annoyed tone.

The ticket agent was taking her time and Jenny and I felt Andrés getting nervous, his pulse had increased and he was breathing deeper to take a breath.

The ticket agent finally tagged Andrés's luggage, gave him a boarding pass and he was ready to go. We only needed Andrés to walk directly to the immigration area.

"If he gets distracted by this line of shops he can probably be tempted to buy and that is that last thing we need now," Jenny said.

The immigration entrance gate was at least twenty shops ahead of us, and that was a lot of temptation. Andrés passed by them all with his head down, occasionally glancing at the immigration entrance. Not once did he stop, not even to look. He appeared to be thinking, concentrating on something.

He reached the immigration line and in few minutes he was handing his passport to one of the immigration officers.

"Where are you going sir?" the officer asked, looking him in the eye.

. "Miami"

"What are you going to do in Miami?"

"I am going for business, just three or four days.".

The officer looked again at his passport. "What do you do for a living?"

"I work for an import and export company."

The officer didn't look convinced. "Sir, please read that note on the board next to you."

Andrés put his glasses on and read out loud. "*Señores pasajeros, si usted trae droga esta es la última oportunidad que tiene para arrepentirse.* Andrés looked at the officer and serenely responded, "I will never carry drugs. Never."

"Good to hear," the officer said and stamped one of the pages of his passport. "You can go."

"Hurray," Jenny and I yelled. We were already inside the immigration area just a few yards from the boarding gate of American Airlines, flight 205, final destination: Miami!

Andrés found an empty seat among the waiting passengers until boarding was authorized. At 6:30 pm a stewardess dressed in white and blue and with a gringo accent called the passengers to begin boarding.

Andrés found his seat, sat down and closed his eyes. He looked tired. Sometimes stress is more exhausting than physical work. American Airlines departed on time and Andrés went directly to sleep.

I couldn't believe I was going home. More unbelievable was the fact that I had survived the paramilitaries, the guerrilla, the drug lords, and the money launderers. I'd seen the dark side of the Columbian army. I'd witnessed negotiations with arm dealers thus confirming they do exist. I saw so much blood only a cliché could describe it––rivers, buckets––; I could've filled a pool with the tears I saw. I'd heard the terrifying sound of bombs falling from the sky above me. I was able, finally, to understand where the money from drugs really ends. I have promised myself I will never forget the faces of those two kids just before they were murdered. I had the honour to meet the most courageous boy I have ever known. And best of all, I made a new friend, Jenny. I saw things in Colombia that I thought were never possible. Looking back it was a journey where I found who I really was and how far humans will go to get and keep us.

The plane landed in Panama City for thirty minutes. A few passengers boarded and the flight continued to Miami. It had been a quiet ride until half and hour before landing in Miami. Andrés woke up sweating and shivering. He leaned his body forward several times then stood up and called stewardess, "Can you bring me an Alka Seltzer," he asked, holding his stomach with his two hands.

"What is wrong with him?" Jenny asked me.

" I think he has gas from the altitude. It's nothing," I replied.

The stewardess came back with a glass of water and two Alka Seltzers. "Are you okay, sir?" she asked.

"I am well, don't worry. I ate too much. *Gracias.*" He didn't look at her.

Soon the pilot announced our arrival at Miami International Airport. I was landing at home with Jenny, but we also knew our time together was shortening. Andrés, still feeling pain and dizziness, grabbed his luggage and was one of the first ones to leave the plane. He came through the exit and passed the first security ring installed by the U.S. Drug Enforcement Agency to monitor all flights coming from Colombia.

"Who are they?" Jenny asked.

"Those are the guys who think you Colombians are the bad guys and their people who use drugs are the victims. I'm, afraid I also believed that before this trip. I'm sorry, Jenny."

Andrés's condition was getting worse. He was unsteady on his feet. He didn't seem to follow the right signs, and eventually he seemed to just follow the crowd and finally he reached the immigration line. His heart was now beating slower . I started to think this was more than stress symptoms.

Some days Miami airport can be very busy, and this was one of them. Several international flights had landed with only minutes between them and this created a build-up of people. Andrés was struggling to stay on his feet. He needed to sit down, his legs were trembling and the cold sweat running down his face and body wasn't helping either. Fortunately five more immigration officers showed up to help the other ten speed up the process. The line finally started to move.

Jenny kept noticing the ups and downs in Andrés's pulse. "He is not nervous. This is something else."

A few seconds later Andres took a deep breath, gripped his stomach tightly with his two hands and fell to the floor. He seemed vaguely aware of what was happening. Then came the seizures. The travellers made a circle around him but no one helped. "Why no one helps him?" Jenny asked desperately.

"Because they are humans. Don't forget they are unpredictable."

"It's an epileptic fit," one said.

"Looks like a heart attack." someone else suggested.

Everyone had something to say but no one helped. Two security guards finally showed up. "Please stand back," one said as he took his phone to call the paramedics. Andrés's wallet and body shook with the seizures, which were now coming seconds apart. White foam came out his mouth and nose restricting his air passage.

"What is happening to him?" Jenny asked, confused.

"I don't want to tell you yet what I think is happening here," I replied.

The two guards had to keep asking the passengers to move away. "This man is in serious condition," one of them said, touching his neck pulse.

At last the paramedics rushed in. Andrés tried to move and had moments of lucidity. "Tell me what is happening to you?" one of the paramedics asked him, as he checked his heart rate. Andrés looked at him.

"I am dying," he replied, white foam still oozing from his mouth.

The two paramedics, helped by the two security guards, moved his body to a stretcher. "*Traes droga adentro?*" one of the paramedics asked gently in perfect Spanish. Andrés couldn't talk any more but he nodded. "Don't worry, we're taking you to the hospital right now. Do you know what type of drug you have inside?" but Andrés had lost consciousness again.

"No. No. This can't be true! I cried out. "Why do drugs have to follow us, just when I am going to get away from it all?" The paramedics were rushing Andrés through the corridors and out a door where a white ambulance and two policemen and a DEA officer waited for them.

"This man is dying," one of the paramedics said, as they put him inside.

"Is the guy loaded?" the DEA officer asked, looking at Andrés.

Alex Barr

"I think so." the paramedic replied as he locked in the stretcher.

"These fucking Colombians," one of the cops muttered, as they both looked angrily at Andrés. I was really getting upset.

"What about your fucking drug addicts," I hollered. "Do you know what they're causing in Colombia?" At moments like this I wished more than ever that I was human and could speak.

Andrés's pulse was too low to keep him alive. His pupils were dilated and his body temperature was dropping. The paramedics were working hard to keep him stable but making very little difference. They were losing him. His pulse was so slow we were not able to feel it.

"You think he died?" Jenny asked with a sob.

"He's alive. The siren is still on."

The ambulance arrived at Jackson Memorial Hospital ER, where a group of doctors and nurses had been preparing to receive him. There wasn't time for questions. Andrés was immediately taken to the surgery where they tried to stabilize his heart. They were able to bring him back to consciousness for a few seconds.

"What type of drug is inside you?" a young doctor asked in Spanish. "Cocaine? Heroin?"

Andrés trembling moved one of his fingers upwards.

"The first one?" asked the doctor. Andrés nodded. "He's got cocaine inside," the young doctor yelled to his other colleagues. He then looked at Andrés. "You will be all right. Close your eyes and rest."

Andrés's clothes had been removed and folded inside a plastic bag and laid on a small chair close to the door entrance. From there we watched Andrés battling for life. They took X-rays that showed the capsules' exact location, which helped the doctors locate all the capsules, including the one that exploded, and completely clean Andrés digestive tract. They all expected the damage to his vital organs would be reversible.

They had also administered a tranquilizer that temporarily cuts the effects of cocaine and would give them time to complete the operation. After the injection Andrés regained consciousness again and it gave him time to say a few words to the nurse holding the defibrillator.

"Please, if I die, tell my kids and wife I love them. I did this for them."

The nurse held his hand and spoke firmly to him. "You'll survive. Try to sleep." There were tears in her eyes.

However, not long after the doctor began the operation, Andrés had a major heart attack. The anaesthesiologist, along with the other doctors, tried hard to stabilize him but during a second heart attack his heart stopped beating. The doctors went through the resuscitation protocol, but Andrés was dead. "We lost him," the Surgeon declared, and removed his gloves. Ten minutes later Andrés was officially declared dead. A second surgeon and two nurses finished removing the cocaine––a total of forty twenty-gram capsules.

I couldn't believe Andrés was dead, and neither could Jenny. "What'll happen to his kids and wife? They loved that father and husband."

Two nurses were still cleaning Andrés, chatting as they worked. One of the nurses was younger; obviously, she was still a student.

"This is the first time I've been part of an operation like this. These really are just the cut-off fingers of surgical gloves," she said. "I've heard about this but never seen it."

"Honey, I've only been nursing for six years, but I've seen this way too much," the other nurse replied. "They fill the cut-off finger half full––twenty grams––and tie it off with dental floss. They put the filled finger inside a second finger and tie it off with dental floss. Theoretically they're resistant to stomach acids, but all too often they fail. You saw the one the doctor held up—the stomach acids had corroded a significant tear and hole. You know how strong the acids are."

"This is so dangerous. Why would he do this?"

"People like this man aren't usually the owners of cocaine. He's just a mule used by drug dealers. He was a very desperate man. He probably had no job, debts with the banks; he's got kids he loves. Who knows?"

How do you become a mule? D'you know?"

"In Colombia it's easy to ask around and find a source for the work. You meet with them and they give you the grape test. They always have very large grapes on a table at the meeting. They watch you eat them. If you swallow them whole, which everyone knows is what they're looking for, then they will consider you for the work. The capsules are also dipped in melted beeswax to help the mules swallow them, but it's not easy."

"One of our instructors told us that thousands of these mules end up dead in surgeries. And thousands more survive but end up in jail for years." The young nurse contemplated Andrés. "How much do you think he gets for bringing in that much cocaine?"

"Not a lot for the risks he took. Probably about $5,000 for transporting the drugs in his stomach from Colombia to Miami."

"That's all?"

The thoughtful nurse looked at Andrés again and nodded sadly. "I'm sure this man felt he had no other choices left."

"Yeah, you'd sure have to be desperate to do this." Both nurses looked quietly at Andrés.

I listened to the conversation. I thought about my time in Colombia and the price that had been paid for my return. Believe me, if I had heard this story before my walk to Colombia, my answer to this would have been, "He asked for it." But not now. I knew, first hand, how many opportunities were lost and how few created because of the drug wars. I saw how a stupid war we finance forces people to do the unimaginable. The nurses covered his body with a white sheet and pushed the stretcher down to the hospital morgue. That was the last time we saw Andrés.

After they left, one of the hundred bills in the wallet said, "I've been in this situation before. Procedures are strict in these cases. The body can't be touched unless there's someone from DEA present and all his belongings will be given to them." As he said this, the experienced nurse came hustling back in the room and grabbed the bag we were in. She peaked inside curiously, but hearing a noise in the hallway, she quickly closed it and took it to a room with lockers and put us in one. As she turned to go, a man in a blue jacket with a DEA stamped on the back came in.

"Good afternoon, mam. My name's Dylan Richelhof, DEA," he said, flashing his ID. "I'm here about the Colombian brought in this morning from the airport. We were notified he died in surgery."

"He's in the morgue. His belongings are inside this locker," she said pointing to it. He had no bags when he arrived." She looked a little intimidated by his serious stare.

"Show me the body and bring his belongings. I'm tight for time."

The nurse unlocked the locker and handed the bag. "Here's the bag with his clothes, wallet, wedding ring, and watch."

Richelhof opened it and laid out everything on a table, then repacked the bag. "Let's go see the body," he said as he walked out of the room and down the hall toward the morgue. Clearly, he knew the way well. The nurse followed him and indicated the stretcher Andrés was lying on. She stood beside it and walked uncovered the body, slowly pulling the sheet downward and to one side.

"Poor man. He asked me to tell his family he loved them if he died. Can you give me his details so I can do that for him?"

Alex Barr

"Don't feel sorry for him," agent Richelhof said. "These Colombians bombard us with their drugs. We're tired of it. They're killing Americans, right here in Miami and across the country. My opinion? He deserves this." The nurse looked at him, shocked.

This DEA agent was getting me worked up again. "Who's he to talk this way? He wants to talk about bombardment and the killing of his innocent drug addicts? I saw with my own eyes the bombs and the arms made in this country being dropped on peasant villages, ripping the skin of innocent Colombians."

"Calm down, calm down. You know he is not hearing you, and he won't care anyway" Jenny said.

The man whipped the sheet from the Andrés body, put a pair of white latex gloves and asked the nurse to help him hold Andrés's right hand so he could take some fingerprints. It was a routine procedure for him, efficiently finished in minutes.

"Keep his body in the morgue until we contact his family, see if they want to repatriate his body. If not, he'll be buried in a mass grave the next week, unless the medical school need some bodies."

Holding the bag of Andrés's belongings, Agent Richelhof looked at the nurse. "Thanks for your time. See you soon," he added with a smile.

He drove to the DEA office in Miami, and in presence of two more agents, he opened the bag and put the watch, clothes, wallet and wedding ring on top of a table and noted. The airline had sent over Andrés's luggage, and the three men went through it, counting and logging in every single article. Then came the wallet. I turned to Jenny "I don't think we'll be together after they search this wallet. They'll probably send me to a bank and deport you back to Colombia."

Richelhof opened the wallet, feeling carefully in all compartments with his finger. He took out all the money and documents and laid them on top of the table. We ended up lying next to photos of Andres's wife and kids.

"His family probably doesn't know yet," Jenny said.

"Four one hundred-dollar notes and one ten thousand-pesos note, Colombian," Richelhof told the man taking notes.

"How much is that shit in dollars?" the other officer asked, pointing at Jenny. Oh man, I was angry, but I couldn't do anything.

"I don't know, exactly," said the note taker, "but pesos aren't worth much. You probably need five of those to buy a cup of coffee." They all laughed.

They put us in two groups—dollars on one side and the single pesos on the other.

"Now what?" I said to Jenny, looking at her lying alone on that cold table.

---

## 22
# The Concentration Camp

AFTER THE LIST WAS SIGNED AND STAMPED BY THE THREE DEA agents, they put all of us––pesos and dollars––inside a small locked metal box. The wedding ring, watch, and documents were sent to the Colombian Embassy, which would arrange to return them to Andrés's wife and daughters. Then we were taken to the offices of the Federal Reserve in downtown Miami where all the money confiscated from drug traffickers, money launderers, terrorists, and thieves is kept. The safe in these offices is known among all bills as the American concentration camp. It's said that inside this safe there's still money confiscated from Al Capone. The DEA officer handed the box to a middle-aged Spanish woman in charge of the confiscated dollars and foreign currencies. He handed her the report and forms for her to sign.

"Please follow me," she said as she guided him to a small booth where they counted and verified the money, privately and without interruption.

He opened the box and said, "Not much this time."

She lifted the ten thousand and looked at Jenny from side to side. "These I know very well. They're Colombian. We've got a bunch of them inside." Then she looked at me, scrutinizing every corner and both sides. She repeated this with the other dollars. "Dollars don't stay inside too long," she said as she closed the box, thanked the officer and walked away with us under her arm.

She reached an enormous security door, punched in the code, and pushed the heavy door to as it clicked open. Before my eyes was the largest amount of foreign currency one could imagine. It was similar to what I had seen in the cartel bunkers, only more. There were bills from around the globe––Arab and African countries, China; you name it, they had it. The noise of all those languages and dialects talking at the same time made me think I'd go crazy staying here. What a racket.

The woman took us out of the box and walked down a central corridor to the end. Looking at her carrying us, all the bills started making comments and looked aggressively at us. "What is this?" I asked one of the experienced hundred dollar bills.

"This is our version of a jail. I was here before. Believe me, this isn't going to be fun. I'm afraid your friend, Jenny, will stay here forever because she is a foreigner. We Americans will be out of here soon."

I was about to say something to him, when those smooth white hands grabbed all us gringos and dropped us in the middle level of one of the stands where the US dollars were neatly piled.

"Hey Benjamin. Benjamin!" I heard a voice calling. "To your left. It's me, Andrew!"

I looked at the bill, puzzled. "Who are you?" Honestly I couldn't remember him.

"I'm the twenty-dollar note Robert used to buy drugs from that Hispanic dealer, Hilario, in New York. Remember he used me to buy dope the second time?"

"Lover Boy! Hey, man, good to see you. What happened to Robert, did you ever hear?"

Lover Boy was quiet, then said, "I stayed with Hilario for a long time after you guys left, and Robert came to buy drugs

Alex Barr

every day. I heard from the bills he brought in that he quit university because he'd failed all his courses. Finally his father kicked him out. And you won't be surprised to learn his girl friend dumped him. He was so hooked all he could think of were his fixes. He's your basic junky, probably on the streets. It was a while ago now.

"I'm sorry to hear this. I could see the kid had potential," I said.

You know, I've noticed that often humans don't appreciate what they have. That kid threw away his youth, his career and his life. And the really sad thing is that he doesn't know the damage he's done to other human beings. I don't think I'll ever understand why humans have such a self-destructive streak. Especially because life can be so great, no matter what.

"Why are you here?" I asked Lover Boy, quietly. "Did you end up in Colombia like me?"

"Nah. You know that the cartel only sends the Benjamins to Colombia because of their high value. I ended up in prison because Hilario was arrested, and part of the confiscated money was sent here. I heard that a month ago Hilario was murdered in prison, the day after he decided to give evidence in court about the Colombian cartels. Humans think it's easy to get into this business. What they don't know is they can never leave. You don't play with those guys."

"I know that all too well, now" I told him.

"Where're the General and Ulysses?"

"They died in Colombia, burned. And please don't ask me how, because I promised myself not to remember all the atrocities I saw in that country." Lover Boy was transfixed.

There was a whole section assigned for Colombian pesos, and Jenny was left next to a stack of them. Some of them looked old and deteriorated; some even looked like they had mould on them.

I passed the weekend in that noisy, babbling world, listening to stupid arguments and insults all around as well as some interesting conversations. It struck me as very similar to the human world. When I realized this I didn't know whether to laugh or cry.

Very early Monday morning, the safe door slowly opened. A woman entered, pushing a small wheeled cart along the middle isle. She stopped at the stand where I was and grabbed all the US dollars sitting there.

"What is happening?" yelled Jenny as she saw the woman put me on to the cart.

"I don't know, but I think they're taking me out of here. I am sure I will see you again in Colombia," I called. "Remember humans are humans. You've been a great friend, Jenny."

That was the last day I saw Jenny. She was condemned to stay inside that prison, and for all I know she's still there, paying for Andrés's mistake. This was not the American dream she expected. I can only hope someday I'll see her again.

Alex Barr

# 23
## To the Bank Again

THE WOMAN TOOK US TO A SMALL OFFICE FOR A SECOND inspection. The bills showing wear and tear and old age were stacked on one side, and the others were stacked with bills of the same denomination. I was again part of a ten thousand dollar stack. Soon we were transferred into an armoured vehicle and driven to a Bank branch in downtown Miami. There we all were examined by a gamma-ray machine, which detected how much life was left in a bill. If the machine detected fifteen percent or less of life left, your chances were you'd be burned, which in some ways was better than slowly rotting in the jungles of Colombia. The ones above fifteen percent were sent to the commercial banks to be put back into circulation and start a new life.

All of us passed the gamma ray, but I was afraid of going back to the streets. What if I went back to Colombia? What if I was used to buy drugs again? Where would I end up? Only the remote possibility of seeing Jenny again gave me the energy to keep going.

Half of us, me included, stayed at the main branch; the rest were sent to a suburban branch of First National in west Miami. I was laid next to a stack of newly-born hundred-dollar bills, full of energy, with clean skin, shiny eyes, no stains, no marks.

Their radiance shadowed me. All my marks, small wounds, and scratches earned during my years of circulation reflected my experience and knowledge. In this we are not so different from people whose journey through life leaves marks on their bodies and personalities, which is what makes each of us unique.

Unlike prison, the bank had a calm, clean environment. The air was cool and dry, no harassment, not much talking apart from some new bills asking me few question about the outside world. Definitely the bills inside the concentration camp are treated as criminals, where the dehumidifying machine never runs, the place is rarely cleaned and no one cares what is happening to them inside.

As expected, the stack where I lay was removed and deposited with Diana, one of the tellers. I was going back to the streets. Diana was a mature woman, maybe in her early forties. Her eyes were red and her nose was runny, and she seemed uninterested in counting money and dealing with clients. I thought she had a cold, but then I heard her tell a colleague that last night her husband had told her he was leaving her and wanted a divorce. "Twenty years we've been married. What am I going to do? What have I done?" she asked her friend as she wiped her eyes again.

Diana finally settled down in a dull sort of way. She was the opposite of most of the young cashiers. She didn't seem to care if the clients were rich or handsome. Clearly, she had no fantasies and as she sadly told her colleague, "I feel like my life is over."

She left some of us on top of the counter in case she needed us. She wasn't exceptionally busy; even the clients seemed to sense from her body language that she wanted to be left alone. However, just before lunch a well-dressed, middle-aged woman with a smile radiating happiness walked straight to her.

"Good morning" the woman said cheerfully.

"How can I help you?" Diana asked, not showing much interest and not looking at her.

"I need to withdraw two thousand dollars from my account." The woman smiled and continued, "My husband is taking me to Europe for our eighteenth anniversary."

*Diana's going to love this*, I thought.

"Good for you," she replied with an edge of sarcasm. "Enjoy yourself because you never know."

The woman was unfazed and just watched as Diana unpacked the ten thousand dollar stacks she had recently put to one side. I was part of the two thousand she grabbed from the top of the stack. She rapidly counted and passed us to the woman.

"I hope you have a good trip," she said as the woman slowly recounted the money and put us in her purse. "Really, I do."

*Yes! I'm going to Europe*, I thought. I'd been there before and images of croissants and ski slopes and the London tube and even the thought of hearing Spanish again in Madrid flashed through my mind.

I checked out her driver's licence and learned her name was Alexandra Lopez. She walked down the Street back to her car. Suddenly life was good again. I was pretty sure, from the look of Alexandra that I wasn't in the hands of a criminal. She looked honest and I was sure I'd stay out of trouble--at least for a while. We drove to her airy, architecturally designed home in Coral Gables.

Alexandra slowly drove into the garage, then walked upstairs to her bedroom. She took out her phone and pressed speed dial. "Hi, honey. I took out two thousand in case we need more cash for the trip…. Okay…Come early. We have to get up at six tomorrow to make the flight."

This was music to my ears. *Europe here I come*, hummed in my head. *I just wish you were with me, Jenny*, I thought with regret.

Alexandra turned off her phone, adjusted the room tem-perature control and lay on her bed. It'd been a long day for me, too. I needed a nap. She closed her eyes and I could tell from her breathing she was almost asleep. I was just closing my eyes when I heard the bedroom door slowly open. *Must be her husband*, I thought. But it was a teenager, about seventeen. Probably it was her son. He walked quietly across the room, keeping his eyes on his mother. He reached her purse that was sitting on a brown leather sofa. The kid looked again at his mom and pulled the zipper smoothly. His eyes shone mischievously when he saw all of us together in her wallet. His mom stirred, coughed lightly and he was out of the room in a shot. But few moments later he was back, quickly stuck his hand inside and grabbed two one hundred dollars notes: the upper one and me. Of the twenty bills resting inside that purse I had the bad luck to be chosen. My dreams of going to Europe vanished the moment those young hands grabbed me. I'd been round long enough to know this was not a good sign. The other bill was a new hundred buck; he was excited at the idea of hanging out with young kids like him.

As the kid slowly closed the bedroom door I looked at the young buck and said, "Hey Junior, don't think he's going to hang around with us too long and don't think he is going to buy books with us. Stealing from his mum's purse, stealing a significant amount of cash, and seeing the look on his face, I have a pretty good idea about what his plans are for us."

Junior didn't pay much attention to me; he was off in dreamland, seeing himself at parties and imaging being touched by young girls. Then he roused himself, "Hey, man, chill out. Save your pessimism, we're going to have fun." Unfortunately the young believe they're more experienced than the old. I was like that too, once.

"Oh, we're going to have a good time," I said.

The boy walked quietly down the hallway away but took the stairs down two at a time. "Bingo!" he said as he put us in his pocket. He took out his phone and speed dialled a number.

Alex Barr

"Trevor. I've got two hundred bucks my mom just gave me. Call Greg and come pick me up. Man, we're going to party tonight."

Junior immediately looked at me. "See he's going to party."

"Yeah, looks like." I said.

Thirty minutes later his friends were honking in front of the house. The kid cheerfully jumped into the back seat of a red Jeep Wrangler and sped off.

"What's the plan for today?" asked the driver.

"I've two hundred bucks; we can buy some good stuff for the veins."

I was furious when I heard the words "good stuff" again. "What are you guys planning to do?" I yelled in exasperation.

The only thing I knew was that "stuff for the veins" means heroin. "Please don't buy drugs. Please don't do this," I screamed in vain. "I know what this will mean. I can't go through all this again," I told Junior. But he just shrugged. He had no idea.

Trevor, Greg, and the kid bought heroin; and once again I was on a voyage of horror. I was walking toward Afghanistan, the world largest producer of heroin.

### THE END

To know more about Benjamin visit
www.benjamin100.com

One Hundred dollar note (Benjamin)

Twenty Dollar note (Lover boy)

Ten thousand Colombian pesos (jenny)

Alex Barr

Fifty thousand Colombian Pesos

Twenty pound sterling (the Queen)

Twenty Dollars Canadian

Fifty dollars (Ulysses)

# About the Author

ALEX BARR WORKED FOR SEVERAL YEARS WITH HUMANITARian relief organizations in war-torn countries and disaster zones. His years as an aid worker and his personal story played an important role in writing this book. Currently he lives in Canada with his wife and two children. Locally his name is well known within the school system and among local organizations where he has given presentations based in part on the message of the book: how purchasing drugs on the streets of North America can devastate a village in Colombia or instigate the murder of an innocent family.